MW01503751

THE SURVIVORS BOOK THIRTEEN
OLD SECRETS

NATHAN HYSTAD

Copyright © 2020 Nathan Hystad

All rights reserved.

No part of this publication may be reproduced, distributed, or transmitted in any form or by any means, including photocopying, recording, or other electronic or mechanical methods, without the prior written permission of the publisher, except in the case of brief quotations embodied in critical reviews and certain other non-commercial uses permitted by copyright law.

This is a work of fiction. All of the characters, names, incidents, organizations, and dialogue in this novel are either products of the author's imagination or are used fictitiously.

Cover art: Tom Edwards Design

Edited by: Scarlett R Algee

Proofed and Formatted by: BZ Hercules

ISBN-13: 9798649071703

Also By Nathan Hystad

ONE

The desolate world was familiar. The way the light refracted through the lake's surface and off the destroyed cities, with stark white bones contrasting against the piles of brown rubble, was all commonplace to Jules now.

She sped across the landscape, her green sphere encasing her as she floated toward her destination. She stopped at the ruins of an ancient metropolis, hovering above it. The four circles formed from stones were partly covered by the long buildings, toppled over onto their sides.

Jules tried to imagine what it had been like before the destruction, but struggled to picture it. The skeletons resembled humans, but when she'd brought a sample back to *Light*, the projections of their appearance had been slightly different: their heads rounder, arms shorter, and legs a bit longer.

"What happened to you?" she asked out loud. Her voice was quiet within her energy field.

And how had a Deity been trapped beneath the ocean? There were so many questions surrounding their current predicament, and they'd failed to uncover answers to any of them.

Then there was Dean. She'd been so sure she could find him all those months ago– confident he'd visit this place, but there was no indication that he'd traveled here.

something dangerous lingered nearby. Jules hadn't been brave enough to breach the water confining the sleeping Deity, but now she felt she was being forced to do so. She was nervous, her hands trembling with anticipation, but she moved deeper into the water. Within her sphere, she could see better, and the farther she sank below the roiling waves, the clearer her vision become.

Jules had no idea what could possibly be containing a god under the water, but she was surprised when she stumbled upon the wooden crate. It resembled an oversized coffin, maybe eight feet long and three deep, and it waved in the water, fastened to something by thick rusted chains on its underside. She floated lower, moving under the crate, and touched the large rings holding the coffin to the chains. She peered down, seeing the tethers continue toward the ocean floor, which was farther than her vision allowed.

Who had put this here? It looked so archaic. She'd been expecting something grand, intricate, and beautiful. A prison for a god, made of crystals and energy, not a wooden box with a tarnished chain.

Free me! The thought boomed in her head so abruptly and powerfully that she shot back with the ferocity of it. Her vision swam as she bobbed in the water, spots in front of her eyes. Blood dripped from her nose, and she felt something in her ear. She couldn't stay here.

Ja'ri. You know what you must do. Free me. The voice was less imposing, and it had used her Zan'ra name. Whatever was inside this box knew her name, or some ancient version of her.

"I can't! I don't trust you!" Jules yelled, wiping the blood onto her sleeve.

Free me and the others. All will be forgiven.

The others? She shivered at the thought of more

hidden Deities out there. "Where are the rest of you?"

You know. The Four know. Free us, and be rewarded.

The box shook violently, a scream carrying into her head. She moved away, her mind aching, her bones succumbing to the strain like they were about to snap. Her eyesight blurred again, but she pressed on, moving farther from the trapped Deity.

She broke free from the turbulent whitecaps, floating into the air. Jules darted to the side, narrowly avoiding another lightning strike, and flew as fast as she could, trying to put as much distance between herself and the angry god as she could. It cried out as she went, the clouds weren't localized to the ocean. They trailed after her, as if attached to her sphere, and she dragged the black storm over the land past the city of ruins and to the lake, where the portal waited.

The waters here were calm. She glanced at the cliff, where the bones of thousands settled in carved-out cubby holes, and continued until she swam into the portal room. The lights glowed along the etched symbols in the walls, and she found *Light's* icon: a star with a streaking mark over it. The god's voice echoed in her mind as she pressed it, returning to the safety of her home.

———————

The luster of being named the newest captain in the Alliance of Worlds had quickly lost its sheen. Seven months later, Magnus' death lingered in the recycled air, palpable everywhere I went. I'd known losing him was going to be difficult, but didn't anticipate it would continue to consume so much of my daily life.

We hadn't been as close over the last decade, with him

running *Fortune* and then *Horizon*, but we'd kept in contact almost weekly over that time. Now I found myself wishing I could take my communicator and chat with him.

"Magnus, you'd be having a fit if you were still around," I whispered, staring out the viewscreen on the bridge. The crew was strong, each of them fiercely positive as we moved through space, heading on my personal mission. So many others were affected by the threat of Lom merging our timelines, even though I was told most of the Alliance board didn't believe it could happen.

I tried to excuse their ignorance. They didn't understand. They hadn't seen what I'd seen. What Mary, and Jules, and Nat… Thinking about her made me more determined to accomplish my goals. She'd remained on New Spero in their farmhouse. Magnus had loved it there, but now his widow was alone, their daughter run off, an ancient Zan'ra possessing Patty. O'ri was dangerous, according to Regnig and Fontem, and I hated that Patty had ever been tied up in this whole mess. She was just a kid.

"Boss, you okay?" Slate asked. He tapped away at his tablet and glanced up, his face stamped with concern.

I nodded, wishing I wasn't sitting here constantly dwelling on our conundrum. My crew needed me, and so did my family. But Magnus' family did too. Dean was out there all alone, scouring the galaxies for his sister, and I wished Jules would finally track him down.

Sergo buzzed from his pilot's seat, and I peered over, seeing him whisper to Walo beside him. Suma was on the right side of the bridge, working diligently at her console, with Rivo on her left.

Loweck was behind Slate and me, running weapons diagnostics. I loved this crew. They'd been through so much over the years, each of them choosing to stay on *Light* with me, regardless of the dangerous mission. Months of space travel had grown so tedious, but together we were getting past the idle times.

The projector ten meters in front of my seat blinked, and a cylinder of light descended from its hub on the ceiling, centering the bridge. The others stared at it, and Sarlun's familiar face surfaced, along with his body. The projection flickered before solidifying. He wore his white uniform and smiled as his snout waved in excitement.

"Dean, I have news."

My blood pumped harder, and I rose, crossing the short distance to stand in front of him. "What is it? Did you find him?"

Sarlun nodded. "Someone has spotted Dean near the Elion system. There's a small station near a mining operation out there, and his ship and his description match."

"Elion?" Slate asked. "What's out there? Nothing but rocks and an unforgiving world, right?"

It hit me. I'd forgotten the name. "It's the place where the Zan'ra language was last recorded. It was how Jules could translate Lan'i's words, that first interrogation with the kid."

Slate frowned. "The time he tried to strangle you?"

I shrugged. "He has issues." I turned back to Sarlun. "Thanks. We're on it."

"Otherwise, how is the mission?" he asked.

I pointed to the viewscreen, and Sarlun's image followed along. "A month out from our next stop. Fontem says we can't bring the starship, so a few of us will be heading from Techeron in my Kraski ship."

"And you still trust this Fontem?" Sarlun asked in front of everyone.

"I have no choice," I told him.

He nodded; his snout stopped moving. He lifted a hand and waved at his daughter. She smiled proudly. They spoke frequently; a nice touch with the added technology of our starship was the ability to communicate from ever-vaster distances, not to mention the portal we had on *Light*.

"We'll be in touch. Good luck with finding Natalia's son." Sarlun's image vanished in a flash.

Walo buzzed something in Padlog before changing to English. "Captain, the portal was just used. Someone arrived."

It had to be Jules. She kept returning to the damned Deity, but she claimed it was sleeping again, no longer pleading to her for liberation. She still worried me. She was pushing herself too hard, trying to become this Zan'ra she knew little about as she chipped away at the complex puzzle around them. How did it all fit with Lom, and could they use her powers to stop the other Zan'ra, as well as Lom's insane plan from another dimension? The entire thing left me with a headache.

"I'll stop by later," I told Slate, who nodded absently. He'd be ending his shift soon, the secondary team coming to work the bridge.

I exited, heading toward the portal on deck two. It didn't take long, but I ran when I saw the Shandra's guards crouched near the room's entrance.

"Jules…" She was on the ground, trying to sit up.

"Get off me!" she shouted, her eyes glowing angrily. The two familiar guards lifted their hands, releasing my daughter.

"She collapsed when she arrived. We dragged her out of there," Keith said.

"Don't worry about it. You did the right thing," I assured them, and helped Jules to her feet. Dried blood crusted her upper lip.

"Papa, there are more of them!" She was clearly excited, but the corridor here was no place to have this discussion.

"Let's bring you up to our quarters," I told her. She clutched me around the chest, and we made the trip as fast as we could. Maggie greeted us at the door, wagging and jumping on Jules' legs.

"Mary!" I called, unsure if she was in at the moment.

She rounded the corner, dashing through the hall as soon as she spotted her ailing daughter. "What happened to you?"

"I went back to Desolate," Jules said. That was the name of the planet where she kept visiting the Deity. The name felt like an omen, and I didn't like it.

"And...?" Mary grabbed her arm, leading her inside to the kitchen, where she snatched a cloth, dabbing it gently on Jules' nose and ears.

"And it woke." She told us about the vision of the beings living their lives in the city, followed by the lightning storm brewing over the ocean. When she mentioned being struck by a bolt, Mary frowned, crossing her arms. "I fell into the ocean and saw where he's held prisoner."

"We don't know he's a prisoner," I said.

"What else could it be? He told me there were others, and that I had to release them all." Jules already looked better, her color having returned.

"How's he contained?" I asked, wondering if these Deities had real bodies, or if they were godlike essences of some kind. Regnig wasn't one hundred percent confident, even though they'd seen a few archaic drawings of the beings.

"He's in a coffin chained to the ocean floor." Jules' face was dead serious; otherwise, I would have thought she was kidding with us.

"A coffin..." I stopped, rubbing my eyes.

"Papa, I have to find the rest of them," she blurted,

and I met her stare. Her hair was messy, dried erratically from salt water, and I pointed to the bathroom near her room.

"Why don't you have a shower and change, and we'll have dinner, then discuss what it means," I suggested.

"Dean, I really think…" Mary started, but a quick shake of my head cut her off. "You heard your dad."

Jules seemed like she was about to say something else, but she stopped herself, taking my advice. I waited until I heard the shower running to speak again.

"She has to stop this. We can't keep letting her travel there alone. It's insanity," I told Mary.

"We have to support her. If we don't try to work with her, she'll just take off like Dean did, and I know for a fact that I couldn't handle that right now," Mary said quietly.

She was right. Jules was too headstrong. She loved us deeply, but she was at that age where she thought she knew everything. Jules considered herself an adult, and she'd gone through more than most people, but I needed to keep an eye on her. To protect her.

This wasn't going to help things, but I had to tell Mary. "Sarlun contacted the bridge."

Mary raised an eyebrow. "Is that so? About Dean?"

I nodded. It wasn't the first time we'd heard rumors about his whereabouts, but so far, the few tips had led nowhere. We'd also learned a few theories about Patty and the Zan'ra boy, but nothing concrete, nor any hard evidence about their location. "Elion system."

Her eyes widened, and she stepped closer. "Do we tell her?"

We were on a direct course to Techeron, where I'd be separating from the rest of the crew, Mary included. I was determined to find Dean before this happened, so that Jules could come with me. Otherwise, she'd never join the expedition, no matter how badly she wanted to see Fontem's real collection.

"We have to, Mary." My hands fell to my sides, and I felt every year of my life as I saw the sadness creeping into her eyes.

"Okay. She won't stop until she finds him."

"And Dean won't stop until he brings his sister home," I reminded her.

"So what do we do?" She slipped her arms around me, pulling me close.

"We do what we always do. Keep fighting the fight and trust Jules will make the right decisions." I kissed the top of her head as she leaned into my chest.

"Like her ending up underwater with this ancient god in a coffin, right?" Mary asked. She was frustrated, but we all were.

"We'll tell Jules about the sighting. It would be smart for her to check out that derelict station at Elion anyway. It's been on her list." I moved toward the fridge and opened it, seeing a few bottles of beer. They were Magnus' favorite. I didn't touch them, pulling out some leftovers to heat up instead.

TWO

Someone had seen Dean. This was it. Jules had a feeling she was finally about to track him down. She was so angry with him. They'd kissed, and then he'd disappeared. He'd even said he loved her, but she didn't have a chance to ask what he meant by it. Did he love her like a sister… was he only saying that stuff because he was vulnerable at the time?

Jules puffed her cheeks and finished packing her bag. It was full of the usual survival equipment, and she opened her bedside nightstand, unfolding the prints Regnig had made for her of the four Zan'ra. She stared at the slightly crude drawings and stopped on hers. The girl had dark hair and bright green eyes. Who had Ja'ri been? There wasn't enough to go on. The one Zan'ra that seemed to have any kind of infamy was O'ri, and that was who possessed Patty right now. He was dangerous.

She wished she could talk with her old friend: find out if the girl remained inside her mind, or if this O'ri had over-taken her, using her like a puppet. Jules wanted to think Patty would be willing to fight it, but the last time she'd seen her, she was too accepting of her fate.

Her door was open, and she looked to it at the sound of a knock. It was her mom, and the sad smile over Mary's face told Jules what type of conversation she was about to have.

"I'll be fine, Mom," she assured Mary.

"I know you will be. I never doubt you, not for a second. But this is Dean, and with how upset he was at losing his sister… then his father. Dean might not be the same boy you…" Her mom paused, stepping into her room. "He's going to have scars now. You may not see them, but they're there, hiding inside his young heart. He needs you more than ever." Her mom's hands rested on Jules' shoulders.

"We all have scars, Mom," Jules said softly.

Her mom nodded her agreement, and hugged Jules closely. "What's your plan?"

Jules slid her tablet from the pack, bringing the Crystal Map application up on the menu. She accessed her saved route, showing her mother the nearest portal to Elion. It was one system over, meaning she needed to procure a ship. "Papa gave me enough credits to find passage out there, but I was thinking of just using my abilities."

"I don't think so, Ju. They're too unpredictable."

"No they're not. It's been a long time since they've failed me." Jules placed her hands on her hips, tapping one foot impatiently. She didn't want to waste any more time. Dean needed her.

"What about yesterday, when you fell into the water?"

Mary had her there. "The lightning hit me. I recovered eventually."

"The ship is your best bet… can we send Slate with you?" her mom asked.

"No! Mom, I'll be fine. I move faster alone." It was Jules' answer, and it was final. She might only be sixteen, but she was a full-fledged Gatekeeper.

"Promise me you'll be cautious."

It was Jules' turn to hug her mom, and she let go,

slinging her pack over her shoulders. "I promise."

Jules knelt, petting Maggie behind the ears before leaving the suite. Mary followed along, chatting about Hugo as if discussing her son would ease the tension. Seven months of searching. Jules' nerves were fried, anxiety filling her every time she thought about tracking Patty's brother. So many things could have befallen him over those months. Maybe he had found Patty and Lan'i.

Papa leaned against the wall near the portal's entrance, holding something in a small pouch. He undid the drawstring, showing Jules the contents. "Take this."

It was the bracelet Professor Thompson had used to steal her powers when the Kold had attacked the Academy. "Good call. Thanks." Jules slipped it into her bag and embraced her dad, who let her go faster than normal. "And save your breath. Mom already gave me the speech." Jules smiled at him, and he grinned in return.

"Good. Remember: Elion, then straight here, okay?" He constantly tried to ensure she didn't go rogue in her search for Dean, Patty, or the Deities.

Now that Jules knew there were other Deities in existence, she had to find them too. And Dal'i, the Zan'ra with the orange eyes. She could teach Jules so much. If they worked together...

"Okay?" Papa echoed.

"Fine. I hear you." Jules nodded to the portal guards and saw they were different than the ones who had helped her yesterday after her collapse. Had that only been a day ago?

The door closed, leaving her alone in the portal room, and she moved toward the beautiful pulsing crystals below the clear table. This entire network of portals was magnificent, almost like a living entity. The Theos had believed they were creating it, but the Shandra stone's power originated from the Deities.

"Imagine their secrets," she whispered to herself. "What could a Deity teach me?" Perhaps the god would smite her from the universe, since they'd killed all but four of the Zan'ra. With the power Jules possessed handling the Arnap, it might have been the right call.

The symbol for Ravios was an interesting one, with a simple bird-shaped silhouette and a wavy line underneath. Jules located the icon and glanced toward the door, making sure she was alone in the room. She pressed the symbol, the room flashing white.

She appeared in the mysterious portal room, and instantly put a shield up, spotting a figure close by. The man was armed, and pointed a gun in her direction from ten meters away. He looked absolutely shocked to see someone arrive here, and almost dropped the weapon.

He said a few foreign words, but Jules didn't comprehend them. One of the newly-unlocked attributes of being a Zan'ra was deciphering languages with ease. It was a skill she was still honing, but after he called out more instructions, she was able to translate what he was saying.

She tested it, using his language in return, the words leaving her tongue feeling too large for her mouth. They came out with a thick accent, but he appeared to understand. "I'm not here for trouble."

He didn't lower the gun. It was dark, almost like it was cast from a heavy iron material, and the man himself was wide at the shoulders, his body narrow. "Where are you from?"

Now they were getting somewhere. Jules noted that the gun's aim began to shift toward the floor. "I'm here on Alliance business. Are you familiar with the Alliance of Worlds?"

He shoved the gun into a leather holster on his hip and

shook his head. "You speak Zecriun. How? And you have a shield generator. Is that technology for sale?"

Jules didn't want to explain it to him, so she took the easy approach. "I've had the translation modifications, and I might be able to connect you with a trader who's willing to barter. I'm Jules. Jules Parker."

If he recognized the name, he didn't show it. The man removed a hat, something that reminded her of an early twentieth-century kind that Papa called "bowler hats." She didn't know what they had to do with knocking pins over with a ball. His hair was long, slicked back, and he smiled, making him closer to handsome. "Artimi Fended. Pleased to meet you, Jules."

"What are you doing here?" she asked, still skeptical of the man's motivations. His skin had a light green tinge to it, but otherwise, he looked quite human.

"It's my turn to stand watch," he said.

Judging by his reaction at her arrival, they didn't have much company. "When was the last time someone came through?"

"A long time," he replied.

She started to move across the room, only now noticing the design of it. The floor was a rich wood, the walls a slate-gray stone. Lights were flickering from digital torches along the edges.

He didn't budge from blocking the exit. She noticed there was a chair, with food containers and water sitting beside it. A cot was centered in the hallway beyond him. He was living here.

"Can I get past you?" she asked.

"What is your purpose on Ravios?" Artimi asked.

"Not that it's any of your business, but I'm just passing through on my way to Elion." She managed to keep most of the annoyance from her voice.

He looked surprised again. "Elion. There's nothing out there for a girl like you."

She fumed at his presumptions but didn't show it. "What do you mean, nothing?"

Artimi put his hat back on and stepped aside, letting her through. "Like I said. Nothing but an old station and some long-abandoned mines."

"I'd still like to go."

"How are you getting there?" he asked.

"I'm going to buy a ship," she replied.

This made him laugh, a sharp mirthful sound. "I happen to have one. It's not for sale, but perhaps you'd care to employ me for a price."

The picture was growing clearer. Whoever Artimi was, he hung out near the portal and tried to con someone into hiring him as a tour guide, or whatever else they needed while stuck on the middle-of-nowhere planet Ravios. "I think I'll take my chances elsewhere."

There wasn't much information on Ravios in the Gatekeepers' network, and the data that had been accrued was at least a century old. All Jules knew was that the locals had interstellar, but rarely vacated their system. And that the people, the Zecrua, weren't very social. Her first impressions of Artimi didn't substantiate those findings.

He followed along behind her as she marched down the narrow corridor leading away from the Shandra, and didn't say anything as she climbed the set of stone steps heading above ground. Most of the Shandra were underground, and she slowed as she neared a double-doored exit.

"What are you waiting for?" he asked.

Jules kept the sphere, not willing to remove it yet. "Nothing." She pressed the button to the side of the doors, and they hissed, separating in the middle. She stepped through, finding a red sky, angry black clouds, and tiny specks in the air.

It was hot, too hot, and she had the distinct feeling she'd traveled to Hell for a moment. Beads of sweat formed on her forehead as she peered around, seeing no other people. Movement above caught her attention again, and she recognized the dark dots for what they were: animals. Flying birds. But they were too big to be…

Something swooped down from behind them, thick talons dragging along the stone ground. All she saw was a flash of red leather, vein-covered wings, and a dripping snout. It screeched, and another arrived, then another, and she stared at the sky as a horde of thousands of the huge winged beasts began circling before diving toward her.

"Now do you want to hire me?" Artimi smiled widely, and Jules nodded.

---

*W*ith Techeron less than a month away, I had a few things to finish up before we left for Fontem's collection, including checking on the Terellion and Regnig's progress. I flew in the shuttle over Haven, thinking how much had changed here since we'd first arrived. I tried not to count how many years had passed. While Mary and I were here that first time, Magnus and Nat had been moving with General Heart toward New Spero in a colony ship.

Back then it was unspoiled, with only a few buildings in a quiet village where the old Deltra Teelon befriended me after a tumultuous beginning to our relationship. Now the city stretched for miles past the actual city center, and towns had popped up in every direction, each with their own communities, schools, store fronts, and local growing zones.

It was nowhere as advanced as New Spero, or even our imaginative colonies on Earth, but it was quaint, with the idyllic smaller-town feeling that many of us had grown to appreciate. So many races had moved here since the creation of the Alliance of Worlds, and with the Academy being the central focus, the population had almost doubled since its inception.

I guided the shuttle above it all, smiling at how far we'd come as an alliance.

The Academy filled the viewscreen as I shifted the craft toward the school, landing near the instructors' residences, opting to visit Karo and Hugo before checking in with Regnig and Fontem. The shuttle settled gently, and I noticed the parking pad was mostly empty at this early hour. I'd forgotten to check what the local time was before departing *Light* through the portal room, but the sun was rising now, and I exited the transport, letting the chilly morning air blow against my face.

I missed the normalcy of living on Haven, but there was no returning to that again. I was the captain of a starship, and with what Lom of Pleva was attempting, and the complexity of the Zan'ra, I had too many things to manage.

Maybe once Lom was dealt with, and Jules, Patty, and Dean were safe, then I'd consider returning to the peaceful life I'd had a short taste of. As I walked toward Karo's place, I shook my head, laughing at the idea of me ever being truly happy on the sidelines. I knew Magnus had planned a retirement in a few years. He'd kept talking about fishing, watching his kids as adults, and enjoying his time with Nat. That had been taken from him.

I tried not to focus on it, but his death always had this natural way of sneaking up on me, no matter the situation I was in. Like he was urging me on, unable to leave my side for some reason.

"Dean, I wasn't expecting you so early," Karo said from behind me. He smiled widely, and I noticed that his cheeks were flushed and he was in workout gear.

"I hadn't pictured the Theos as the running type," I told him.

He patted his stomach. "How do you think I'm able to eat so much pizza?"

We walked to his door, and he unlocked it. Hugo sat at the table, his back to me, and he chatted with Karo and Ableen's four kids. They were joking and laughing, and it melted my heart to see my son in such a caring household. This was vibrant, a family atmosphere that would do Hugo well.

"Hello, Mr. Parker!" one of the quadruplets said. I thought it was Barl, but I hadn't been around enough lately to watch them grow up.

"Kids, good to see everyone."

Hugo was out of his chair, rushing toward me, and I lost my breath as we collided, squeezing in a tight hug. "Dad! What are you doing here?"

I glanced at Karo, and he shrugged. "I thought a surprise would be better."

"Are you taller?" I asked Hugo, even though he'd visited *Light* just two weeks ago. I couldn't believe how big he was getting. He was already stronger and more agile, and I thought the training at the Academy was doing wonders for the boy. Before this, all he'd been interested in was video games.

"Dad, I aced my portals exam!" he shouted, and I walked him to the table, arm over his shoulder.

"Is that so?"

He took his seat, and Karo Jr. moved aside, offering me a spot. Ableen entered the room, carrying a jug of juice, and smiled at me. "Dean, so good to see you," she said.

"Likewise. Thanks again for letting Hugo stay here. I know he can be a bit of a handful," I said, receiving an eyeroll from my son.

"Nonsense. I wish these four were as polite as he is." Ableen winked at Hugo, and he laughed as he returned to his breakfast.

Karo gestured toward the food. "Can I offer you something?"

"Sure, why not?" I grabbed a plate and dug in, chatting with the kids and the Theos adults, learning about what was happening at the Academy, but never fully able to concentrate. Not with the looming threats over my head. At that moment, *Light* was moving toward Techeron, and I still had far too many things to deal with before we figured out how to prevent the timeline merge.

"Time for class, kids," Karo said, and they all groaned, rushing away from the table and leaving it in a total mess. Hugo stood and started to clear the plates.

"Hugo, don't worry about that today. You'll be late," Ableen told him.

"Thank you. Dad, will you be here later?" Hugo asked.

It broke my heart, but I had to tell him. "No. I can't stay. You're coming next weekend, though, and your mother can't wait to see you." I wanted to tousle his hair, but it was combed nicely: another new thing about him I hadn't noticed before.

"Will Jules be there?" he asked.

"She should be," I told him.

"Is she… okay?" Hugo's big eyes stared at me, and I didn't want to lie to my son.

"Not quite. Soon."

He nodded solemnly and exited the room.

"Is it that bad?" Karo asked when none of the kids were around.

"She hardly eats. She's so consumed by all of this." I slumped in my seat and poked at a pancake with my fork. "I think if she can just find Dean…"

"It won't be over, even then. She needs a teacher," Karo said.

"A teacher?"

"Her powers are growing, Dean. Becoming more focused. You know what she's capable…" Karo stopped as the kids entered, each with a backpack over their shoulders. We said our goodbyes, and I witnessed how excited Hugo was as he darted off to his classes. The Theos children were almost in their final year, but they treated my son like one of their own brood. It was nice to see.

When they were gone, we started to clean up. "I know what she can do."

"Do you?"

"Well, I've seen some of it. That other girl, the one with the orange eyes… she could project herself." I stacked the dirty plates near the sink and leaned against the cabinets.

"You need to find her," Ableen said.

"Jules is trying, but how?"

"The Crystal Map formed two new locations around the same time as everything transpired last year. Sarlun refuses to let anyone investigate yet, but there has to be a reason. This hasn't happened since Jules fixed the portals more than a decade ago," Karo said.

I hadn't paid much attention to the Crystal Map over the years, not as much as I should have, but Jules kept a close eye on it. "I've heard about the new locations, but with everything happening, we haven't even talked with Sarlun to discuss them. What do you think their presence means?"

Karo loaded the dishwasher, placing the glasses in the top section while he spoke. "If Jules was the only one able to mend and expand the portals' reach, then I have to assume that another of the Zan'ra is responsible for these two."

"You're right. But what if it was Lan'i, or this O'ri within Patty?" I asked.

"They showed up before all that. I have to presume it was the other, the one…"

"Dal'i. And you think she could be Jules' teacher?" I asked, assuming what their answer would be. The married Theos couple nodded as one. "Okay, I'll talk with Jules about it when she's back."

"Where is she?" Karo asked, and I told him about Elion.

"I know you trust her, but it must be scary traveling around the universe on a solo mission like this. Trying to find Magnus and Natalia's son out there is like finding the thinnest needle in the largest haystack ever created." Karo paused and met my gaze. I saw pity in his eyes.

"She's up for the challenge," I assured him. "Anyway, Ableen, I'm about to visit with Regnig and Fontem. Do you mind if I borrow your husband for a few hours?"

She rested her cool palm on my forearm and smiled. "Any time." She wore a long dress, bright yellow star patterns over a navy-blue fabric. It was something Jules would like. Thinking about her made me wonder how she was doing, and I hoped she'd acquired transportation to the old Elion Station by now.

THREE

"*W*hat the hell are those?" Jules ran, her hands resting over her hair, knowing it would be futile against the swooping creatures.

"Those are the Frynu." Artimi was in front of her, sprinting along the side of the empty street. She could hear her own heavy breaths and the shrieking from the cloud of Frynu high in the sky.

Jules had so many questions, but she'd hold the inquiries until she wasn't running for her life. A few more arrived, landing on top of two-story brick buildings. They cawed at the pair of humanoids darting past them, but didn't move to attack.

She wondered where everyone was, and why the entire city appeared vacant. Jules infused more of her energy into her core, feeling the burning in her lungs subside, the ache in her legs ease. Artimi slowed his quick pace as they came upon the end of the street, and he turned left, waving for her to follow. The ship was landed in a parking lot, a few rusted wheeled vehicles sat near it.

It looked like a hunk of junk. They stopped as they neared the vessel, and Jules shook her head. "There's no way I'm getting in that thing. We'll die!"

Artimi had the decency to hide his emotions at the hurled insult. "It's a fine craft. But if you'd rather take your chances with the Frynu, be my guest."

She glanced at the sky, the red sun blazing fiercely. It blacked for a moment, the cloud of these creatures slowing and blocking the star in an eclipse. She shivered despite the heat and begrudgingly nodded. "Fine. But I'm not paying you if this thing implodes."

He activated a ramp, and they climbed the few steps, Jules hearing significantly more monsters gathering behind them. One was close, flapping its leathery wings, and she stuck her hand out, ready to obliterate it if necessary. The door slid shut, the monster striking the hull with a resounding thud.

The ship had a discolored exterior, with miscellaneous craft panels placed together in a mismatch of metallic shades. It was shaped like a shuttle, but five times the size, and she was impressed by how pristine it was inside.

"Will this suit your remarkable needs?" Artimi asked, grinning at his own comment.

"Fine. Take us out of here." The cargo hold was lined with neat rows of crates, and Jules noticed there was a locked energy container with various guns behind it. Jules followed him through the ship, toward the cockpit, which was roomier than she'd expected.

Now that the rush of arriving on this planet had subsided, she couldn't stop thinking about Dean. The news of his arrival in the system had reached them a day ago, but that was enough delay for him to be long gone.

"Any particular reason you're heading to Elion Station?" he asked curiously.

She watched as the strange man initiated his ship's start-up process, and jumped when something moved behind her. A robot stepped from a charging station and moved past her without comment as it took the seat next to Artimi.

Her pilot glanced back, frowning. "Not going to tell me? Fine, but you'll have to return somehow. There's nothing at that station, I'm telling you. You won't want to be stuck out there."

Jules didn't tell him that she could fly or move through space without the need of a ship. She was only doing this because of her parents. They might not be wrong, though. The last thing she needed was to lose her powers out here somehow and end up a frozen popsicle while Dean gallivanted through the universe alone, searching for Patty.

"I'm looking for someone," she whispered.

"Someone?"

"Yes. His name's Dean, and he's been spotted in Elion," she told him.

"I see. Lost love." The ship rumbled, lights flashing on the strange dash. She'd never seen something like it, with tiny flames glowing behind buttons and dark metal frames.

The cockpit had a bench behind the pilot's seat, and Jules sat there, observing through the viewscreen. More of the Frynu had arrived, and there had to be a hundred of the freakish beasts outside, their small beaks opening and closing, pulling their red flesh tight over their faces. It was unsettling.

"Can you tell me about this place now? What happened to Ravios?" she asked as their ship rose from the ground, heading up into the dark and angry sky.

"One of my people, the Zecrua, traveled to a distant world. You see, we have a general rule not to venture too far from home. We've seen the feeds a million times. As soon as you start joining coalitions, or making trade deals with other races, you're opening the door for war. We didn't want that," he said, focused on his task.

"There are a lot of good things that come with expanding your borders," she advised him.

He peered over at her, a smile on his face. "Aren't you a little young to have philosophical ideologies?"

She stifled an eyeroll and urged him to continue. "I have a feeling there's more to your tale."

"As it happens, one woman, along with her fool of a husband, decided to disobey our rules, and they traveled distantly, landing on some unknown world. It was devoid of intelligent life, or so they thought. They stumbled upon two creatures living in the wastelands. They were fragile, freshly out of eggs, their shells still within a mile of their location. This duo took it upon themselves to bring these two creatures home with them, to care for the babies."

Jules knew where this was going and didn't interrupt his narrative.

"They came here and kept the strange animals to themselves, nurturing them, until they grew larger than their caregivers. They noticed the eggs behind their house too late," Artimi said as the ship broke from the atmosphere, the star no longer red and imposing like it was below the ozone layer.

"How long ago was this?" she asked.

"Fifty years. After their first attacks, an entire town was nearly eaten. They grew from there, reproducing faster than should have been possible. They were a bane, a horrible plague on our people, and now we've abandoned Ravios." Artimi went silent, and Jules heard the robot beside him whirring and beeping gently. Its clumsy fingers moved over the keys, flipping switches every few minutes.

"Then why were you really there?" she asked.

"Where?"

"In the portal room."

"The what?"

Jules realized the word *portal* didn't translate, and she tried the other name. "Shandra?"

"I told you. I was hoping to sell…"

"Enough lying, Artimi." She felt the ability to be straight with this man. Her first instinct, at seeing him with a gun pointed at her, had been to not trust him. But as they interacted, she was starting to like him.

"Fine. I'm waiting for someone."

"Is that why you had food and a bed at the Shandra?"

He nodded, not answering.

"Who is it?" she asked.

"My brother."

"And… "

"He departed with everyone years ago, and we were separated on our ships. We made a deal to return here, to the Shandra."

"When was he supposed to show up?" she asked.

"Too long ago. I don't think he's coming," he told her. "We sent off ten ships, and our envoy was attacked halfway to Neeriox Twelve. We were separated, and these guys… they used a wormhole weapon against us."

Wormhole weapon? That was new. "You got lost?"

He shook his head. "Not me, but my brother's ship did. Two thousand people. He was with his kids, his wife."

The ship shook, the floor vibrating as they neared what appeared to be rows of debris. "How long until we reach Elion?"

Artimi peered at his robot, who spoke with an oddly-tuned voice. "We are fourteen hours from our destination," it said, sounding like a woman. Jules grinned in response to the feminine tone.

"What, she can't be a she?" he asked with a laugh. "Say hello to Betheal."

Jules smirked. "Hi, Betheal. I'm Jules."

"It's my pleasure to meet you," the robot said. Jules still found speaking another language so peculiar, but the more she used the ability, the easier it came.

"Artimi, can you tell me about these enemies, the ones that attacked your people?" she asked, settling into the seat as their clunky vessel darted through the specks of debris, each piece glowing as it burned into their shield.

"What do you want to know?" he asked.

"Where they came from, and how the wormhole weapons worked." Jules' intuition told her something about this was important: that she hadn't met Artimi by chance, but by fate, or the universe, or whatever it was that oversaw them.

"It's a heavy topic, but sure, it'll help pass the time." He started talking, and she listened closely.

———————

"Regnig, I think it's best if you join us," I told him again, trying to keep the urgency from my voice.

He shook his little head, his beak shifting open. *Dean, I think it's a younger man's endeavor.*

"I have an idea," Fontem said, and we all listened. "We can use the portable doorways and activate the other side when we arrive."

"Why didn't I think of that?" I asked, muttering to myself. I'd suggested it a half hour ago.

Regnig's tongue flicked out, and he grabbed one of his canes, hobbling over to the kitchen behind us. *I will think on it. I do long for some adventure, but I fear my knees have been acting up again. Some days are better than others.*

"Have you had anyone examine you lately?" Karo asked him.

Regnig paused, glaring at the Theos with his one large eye. *Such as a physician?*

"Sure, a doctor," Karo replied.

Never trusted them.

From what we could gather, Regnig was hundreds of years old, so he was probably doing fine without them, but I didn't say so. "You'll join us, then?"

He poured another tea, and I went to help him, refilling the rest of our cups.

I'll join you. It has *been getting a little stuffy down here.*

It was a rare occurrence to hear the small birdman complain about being in his libraries, and I smiled, knowing he was growing more used to spending time with people. He and Fontem had been working closely over the last few months, not to mention his consistent visits with Jules.

"Good. I'm glad you're coming," Fontem said.

"When's the last time you were there?" I asked the artifact collector.

"Probably four or five years before I was abducted," he answered.

"And you're sure no one will have found it after all this time?" I pressed.

"I doubt it."

"You realize that Polvertan located your other cache, right?" I couldn't help but mention it.

Fontem smiled and nodded. "I know. I should never have placed the Delineator in there, either. I'd stored it there because I didn't have a chance to head to my final destination with it."

"If we hadn't found it, I'd be dead." I thought of the device opening, shoving Lom of Pleva through it, and grimaced. I wished I'd managed to kill him instead. "Now that Regnig is coming, where are you with your research?"

We've determined there are references to merging timelines, only in smaller cases. There was a scientist tens of thousands of years ago, on a world called Ephor, who managed to test a theory on this, sealing himself in a time-proof isolation chamber. His name was Hanrion. He used a device similar to the Delineator, though much more basic. It allowed him to pause himself by seconds. He did this ten times, so the story goes, and then used another device to blend them together. This resulted in the scientist having ten different memories of that experiment, each slightly longer than the other. Regnig paused and took a sip of his tea.

This was bad. "What happened to him?" Karo asked.

He exited the chamber, transcribed his notes over the next few hours, told his assistants he felt fine, and went home.

Fontem swallowed hard, preparing for what came next. He glanced at me over his teacup and finished the tale for Regnig. "They found him the next day, dead in his bedroom."

"By his own hand?"

"That's how they recorded it." Fontem set the tea down and passed me a tablet. "If Lom found a way to build a device like this, we think he must have created something similar to Hanrion's gadget."

"Meaning we might want to check out that planet. Where is it?" I asked, looking at the tablet. I almost laughed but couldn't bring myself to. "The Arnap obliterated them thousands of years ago. This is our luck."

"They appear to have vacated the system far later, leaving it empty. We could check it out. There's a portal on Ephor, one Sarlun said was on the original no-fly list," Fontem said.

When we'd first started using the portals, half of the symbols were hidden. This was because they were deemed too dangerous for travel, or they were unexplored. With Jules patching the entire Shandra network, it had opened up a floodgate of locations, many never before seen. Most of the inhabitants on the planets with one of the crystal-powered portal rooms were unaware they held such treasure.

It was part of the reason we'd created the Gatekeepers' Academy. We needed to catalog and record information on thousands of planets. We were about twenty percent through even now.

"We haven't been there before. Who knows what we'll find?" I asked.

You do have nearly a month before Techeron. And Jules is always telling me how bored you are on these long journeys. Regnig blinked and passed what I figured to be a smile over his beak.

"Fontem, what do you think? Bring a team? See if we can find Hanrion's lab intact?" I doubted that was possible, after countless years and an invasion by the deadly Arnap, but it was worth a shot. If we could identify information on how he'd merged these timelines, we might be able to prevent Lom from doing the same.

"I think it's a good idea, and I've been cooped up in libraries for too many months. I'm starting to long for some adventure myself." He stood, stretching his back.

I rose too, shaking his hand. "Good to have you on board. We'll bring the team. Slate for muscle, Suma for brains." I almost felt bad for thinking of my good friends in such narrow lanes, but they'd be insulted if I didn't.

Be careful. Anywhere the Arnap once were could be dangerous.

We started for the door, but I stopped, remembering something Jules had said before she left. "Regnig, Jules spoke to the Deity."

She did? How is this so?

"You've heard she keeps going to that damned world she calls Desolate, right?"

He nodded.

"He was activated and told her to free them all, implying there are more. I need you to research any other planets with that symbol, the four circles with the X over them, and anything else that might help our search," I suggested.

I have been working on it but have been more focused on the Zan'ra and time travel challenges. I will shift to this. Are you planning on doing what it asks? Freeing them?

I shook my head. "I'm undecided, but I want the option." I hated how many moving pieces there were to our current situation. Old gods, a powerful enemy with unlimited resources trying to merge timelines for revenge, and my daughter learning about the Zan'ra and struggling to find her friends.

I glanced at Karo as we started to leave, knowing the Theos were an important piece to the universe. He'd been surprised to hear there were anything called "Deities" even out there, and that had shocked me. The universe was a vast place, where ancient gods thrived and died and never crossed paths.

I stopped Karo at the elevator's exit. "You want to come with us?"

He acted sheepish, staring at the ground. "I'll have to ask my wife."

----

*T*he chiming from the cockpit woke Jules from her light slumber. She'd been dreaming: of four circles, the X, and Patty with glowing purple eyes. The last thing she'd seen before opening her eyes was Dean trying to breathe, his face turning blue.

"Dean!" she called, sitting up straight.

"You're okay," Artimi said from ahead. "We're nearly there. You were talking in your sleep."

She wiped her mouth with a sleeve and stared out the

viewscreen. There were twin moons to either side, orbiting a dark brown planet. It didn't appear as though there was any water on the surface. "Is this Elion?" she asked.

Betheal, Artimi's robot, answered, "This is Elion. Current population listed at nineteen thousand four hundred and seventeen."

"That's not many for an entire planet," Jules muttered.

"If you've ever been there, you'd say it's more than enough." Artimi almost spat the words.

"What's it like?" She leaned over his seat, trying to garner a better view.

"Dirty. It had a solid century of disasters, volcanoes, tornados… anything you can think of, and it left the world a husk of what it once was. The oceans dried up, and now, the people fight over the remaining water catchment stations. It's bad."

"Why doesn't someone help them?" Jules thought the Alliance of Worlds would.

"It's too far gone. You try landing nearby, they'll tear you apart," he said, as if he had firsthand experience on the surface.

"They can't be that bad."

"Well, they are, and then some," Artimi added.

"Where's the station?" she asked, wishing she was floating through space alone, without the company of this loner and his robotic partner.

"Ahead." He pointed to the radar screen, and she spotted the small blinking indicator light. Was Dean still there?

Something didn't sit right. "How could someone have seen my friend out here? If the world is full of trouble, and the station is derelict…"

"There's a secondary station, one people like me use when passing through. Ship components, food supplies, weapons…"

"Like a junkyard trading post?" Jules asked, feeling the sting of the comment.

"Sure. Something like that. All I ask is that you be cautious when we arrive. There's no other post like this for four systems, so this one gets more traffic than you'd expect," he told her.

"We're not heading there. We need to hit Elion Station first," she ordered him.

"Look, I need supplies, and you're supposed to pay me. We're making this deal first, then we'll see if your boyfriend is hiding in the old space station, okay?" Artimi's voice lowered, and he frowned deeply, indicating there was no other option.

"Fine, but let's make it quick."

They continued the rest of the trip in relative silence, Jules watching for signs of the older space station in the viewscreen. She thought she spotted it to her left, but at that moment, Artimi changed trajectories, and their destination came into view. Another ship coursed above them, large thrusters pulsing as it moved for the docking bay.

The station was unnamed, according to her pilot.

"What do you call it, then?" she asked him as he slowed propulsion, moving toward an empty dock.

"The Hub." The ship latched along the upper ring over the floating structure. It didn't appear special; it was clearly visible where the original station had been erected and where the proprietors had added onto it over the years. To her shock, there were over twenty vessels parked here, and she even recognized a Padlog ship among them. She wondered what one of the Alliance of Worlds members was doing at such a shady establishment.

The station had three rings around it, rotating for gravity. Jules followed Artimi as he stalked through his ship, heading for the exit. Betheal remained in the cockpit as per his instructions and had silently returned to her charging port.

Jules glanced at herself, seeing the pristine white uniform of the Gatekeepers.

"Do you have anything… less conspicuous to wear?" Artimi asked.

With his matching suit and bowler hat, she thought he might be the one that stood out between the pair of them. Jules shook her head. "This is everything I brought."

"That won't do. Let's see what I have." Artimi rummaged through several crates, casting lids aside as he searched through them. She had half a mind to leave, exit the station, and float over to the other one, but she needed to show some patience. That was what her mom would tell her. Papa would be thinking the same thing as her.

He returned a few minutes later with a black cloak constructed from patches of leather. It was lighter than she'd expected, and Jules slid it over her shoulders. It draped to her shins, and she kept the cowl off her head.

"Now, for those eyes… try these." He pulled tinted goggles from his pocket, and she groaned.

She placed them over her head, adjusting the strap so they stayed secure. Everything turned a few shades darker.

"Perfect. I can't tell you have glowing green eyes. Which, you'll notice, I haven't harassed you about." He shifted on his feet, hands finding his hips. "Last part. Time to talk about our payment."

"What's fair to you?" she asked, surprised he hadn't negotiated before the trip. She could have been lying to him. Then she'd be stuck, or at least, that was what he would assume.

"I was thinking a thousand credits," he suggested, his expression impassive.

It was a lofty sum, but Jules didn't have time to barter.

"Look, all I have is this." She reached into the cloak and to the front pocket of her uniform. Her hand clutched one of the Inlorian bars, and she pulled it out, leaving two behind.

It was the first time she'd seen the façade of the confident pilot falter. His eyes narrowed, and she noticed his hand move toward the gun at his hip, as if this were a setup. She was prepared for an attack, but none came.

"Where did you find that?" His voice was small.

"I'm surprised you even recognize it," she told him.

"That's my ticket out of here," he said, with a slight waver to his words.

"What about your brother?" she asked.

He took a step toward her, making her take one back. "He's gone. I've been here too long, and I needed you to remind me there was more than that cot and those four walls."

"Gather your supplies, we ask after Dean, and then you bring me to the station. If I need to leave, you take me to Ravios, right?" Jules wasn't going to enjoy returning to the place littered with huge insatiable demons, but she'd be okay.

He jutted his hand out, palm up, and she slid the bar into it. He gripped it tightly, clutching it to his chest. "Deal." Artimi tipped the brim of his bowler cap to her, and the bar disappeared into his coat. "Time to go." He pressed the ramp open, and they emerged from the ship onto the docking corridor. The space was cramped and dark, and they entered the central station after crossing the one-hundred-meter throughway.

"You know where you're going?" she asked, squinting behind the tinted lenses. She was sure she looked stupid, which would normally matter to a teenage girl, but he was right. Out here, she needed to be more cautious.

The circular room was empty, but someone sat behind

a desk. It had scales and two heads, each with a flickering angry tongue lapping at the air.

"Business?" both heads asked in unison. They spoke the same language as Artimi, telling her they knew him.

"Supplies," he said. The heads bobbed up and down, and it keyed something onto a screen.

A light flashed, sending a scanner beam over the two of them, and Jules flinched as it receded.

"Common procedure. They want to control who's on and off the station at all times," he whispered as they walked past the desk toward an elevator.

The large metal doors were tall enough to accommodate all sizes of visitors, and they slid shut with a bang. Gravity almost vanished as they lowered, Jules' feet nearly lifting from the floor. Artimi observed it with quiet acceptance, and soon they stopped, the doors opening to bustling activity.

"This is the central Hub, where everyone sells their wares. Keep close. Don't try to stand out in any way. And whatever you do, don't take those goggles off," he ordered her.

Jules didn't like being bossed around by the stranger, but it was his arena, not hers, so she'd have to listen to his suggestions. There were so many unfamiliar beings here, from lizard-like people to an entity in a gaseous state. She heard its thoughts as it moved through her without seeming to care.

"Where do you hear news?" she asked.

"Everywhere." The room was round, and the vendors had small unlabeled storefronts, as if anyone visiting would already know what each of them held. This one had what appeared to be a bald woman, her skin flaking like she'd had a terrible sunburn.

"Artimi, what a pleasant surprise," the woman said, her

voice high and airy.

"Nuul, meet Jules. I need some goods," he said.

"The usual?" she asked.

Jules peered over the counter, where numerous stacks of square canned goods were stamped with alien labels.

Artimi shook his head. "Better triple it, and… I'm trying to help Jules here track someone down."

"Is that so? And do you think I'd know anything about that?" she asked. Her skin was pink, and more flakes fell, being replaced by others. Jules had never seen anything like it.

"Nuul, you know everything around this place."

Jules smiled as she watched Artimi butter up the vendor. She leaned toward them and put a skinny hand to her mouth. "It'll cost you."

Artimi smiled, sliding the Inlorian bar onto the table. "I hope you have change."

FOUR

"*A*re you sure this is such a good idea?" Mary asked. Our place felt so empty without the kids. Maggie was at my feet, snoring on her side, but otherwise, it was deadly silent in our suite.

"Is it ever a good idea to go wandering to a planet once occupied by the Arnap?" I asked, mostly joking, but Mary didn't seem to find amusement in my words.

"I'm coming with you," she said. She sat close, our knees touching, but she pulled away as if she were angry with me.

"You can't come, honey. Jules might return home, and if anything happens to…"

She grabbed my hand. "Don't say it. You'll be fine. I'm not worried about that. Slate's with you too, which eases my mind a bit. Honestly, I don't even want to go. I'm tired of doing this."

"Doing what?" I asked.

Her arm raised, her finger circling over her head. "This. All of this. First it was saving the world, then finding the Theos, then stopping Lom, and now we're talking about time travel and Deities. It's too much, Dean. All I wanted was to work on the board of the Alliance, make a real difference. And here we are, you the captain of *Light,* and look at us…"

"Mary…"

"Let me finish. You're leaving again. Jules is God knows where, and Hugo's at the Academy—not because we want him to become a Gatekeeper, but because we're scared to bring him into danger with us. This can't go on," she said, a single tear falling over her cheek.

"We don't have a choice," I told her.

"Why does it have to be us? Why can't someone else do it?" she asked.

"Because Jules has the essence of a Zan'ra inside her, and I'm a Recaster." I said the last quietly. "And you said you wanted me to become the captain of this ship."

"That was before I knew what was going to happen. We were supposed to drop off some friends we saved from the Collector. They were diplomatic missions, and I thought I might be able to talk a few of them into joining our Alliance, expanding our reach. But now… there's too much at stake," Mary said. She rarely spoke like this, and I could tell she'd been thinking about these things for a while. Bottling them up.

"Do you want me to stay here?" I asked.

"No. Go to Ephor, find Hanrion's lab, and learn what you can," Mary said.

I wiped her tear streak away and kissed her softly. "I will."

"And finish it. I'll help Jules find Patty when she brings Dean home, and together, we're going to end this once and for all," she told me with resolve.

"And after that?" I asked, wondering if this was my last chance at adventure.

"We'll talk," she said, finally breaking and giving me a smile.

"I'd better go," I told her.

She helped me gather my suit and supplies, and walked

with me as we headed toward deck two and the ship's portal. Slate and Suma chatted with the stationed guards near the entrance, each in their EVAs. Fontem and Karo were just inside the doorway, suited up as well.

"Boss, you look rested." Slate glanced at Mary. "We'll be home soon."

Mary set a hand on his arm and nodded. "Make sure of it."

I was leaving my wife alone on the ship, with most of the bridge crew coming with me. Loweck was in charge while we were absent, much to Sergo's chagrin. Somehow the ex-thief expected me to give him autonomy in my absence.

I said my last goodbye to Mary, and we all gathered near the glowing crystals, the green color reminding me of Jules. The door closed, and we stood in a circle around the table while Suma found Ephor's symbol. We knew next to nothing about the world, since the Gatekeepers hadn't catalogued it, and we were solely relying on Regnig's information. We had an old digital map on a tablet Fontem held, which we should be able to decipher once our drones took to the sky.

Suma's snout wiggled beyond her helmet's visor, and she stared at me. "Captain, are we ready?"

"Let's do it."

The room went bright, but the whiteness didn't fade for me.

I wanted to leave, to join the others on Ephor, but was stuck behind, somewhere between the portals. It had been years since this had happened to me, and I looked around the white expanse, searching for a sign of the older me.

"Hello!" I shouted, but the words didn't echo. Quite the opposite. It sounded like I yelled against an acoustical wall.

I gazed down, seeing my feet weren't planted. I floated in the void, not as fearful as I had been before.

A dot glistened in the distance, and I called to it again, with no response. It felt like ten minutes before the figure arrived, stepping towards me. I waved at it, thinking it had to be the same Not-Dean that had visited me previously.

"What kind of riddle do you have for me this time?" I muttered under my breath.

Something was wrong. The starkness of the void began growing darker, and I caught the outline of the figure as it neared. This person was huge. It was hard to tell from this distance, but I guessed he was at least two feet taller than me, twice as wide, and it clicked.

"Lom…"

His scarred face twisted in a half grin, since the other side was made of metal. He wore a black shirt over matching pants, covering the metallic parts of his cyborg body. "Dean Parker," he said, his voice grating and deep.

"How are you doing this?" I asked.

"You should ask yourself, since he's the one I tortured to figure it out." He smiled again, and I cringed at the idea of Lom with older Dean, forcing information from me.

"What do you want?" I asked, trying to act calm and sure of myself. I felt the polar opposite. My heart raced, my hands trembling.

He was close enough for me to witness his terrible expression. His smile made me sick. "I just wanted to see you, Dean. One more time."

"So this is it?" I asked. "Finally retiring?"

"Always quick with the jokes." He lingered a good ten meters from me, hands at his sides. "Do you remember what I said that day?"

I thought about them, each word etched into my memory.

"I'll take your beaten body and make you watch as I kill your child, then your wife. You'll view it all from above as I destroy New Spero, and then, as I hunt every damned human out there, you'll be by my side, broken, without a tongue to argue, with no hands to fight. You'll watch your people all die, and then, only then, will I consider letting you join them."

So much had happened, and Jules had just been born. Sixteen years had passed, but I knew those words like he'd spoken them yesterday. I wasn't going to offer that, though. "Was it something about wanting to go on a trip through time?" My tiresome jokes were going to catch up with me one day.

He smiled again, waving a long finger at me. "I meant every word. Don't think that anything's changed, Parker. I *will* kill them all. And you *will* watch."

I shivered but tried to regain my confidence. I had no idea if he could harm me in here, but I didn't think so, or he'd have acted by now. "We'll deal with that when the time comes," I told him. "In the meantime, why don't you get a good look?"

His half-brow furrowed, the other side metal and un-moving. "At what?"

I sneered. "At the guy who's going to kick your ass when we meet again."

He laughed, the sound slight, growing in volume with each passing heartbeat in my chest. "You are something, Parker. This version of you thought he was funny too, but his fingers broke just the same. His eyes burned precisely like yours will."

The darkness around him began to fade, and his form slowly floated away from me. His time was up. I needed more information, something to go by.

"They betrayed you, you know. Did you really think we couldn't find out how you were communicating with them through time?" I asked, trying to sound casual.

He shook his head, and I heard him muttering something. "…trusted a Padlog…"

I tried not to look shocked at the revelation and instantly thought about Sergo. I'd left my bridge crew nearly empty-handed, and two of them were Padlog.

Lom continued moving, the white void brightening until I could no longer see him. When the light dissipated, I saw my friends huddled over me. I was on the ground, hard-packed dirt breaking my fall.

"What happened, boss?" Slate asked, concern etched on his face.

I sat up, feeling totally fine other than a trace headache creeping through my brain. "It was him."

"The Not-Dean?" Suma asked, stepping back to give me some room.

"No. Lom of Pleva."

---

*J*ules and Artimi were in the storage room behind the vendor's storefront, and Nuul arrived, wiping her hands over a blue smock. Flakes fell off her fingertips onto the floor, and Jules watched them drift upwards as a vent blew air.

"I'm Maulo. I take it you haven't seen one of us before?" she asked Jules in Artimi's language.

Jules shook her head.

"We molt every seven years. Basically, we rejuvenate each organ, starting fresh. I'm about a third of the way through, so you'll have to excuse the mess," she said, smiling. Jules noticed she was missing all her teeth.

"I didn't mean to stare," Jules said truthfully.

"It's okay. So you're searching for the human?" Her

gaze lingered on Jules, who nodded.

"He was here two days ago. Was asking if someone could bring him to the station. I think Loplin helped him out."

Artimi smiled. "Loplin? Knowing that guy, they're still on their way. His ship is a piece of junk."

Jules didn't remind Artimi that his ship wasn't all that great either. "Did you hear his name? See what he looked like?" It had to be Dean, but she wasn't taking any chances.

"Young. Light brown hair, a smile that's sure to attract a few human girls," Nuul said lightly.

"That's him," Jules confirmed. "Come on. Time to go." She stood, but Artimi remained seated.

"Not so soon. We haven't finished our drinks yet." He sipped from a brown bottle, and Jules smelled a fragrant beverage.

She stayed standing but decided to ask another question. "Nuul, if you hear everything, has anyone mentioned someone out there with glowing eyes?"

Nuul brushed at her arm where a piece of her skin faded to gray, sending it to the floor. "I've heard a few things. Apparently, there's a daughter of some Alliance leader with green eyes. I can't believe the rumors around that one, though."

Without moving her head, Jules glanced at Artimi, curious if he'd break their confidence. When he took another drink instead, she spoke. "Why? What makes you question it?"

"The fact that she can fly, and she fought off Earth's invaders when the Kraski attacked. That she's destroyed an entire Arnap fleet. Two hundred thousand of their people." Nuul snapped her fingers loudly. "Gone. Poof."

Jules wanted to tell her it was only twenty thousand, and that she'd been born years after the Event, but kept her mouth shut. "Anything else? Anyone with other colored eyes?" she asked tentatively.

"You are an inquisitive one, aren't you?" Nuul rose, smiling at Artimi. "I think it's time to go."

He shook his head. "We paid you well. Better than well. Answer the girl's questions."

She sighed. "Sure. Guy came here last month, said he was heading through the Golnex system. Apparently, the locals saw a pair of them searching in the mountains. Didn't talk to anyone, and when they were approached, the two attacked, injuring five or so."

Jules' chest tightened. That was them. "Where was this?"

Nuul shrugged. "Golnex system, like I said. Not sure about the planet."

"Did they find what they were after?" Jules asked. If they were searching for something, she had a feeling what it was. The Deities.

"No way to tell. Is that about it?" Nuul was called from the front, and a man poked his head in the back, asking for her help. "Take care of yourself, Artimi. Thanks for the business. Bring another of those around, and we'll be even closer friends."

She left them alone, and Artimi placed his hat over his slicked hair and set the bottle on a wooden table beside his chair. "Are we good?"

Jules nodded. Without this man's help, she wouldn't have heard this tidbit. "Can we get out of here?"

"I'm on it."

Ten minutes later, she and Artimi were at the ship, and with Betheal's help, they loaded the ten crates of supplies up the ramp and into the cargo hold. Jules wiped her brow as they finished, and removed the tinted goggles as the ship sealed closed.

"What are you?" he asked.

"You don't want to know," she told him.

"Fine, but I'll figure it out somehow."

"What are you doing with all this stuff?" she asked, thinking about his nest near the portal.

"It's time to move on. There's more for me than waiting on someone who's not coming back." He left her there; Betheal walked past her as they moved for the bridge.

A few moments later, Jules felt the rumble of the ship's engines in the pads of her feet, and she finally wound her way to her seat, hoping like hell Dean was still on Elion Station.

The trip should have taken an hour, but there was debris from an errant asteroid that the locals had decided to break apart rather than redirect. Artimi guided his ship slowly, claiming he didn't want any damage to his shields, especially to the hull.

Jules thought some dents might be an improvement but kept her musings to herself. Artimi probably wouldn't appreciate the joke.

She felt different now, lighter than she had since discovering Uncle Magnus was dead. She was close to Dean, she knew it.

Finally, it came into their viewscreen, and she hopped up from her seat when she spotted the docked ship along its outer edges. The station itself was completely dark, making it difficult to see the outline against the black space beyond.

As they neared it, she understood the shape better. It was comprised of four towers, each connected by large passageways along the top and bottom. In the center of the station, there was a giant sphere. The entire thing was unique, unlike anything she'd ever viewed.

"Welcome to Elion Station," Artimi said with a

flourish.

He neared the docking bay where the compact vessel of Dean's hired guide sat, lights dimly glowing from the small thrusters behind it. As they moved to the edge, Artimi's ship almost bumping into the station, Jules found her happiness converting to something else: anger. She was mad at Dean for leaving her. He'd abandoned his own mother in her time of need, and he had to see how foolish and selfish that was.

She choked back her emotions, clenching a fist as she watched Artimi attach the ship to the old dock system.

"You're going to need to wear a suit," he told her. "There's been no gravity, no air recyclers on this thing for the last fifty years or so."

"I won't be needing the suit," Jules said, not wanting to wait the additional five minutes it would take to strap into an EVA.

Artimi lifted from the pilot's seat, and turned to face her. "Okay, I don't understand how you're going to…"

She sent her sphere out, green light crackling in a perfect circle around her.

"I keep forgetting you're not…"

She waited for him to say "normal" or "human", but he stopped short.

Something chimed from the dash, and Betheal used her clunky fingers to tap at the screen. "Sir, there's incoming."

Artimi bent over the console, muttering under his breath. "Damn it. Three incoming vessels."

Jules saw the dots blinking across the screen slowly, in their direction. "What kind of ships?"

"Does it matter? No one should be out here… not this far out, and not to Elion Station. No one gives two credits about this place; they haven't for years. Why, all of a sudden, is it so important?" he asked.

Jules noticed his hand wasn't far from his gun. "I have no idea who that is," she told him.

"Sir, I have identified them as Padlog," Betheal said.

"Padlog?" Jules recalled seeing one of their ships at the last station, but she hadn't spotted any of them in the market. "We're in an alliance with the Padlog. They wouldn't want to harm us." Would they? Papa would tell her to be cautious, that anyone could be turned under the right circumstances, and that any faction of a race could go rogue. Jules was confident the Supreme wouldn't turn against them, but that didn't mean all of his people thought the same.

"Either way, they'll be here in..." Artimi's fingers keyed the dashboard, "...forty minutes."

"Then we'd better hurry," she said, running down the corridor toward the ship's exit. She used the ramp, sealing the airlock off first. Artimi arrived, banging on the round window.

She read his lips and briefly heard his words. "Get back in thirty minutes or I'm leaving without you!"

Jules stepped onto Elion Station, wondering where Dean was.

FIVE

*E*phor wasn't what I'd expected. The place had long ago been invaded. Hanrion had been around tens of thousands of years ago, so I didn't expect to find much, but if there was a clue about how his time travel testing case worked, it was here.

The portal was hidden, concealed in a remote valley ten kilometers from the nearest city. We'd considered bringing the hoverbikes, but without knowing the terrain, we'd elected to use the hoverpacks instead. I had never been overly comfortable with them, but Slate was an old pro.

I still remembered using them for the first time on the ice world where we'd found the clue to the Iskios' location as we searched for the Theos. That hadn't ended well, so I hoped this journey would be a lot smoother sailing.

The valley was cold. Snow drifted from the thick cloud cover, blocking any signs of the system's star. Bare trees enveloped us, their leaves rotting on the forest floor. I listened for signs of wildlife, but heard none.

"When did the Arnap invade?" I asked Fontem.

"We aren't sure. It's been thousands of years, Dean," he told me. "There shouldn't be anyone living here now."

"This place gives me the creeps," Slate said.

Karo had remained silent, and he stood ahead of us, staring towards the valley.

"Suma, what do you think? Head for the peaks in that direction?" I pointed to where Karo was looking.

She nodded. "Use the packs, scope our destination. There should be a city about twenty kilometers ahead." She showed me her tablet, and I saw the rough map with the handful of landmarks etched on it.

"And Hanrion?" Slate asked.

She touched the screen farther out, a distance I judged to be at least three hundred kilometers. "That's going to take a while."

Slate patted the discreet hoverpack strapped to my shoulders. "Not as long as you think. How come we can never find a world to visit that has warm weather and sandy beaches? It's always snow, or prison worlds, or ghost wraiths… remember the size of those mosquitoes when we tracked down Polvertan?"

I laughed. "You're right, Slate. Next time we have to send the team out, you get to pick the location, okay? I think it's called a vacation."

"Dean Parker at a swimming pool, reading a book. That's not something I can picture," Fontem said.

"You're probably right. I'd be at the beach instead. Enough kidding around. We have a job to do here. Once we locate Hanrion's city, we need this information. It may be the only way we can fight what's coming." Lom of Pleva had been too real. Seeing him after all this time had solidified my fears. He still wanted to kill my family, not to mention every last human. This information might prevent that from happening.

Slate was the first one to power up his pack, the thrusters glowing as he used the hand-held controls, launching himself twenty meters into the air. I went next, and heard Fontem shouting in his native tongue as he fumbled with the controls.

Suma was proficient with it, and Karo was the last to rise from the ground, remaining behind us. He was oddly quiet today, but I knew it had been a while since he'd left his wife and children like this, so he was adapting to the moment.

Part of me longed to feel the wind against my face as we flew through the valley, but not wearing a helmet would have been foolish. The air was breathable, according to Suma's tests, but we kept the helmets on, hoping we didn't need their protection.

We flew in a line now, all five of us, staying a few meters from the ground in case one of the units malfunctioned. We wouldn't have far to fall. The valley turned, and the majestic mountain ridges beside us grew in height, the tops of these peaks snow-capped. There were a few red trees here, something similar to Earth's conifers. They stood like tall auburn Christmas trees along the mountainsides.

Eventually, we had to rise with the inclining slope, and after a few minutes, we stopped at the top of the ridge. The first city was in the distance. One by one, we landed, our boots puffing up snow as we hit ground.

Slate was the first to pull binoculars, and he spoke clearly through my earpiece. "The Arnap were definitely here." He passed them over, and I gawked at the sights.

Half of the city was a crater the size of a canyon. Around it were a couple of giant vessels, the same kind we'd seen through the wormhole a few months ago: the Arnap warships Jules had torn apart with nothing but her mind. "Think there's anyone around?" I asked.

Suma held another pair of binocs up, seeing what I saw. "I doubt it. They probably settled their ships nearby, and maybe those ones were damaged in the initial invasion. Happens all the time. Someone attacks and suborbital defenses kick in, taking some of them down. The Arnap likely used residual pieces and components to repair other vessels, leaving these behind."

Slate nodded along and turned to us. "Keep going?"

I considered checking this city out, but our destination lay a couple hundred kilometers away, and I'd promised Mary I'd be as fast as I could. "Let's move." I hit the sky first, the pack becoming more comfortable the longer I used it.

We traveled around the city on the off chance anything was there, watching and waiting.

It went fast, and in another hour, we'd passed by two huge lakes and found our destination along the second body of water's shoreline. This was no city, not like the first one we'd seen, and there was no evidence of an attack. The buildings were in ruins, disintegrated by thousands of years of weather. Most of the structures seemed metallic in nature, but even they had turned rust-brown, sun-paled, and unkempt.

I couldn't picture the locals since I had no viable description of them. The streets were overgrown with vegetation, trees jutting from the fronts of buildings, leaning toward the water. I tried to guess the population and deemed it had been a village of maybe five hundred at its peak.

This was where Hanrion had worked, doing high-level time-travel experiments long before humans were banging clubs against woolly mammoths.

The buildings were without windows, making them akin to old dystopian complexes. Not very inviting.

We landed along the water's edge, and the eerie feeling continued to course through me. Judging from how silent everyone was, I wasn't the only one experiencing this.

"What is it?" Karo asked, staring at the nearest six-story structure. The wind had stopped, and everything around us was totally calm. I peered at the lake and noticed it was as still as a sheet of glass.

Fontem stepped toward the building and paused, speaking into his mic. "It's time. There's something disrupting it." He stepped closer to the building, and it happened.

Suddenly, Fontem was behind us.

"What the hell was that?" I spun around, searching for him ahead, but he was gone.

Fontem lifted his hand, wiggling his gloved fingers. "It… I was in there. How long was I gone?"

My words caught in my throat, and Suma answered for us. "Fontem, you weren't gone. You were there, warning us that something was disrupting time, then you were behind us."

Fontem fell to his seat, sitting in the pebble-covered beach. "I was in the village for at least an hour. Alone. You weren't there. I couldn't find any of you."

I peered toward the building and started forward. Slate grabbed my arm. "Boss, you don't want to do that."

I shrugged him off. "We need to see what's inside. Fontem, what can you tell me?"

He stared at the complex a hundred meters ahead.

I crouched near him, grabbing his EVA by the collar. "What did you see?"

"I don't know. I went inside, but… I think someone was in the time bubble," he absently answered. It was like he wasn't fully present.

"Who?"

"Hanrion, maybe?"

I hiked over to the last line Fontem stood at before disappearing. "Suma, what do you think could be causing this?"

She wiggled her snout. "I have no idea. If Hanrion created a time distortion, it might have settled here after he died."

I glanced at Fontem, who was still seated, mumbling to himself. "Was it dangerous?" I asked him. He blinked and finally looked up, and I wondered if he'd even heard me. "Fontem. Was it dangerous?"

"I… don't think so."

I took a step forward, and then another. I heard Slate call out, but it was too late. I entered the time bubble.

———————

*J*ules wasn't a stranger to working without gravity, and with her abilities, she made quick work of the first corridor. She hovered in the center of it, floating to the door. The power was off, and had been for years, but all it took was a sprinkle of her energy shooting from her hand to the keypad to bring it to life. The old door split open from the middle, and she continued on.

The station wasn't that intimidating, and she considered the shape of it. She was near the outer edge now and would be arriving at one of the four towers if she continued. She could scour it and move to the next. Jules guessed this could take an hour, maybe two, and Artimi had given her thirty minutes. She'd already wasted five of them getting here.

Jules activated a light drone, clipping the lower half to her jumpsuit. She let it leave her sphere, sending it ahead, and floated after it as fast as she could. The pathways connecting the towers were metal: walls, floor, and ceiling. No art. No screens. No windows. It was built for function and nothing more.

She wanted to call out for Dean, but not yet. Wherever he was, he wouldn't be able to hear her muted demands from this hallway.

Jules came upon another door and did the same trick, entering the first tower. The room was large, with an elevator in the middle of it. No stairs. She floated in a circle around the space, discovering nothing useful. Instead of moving on, she entered the elevator doors, finding them absent of a lift.

She floated up the shaft, the drone illuminating the way above her. She tried the next floor, and the next, until she reached the elevator box. She used her powers to cut a square entrance out of the bottom section and pushed it aside, the section floating in the zero gravity. Once she was on the top floor, she scrutinized the room.

There was more here. It looked like there were rooms: at least two dozen small bedrooms, most of which had been picked clean. Nearly everything around the old station had been removed, likely by scavengers over the years. The place was almost entirely empty, making her search that much faster.

What time did she have remaining? Twenty minutes? Fifteen?

She was focused on the task at hand: locating Dean. Jules entered the next walkway and raced to the next tower, finding much the same. But at the third one, she paused, hearing noise through the elevator shaft.

Jules entered it, lowering toward the source of the sound.

"You can't leave. I haven't uncovered it yet." Dean's voice was muffled, and Jules pried the shaft doors open to see him in an EVA, holding the wall with his left hand.

"Dean!" she shouted, and the look on his face said it all. She'd been worried that he'd be angry at her for tracking him down; that he'd resent her, or that he didn't care about her. But the softness in his eyes, the smile that hit his cheeks, told her otherwise.

"Jules…"

"Who's this?" the other man asked. He was short and stocky, with one arm.

"Loplin?" Jules asked him.

He nodded gruffly, his tusks clicking against his face-mask. "What's it to you?" He spoke a rough English, which surprised her.

"You're free to go," Jules told him dismissively.

Loplin didn't need to be told twice. "Crazy kid. Dragging me out to Elion Station. There isn't anything here…" He exited abruptly, bounding from the walls down the corridor.

"Jules. How did you find me?" Dean asked, his smile gone.

"I have my ways." She floated toward him. "We need to leave."

"Why? I haven't seen anything out about the Zan'ra here yet."

"It doesn't matter. I have a lead," Jules told him. She stared at him and saw how tired he looked. It was hard to tell in the bad lighting, but he was paler, maybe thinner in the face.

"I haven't checked the center section yet," Dean said. "Maybe there's something about their homeworld…"

"There are three Padlog ships destined for here, and Artimi doesn't think they're friendly." Jules floated right in front of him, grabbing his arms.

Dean didn't resist. "Who's Artimi, and why would we run from the Padlog?" he asked.

"There's a lot developing right now, and you'd know that if you'd stayed with us. We could have done this together. You've spent seven months chasing Patty, and I've had to follow your trail," Jules said, unable to stop herself. This wasn't how she'd pictured their reunion.

He shook her hands off. "I didn't ask you to find me. Did you ever think that Patty wouldn't have been taken if it wasn't for you…?"

He seemed to be aware of his words the second they left his lips, but the damage had been done.

Jules turned, starting away.

"Look… I'm not blaming you, Ju."

She stopped, fuming. "Then why did you leave? Why did you leave your friends, your mother… me? I needed you too, Dean. Auntie Natalia needs you."

"I had to leave. If I'd stayed there, I'd have gone insane. My dad's dead. Patty's gone! I couldn't sit around *talking* about it," he said, this time quietly.

"True, but we could have done it together."

Dean's head hung down, and he looked much younger in his EVA than she'd thought of him in her mind since he'd vanished. "You said you had a lead."

She nodded. "I do. They've been sighted. We'll start there. Just come with me."

"Where?"

"Home."

"I don't know where that is anymore," he admitted.

"You can feel sorry for yourself later. For now, we have about five minutes to return to the ship I've rented before Artimi leaves without us," she told him.

"We'll never reach the dock in time," Dean said.

She extended her sphere, enclosing Dean inside, and began circling through the corridor, with the drone guiding their route. It went quickly, and she burst onto the ship as the vessel's engines roared fully to life, and closed the ramp, shutting her energy sphere off, spilling Dean to the cargo hold's floor.

He sat up, unclasping his helmet and letting it fall to his side. "That's one way of doing it," he said.

Jules helped him to his feet and couldn't refrain any longer. She wrapped her arms around him, squeezing him tightly.

"Jules, you're…"

She kissed him, not willing to let the moment go. It was quick, not filled with passion, but worry and love. When they broke apart, he stood there silently.

"You missed my birthday," she told him.

"I'm sorry."

"It was my sixteenth. Can you imagine how much fun that was with Hugo, Mom, and Papa? I didn't even wear a dress… not that I wanted to."

"Right. Again, I'm sorry. I…" Dean ran a hand through his hair, which was longer again. "I was possessed by this idea of finding her."

"And then what? What were you going to do?" Jules asked, tapping her foot impatiently.

"I was going to bring her home."

She thought even he didn't believe that story. "How? She has O'ri's powers now. She wouldn't have agreed to it. She could have killed you."

"I wanted to tell her about Dad. She needs to know," Dean said firmly.

Jules shook her head. "Promise me you're done going solo. It's going to get you killed. Then I'd be alone."

He shrugged.

"What would your mother do? Do you ever think about anyone but yourself?" Jules hated having to say it, but it was how she felt.

To her shock, Dean didn't defend himself anymore. "You're right."

"I take it we're done here?" Artimi walked into the room with his arms crossed.

"You bet," Jules told him.

Artimi started to walk away. "Good, because the Padlog have arrived."

Dean's head tilted to the side. "Who the hell is that?"

"That's Artimi. He's from Ravios… or his people once were. Until someone brought two demons home with them…"

"Demons?" he asked.

"Never mind. Come on, I'll introduce you." Jules took his hand, running to the cockpit. It was much less roomy with her and Dean on the bench behind the pilot's chair, but she didn't mind being in a confined space with Dean, even if he had bailed on her and his family in a time of need. He was doing what he thought was right, and that was something Jules understood more than most.

"Hold on to your hats. We're making a run for it," Artimi said, punching the engines to full. As Dean flew back in his seat, Jules remembered that he couldn't understand Artimi, since he was speaking another language. She glanced apologetically to Dean as they darted from the station.

"The Padlog are activating their weapon systems," Betheal said, altering the image on the viewscreen to show Elion Station from a camera on the rear of their ship. The three vessels fired at the station, destroying it with ease.

"What just happened? Why would the Padlog want to blow that place up?" Dean asked.

"I'm assuming someone ordered them to do it," Jules said.

"For what purpose?"

"We weren't the only ones that heard you were there," she told him, thinking about the Padlog ship docked an hour or so away. "Artimi, take us to Ravios. No stops."

"Consider it done," he told her.

Dean paled as her words sank in. "Are you saying the Padlog were sent there to kill me?"

She nodded. "That's what I think. Maybe me as well. I don't know how much information they have."

"And who's feeding this to them?" Dean asked.

"I don't know, but I have a feeling Lom is involved."

Dean mopped a hand over his face. "Where did you find this guy? And how are you speaking his language?"

"Artimi's a friend now. And you can thank my being Zan'ra for that particular talent. He'll bring us to Ravios, where we can use the portal to get to *Light*."

"You haven't heard from Patty at all?" Dean asked.

"Nothing."

"Where's Mom?"

"New Spero. She's been mourning you too, you know."

Dean nodded. "I'll go see her."

"Good."

"Jules?"

She waited expectantly.

"Will you come with me when I visit her?" Dean asked.

Any other time and Jules would have been thrilled at being asked, but now, she felt like it might be invasive. But she had to support him. He was in a fragile state and needed her more than she needed him. That might not have been fully true, but she didn't want to admit that. "Of course I will."

"Setting course for Ravios," Betheal said.

"Do you want to get some sleep?" Jules asked Dean, but he was already drifting off in a seated position. She wondered about the last time he'd been comfortable enough to close his eyes.

SIX

*F*or a moment, I was alone in the village, but the surroundings had changed. The structures were no longer rusted, overgrown with green growth. It was as if I'd traveled thousands of years in the past. Something akin to a bird chirped from a nearby tree, and the grounds were trimmed. Colorful flowers grew in familiar clusters along the walkway leading to the first complex, and I smiled at the sight.

"Dean, you have to stop doing stuff like that." Slate had followed me, and I saw Suma beside him.

"Fontem said it wasn't dangerous, so I took a chance," I told them.

"Just don't tell Mary, okay? She'll kill me." Slate walked ahead of me, his pulse rifle tracking the air in front of him.

"I don't think you're going to need that, you big oaf." I set a hand on the barrel, lowering it.

"Famous last words," Slate mumbled.

Suma pointed at the building. "This is crazy. I've never heard of something like this. Fontem obviously has, since he called it a time bubble."

"If this is a different time, where are the locals?" Slate asked.

I shrugged. It was a good question, but we needed to investigate first. "Is he going to be okay?" I asked Suma.

"We left him with Karo to stand watch. Fontem was emerging from his daze. It seemed like the time shift had some psychologically adverse affects," Suma said.

"No kidding. He was out of it," Slate whispered, staring to the top of the building.

"Let's move. He said he spent an hour inside here, but no time passed on the other end. To them, it'll be like we never departed, so we can take our time, search this place properly." I pointed over the sidewalk that led around the building. "Let's avoid the obvious and start at the other end of the village."

Slate nodded along, silently agreeing with me, and we walked past the first tallest structure and down the middle of a paved street. This roadway had appeared like rubble, with a proper forest growing from it in our timeline, but here, it was pristinely maintained.

We heard something, and my pulse pistol found my grip in a split second. Slate stuck a hand out, stopping us, and he stepped in front, holding his gun up.

An animal darted into the street a good two hundred meters ahead and paused, staring in our direction. It was almost deerlike, but with six legs. A longer tail flitted warily before it scurried to safety.

"That's probably what Fontem heard. I doubt Hanrion is still here," I told them, but why else would this bubble exist? Maybe I was wrong.

The village was smaller than I'd thought. Maybe, in our time, it seemed that way because of the immense overgrowth. The nearby trees had spread hungrily to the beach, filling the town out, but here, with everything so manicured, it felt intimate.

"I don't think this is a village," I told them.

Suma slowly spun around, taking it all in. "It's a research facility. Far enough from the cities. Fresh water.

Nice climate."

I hadn't even noticed how much warmer it felt than the portal valley, but there were no flakes in our time or in this shift. The sky was clear; a few white clouds drifted above us lazily, making me think of weekends as a child. I used to read a book near the farmhouse, sitting under the same oak tree I'd found Jules using frequently as a young girl. I remember resting with the book opened, leaning against my chest, as I stared into the sky, watching clouds coast and spread apart, morphing into shapes my mind imagined as something formidable. Sometimes I'd see a dragon spewing fire from her mouth; others I'd witness a train racing overhead, exhaust billowing from its smokestack.

These clouds held no such shapes, and I brought my attention to the task at hand.

"Not my type of facility. No windows on any of the buildings. I hope they get outside time for good behavior," Slate joked.

We continued on, finding the farthest structure from the shoreline. It was two stories or so high, and the doorway was almost hidden along the wall. We had to walk around it a second time to notice the indents of the handles.

I shrugged. "Who's to say everyone's entrances need to be identical?"

"I suppose, but this looks like they wanted to deter entry," Suma suggested as she pulled on the door. It opened smoothly, and inside, the room was bright. I shielded my eyes as I entered, letting my visor's tint acclimate to the change.

We spent the next ten minutes scouring through the building, but found it devoid of life. It all seemed so human, with chairs and desks, but everything was just a little off. Their chairs had six legs instead of four. The desks were odd geometric shapes; rather than being square, round, or rectangle, they were ovals or obtuse triangles. Artwork lined the walls, but it was almost three-dimensional, with deep grooves and peaks of color.

We found basic bedrooms, what must have been bathrooms, and an oddly laid-out kitchen.

"On to the next one," Slate said, heading for the exit. The moment we returned outside, I spotted the form near the central building, the largest complex in the region. At first I thought it might be the animal again, but no, it wasn't walking on six legs. It was on four, two long arms dangling by its sides as it remained completely still.

"Do you see…" I started to ask.

"I see it," Slate replied. "It has clothes on. That's no wildlife."

I took a chance. Regnig had been able to add their language to our translators, having read enough from their old texts, and I spoke using it as we walked over the cobblestones toward the figure. "Hello. We need your help." The words echoed in the language of the Ephor people. I had no idea what they were called.

I couldn't make out his face, if that was indeed the inventor of the time bubble we were in, but he didn't move or reply to me.

We slowed our pace, and when Slate started to raise his pulse rifle, I shook my head, silently ordering him to stand down. We weren't going to get anywhere with the local if we scared him off.

"I'm Dean Parker, and we seek your assistance on a dire matter," I said, letting the translator work. For a moment, I thought it might not be working properly, but as we closed in on the four-legged being, he spoke to us.

"You aren't supposed to be here." His words repeated through my earpiece.

We closed in on twenty meters, and I finally had a better look. My first thought was of the fantasy books I'd read as a kid, the ones with centaurs: men on the top, horses on the lower half, but that wasn't quite right. His legs were clothed, and his torso sat directly in the center of the four legs. He wore gray pants, his shirt white, long arms extending past his waist almost to his knees. He had no tail I could see, and his face was flat, with bulging round eyes and a slit of a nose. His mouth was a small oval, and it scarcely moved as he spoke.

Two circular ears jutted from the top of his head. They wiggled when I spoke to him. "We came seeking Hanrion. Is that you?"

"I am Hanrion. You aren't supposed to be here."

Suma stepped forward, hands up in a peaceful gesture. "We heard you were dead. How did you do this?"

"Do what?" he asked.

"Create this place."

"I did not create it, only harnessed it," he said, as if that was all the explanation necessary.

"Can we speak somewhere?" I asked him calmly.

He grumbled in response. "You should leave. I scared the other one of you off last year. Did he send for you?"

Last year? "Do you mean Fontem?" I described the Terellion to him, and his ears twitched.

"That is the one."

"Hanrion, I don't begin to understand this time distortion, but you sent him from here less than an hour ago," I told him.

His pupils shrank, almost as if they'd entirely contracted, then returned to normal. "That cannot be. I recall distinctly... I've been working for the last year, trying to firm up my boundary. I think I can finally seal it up."

"What do you mean, seal it up?" Suma asked.

"Occasionally, someone lands on Ephor, and the explorers tend to find my sanctuary here. Some go mad at the effect it causes; others become angry. Rarely do I let one escape, because I need time to figure it out. I can't have someone coming to disrupt my research." He stepped closer, moving from the edge of the complex. Slate clenched his jaw but refrained from moving.

"Let one escape?" I whispered it, but the translator was still on.

"You understand, right?" he asked.

I didn't like where this was headed. "Did you *let* our friend go?"

"No. I was busy, didn't know he was here until it was too late. I couldn't catch him in time," Hanrion said.

"We aren't here to stop you from working on your experiments. We need your assistance," I told him.

"I don't have time to help you," he said quickly.

Suma waved her arm around. "It seems to me you have all the time in the world."

"You'd think that, but you'd be surprised at how long it takes to gain traction with my research. Forty thousand years, and I'm still barely scratching the surface," he said. His eyes darted from side to side, and my stomach dropped. He was out of his mind. All these years of working in this time bubble, in isolation, had driven him mad. Perhaps it had started the day he'd merged with those other versions of himself, and it made me wonder what would be done to everyone in the universe if Lom was able to duplicate Hanrion's experiment, only on a massive scale.

It would likely drive each person in existence, every animal, completely mad. I had to play on this; it might be the one way to get through to the scientist.

"What if I told you that there was someone out there, in another timeline, who's working to merge every single thread of time in an effort to destroy everything we know?" I let the words translate, and Hanrion froze, a sense of clarity passing his flat expression.

"Why?"

"Because he's a real jerk," Slate answered.

I laughed lightly. "He's angry. Doesn't care about anything but revenge and will stop at nothing until it's done. We need your assistance."

Hanrion considered this, and I noticed his ears bend as he spoke. "If that occurs, my own time stasis may be affected. I couldn't continue my research." He scratched at his head. "Perhaps I can help."

I knew catering to his own sense of personal interest would do the trick.

"What do you need from me?" he asked.

Suma moved toward the complex. "Can we see inside?"

He paused but eventually turned, motioning us toward the entrance. "Don't touch… anything."

———

*A*rtimi lowered them through Ravios, and Jules watched as the clouds of demons swirled through the sky, gliding toward his ship.

"You weren't kidding about these things," Dean told her, never breaking his stare at the viewscreen.

A couple of them bumped into Artimi's shield, slightly adjusting his trajectory, but he didn't seem overly concerned. "I wish I could go with you guys," he said at long last from the pilot's seat.

"Why don't you?" Jules asked, getting an inquisitive frown from Dean. He couldn't understand them as they spoke in Artimi's tongue. "You could see what a real space-ship looks like. *Light* is most impressive."

"I don't doubt it, but I should return home to my family. Tell them I'm okay," he advised.

"If you ever need somewhere to"—Jules wanted to say *hide out*, but caught herself—"visit, go to Haven. Everyone is welcome." She leaned over Betheal the robot and opened a screen, using her finger to draw the symbol. She made sure Artimi witnessed the image and saved it, and she settled in her chair as the pilot landed them as close to the portal entrance as possible. The streets narrowed ahead, making it impossible to land within three blocks of the Shandra. She remembered the way back and rose, leading Dean to the exit.

Artimi followed and observed her as she hovered her palm over the ramp release button.

"Thanks for everything," she told the man, and he removed his bowler hat, tipping his head.

"And thank you for the Inlorian bar. I'll be able to do some good with it." He'd received a lot of change from the vendor Nuul, but Jules was certain he'd been swindled of Alliance market value. But he seemed content with the arrangement, and she couldn't fault him for that.

"Wait. You need to explain how to find one of these wormhole weapons your brother was attacked with," she told him.

"Do you really want to know? They aren't the friendliest of sorts," Artimi advised her. Jules nodded, and Artimi's shoulders relaxed, telling her he'd finally relented. "Fine." He turned, heading toward a locked vertical storage container. It was as tall as the ship's cargo bay, and he used a thumbprint to open it. Artimi stepped between Jules and the contents, as if hiding them from her prying eyes, and he slid out a round tablet. "Everything you need is on here."

Jules tucked it away, smiling at him. "It's been fun. Thanks again."

He closed the container and leaned against it. "Be safe."

"Dean, you ready?" she asked, still elated at finding the boy. Jules would watch him like a hawk over the next while. She'd never let him out of her sight.

She spread her sphere around them both and hit the button, racing down the decline and toward the Shandra. Some of the demon creatures spotted them as they rushed through the center of the street, and a few shrieked, swooping toward her. She lifted up, easily evading them, and a minute later, they were entering the portal room's opening.

Artimi's cot and supplies were still blocking the entrance, and they stepped over them. Jules had Dean, and she was about to bring him home to *Light*. Even though all wasn't right in the universe, her personal solar system felt deliriously content.

She took Dean's hand, bringing him to the table.

He glanced up at her, sadness and grief lining his eyes. "I *am* sorry about everything. I…"

"Don't worry about it. We're together. We can find Patty," Jules told him, adding, "I promise." It wasn't a phrase she would use without credibility. That was one thing Papa had taught her: never make a promise you can't keep. And she wasn't about to start now.

"Thanks. That means a lot."

Jules smiled as the crystals glowed bright green, matching her eyes, and she found *Light*'s symbol on the clear table screen. She pressed it to life, and took him home.

"$\mathcal{M}$om, we have to leave for the Golnex system. Patty and Lan'i were spotted there not long ago," Jules said.

Her mom shook her head emphatically. "Listen to yourself, Jules. We don't understand anything about the Golnex system, and how old is that news?"

Jules averted her gaze, folding her hands in her lap. Dean was beside her on the couch in their suite, and Papa was noticeably absent. "I don't know."

"Then it's old. Weeks, months, even if it just reached the rumor mill at the space station near Elion. I empathize that you want to find your sister, Dean, but you can't be chasing ghosts. You have to change your strategy. Lure them in," her mom said.

"Mom, that's not…"

Dean tapped Jules' leg, cutting off her train of thought. "Maybe you're right, Mrs. Parker. Jules, what if we found a way to give them what they want?"

"And what do they want?" Jules asked.

"To be free. To have power." Her mom started listing things off. "To reunite the Four."

"Do you think that's it?" Jules asked. They'd discussed it before, but never with so much clarity.

Her mom smiled at her, a warm look despite the circumstances. "Lan'i's memories of hiding from the Deities would be a lot fresher than the others', since he'd been trapped by the Collector. The Ja'ri that's inside you…" She stopped. Jules' mom hated accepting there was some ancient being living in her daughter.

Jules wasn't sure if that was how it worked. There were a few times her body had grown possessed, like when she'd discovered the strange round portals like the one in the Nirzu valley, but Jules was confident she was in control of her destiny. If that was the case, it meant Patty could control herself too. They only needed to convince her of that.

"Go ahead, Mom. Finish your thought."

"I think you need to find the last one. It's time," her mom said, mirroring her own thoughts. She'd wanted to solve that over the last half-year, but her first priority was bringing Dean home. Now that she had him at her side again, Jules could focus on the next mission.

"Dal'i is out there somewhere, and she managed to project to me. There has to be a way for me to track her," Jules said.

Dean jumped up, slapping his thigh with a palm. "That's it! If this Zan'ra was able to find you, then you can do it to locate Patty!"

Jules tugged his arm, bringing him to the couch again. He landed with a thud. "Don't you think I've tried that already? That every time I close my eyes, I'm trying to find them, to see if there's something drawing me to Patty?"

"I guess."

"You would have known if you hadn't run off abandoning us," Jules muttered. She'd thought she was over it, but in the heat of the moment, it was evident she needed more time to forgive him.

"I said I was…"

Jules cut him off again. "Sorry. I get it. You're sorry."

Her mom's face kept a strained expression as she broke the awkward silence. "Anyone want more tea?"

"No. We're good," Jules answered for the pair of them. "Where's Papa?"

"Checking out a lead. Numerous travel experiments were conducted on a world called Ephor that might help us," Mary said.

"Will he be home soon?" Jules asked, wishing she could talk with him. They'd been so focused on their own things that their plans had followed different paths. But if anyone could figure out how to reach Dal'i, it was Dean Parker.

"I hope so," her mom said. "We'll find a way for you to locate Dal'i. That's the key. Learn how she tracked you and we can trace the others, and I have a feeling we'll need to do it soon."

"And the Deities?" Dean asked.

In all the excitement, she'd almost forgotten about them. *Free me.* The voice rang in her mind as soon as she thought about the underwater coffin. Where were the others? "That's it. Mom, they want to kill the Deities."

"Are you certain?" she asked.

"No, but doesn't it make sense? Once there was an entire race of us, the Zan'ra, and only the Four managed to escape. Now the Deities are trapped underwater. Who do you think put them there? It had to be O'ri, and perhaps the others. They must have planned the whole thing," Jules said. "I wish I had Ja'ri's memory."

"No you don't. We don't want our Jules letting someone else into her mind," her mom said kindly. "How about you bring Dean to New Spero to see his mother tonight? I've already sent word you're here, Dean."

He nodded slowly, accepting her words. "She's going to be so pissed with me. I'm a horrible son."

Her mom rose, meeting Dean by the couch, and she pulled him into a hug, a hand resting on the back of his head. "You were trying to help. You were hurting, and needed to find your sister. Your mother will be thrilled to see you. And if she's angry at first, let her be, okay? It'll pass."

Jules smiled at the sage advice her mom was giving the boy she loved.

"Thanks, Mrs. Parker," Dean said, heading for the exit.

Jules' mom grabbed her arm, keeping her behind. "Be cautious. He's a flight risk. And you… are you positive everything is okay? I know a lot is going on, and it's not an easy time, but like I just told Dean, this too shall pass."

Jules slumped to the couch, chin to chest. "I don't think I have the energy for all this, Mom."

"Of course you do."

"How can you say that?"

"Because you're a Parker." Her mom winked, making her laugh.

"You've been with Papa for too many years," Jules joked. "I'll bring Dean to New Spero and stay the night, okay?"

"Sure. I'll fill your dad in when he's home."

Jules rose again, jogging to her room to gather a few things before meeting Dean at the door.

A few minutes later, they were back inside *Light*'s Shandra room, heading for New Spero for the first time since Uncle Magnus' wake.

SEVEN

I was completely shocked and out of my element. What-ever I'd thought might lie inside this windowless metal-walled complex, I was wrong. Dead wrong. There were dozens of people inside, and it took me a moment to real-ize they were all versions of Hanrion. Different ages, but it was clear as day that they were him.

Suma clutched my arm and tugged me close. "He's a madman."

"We still need his help," I reminded her quietly.

"This is what I'm working on," Hanrion said.

"What are we looking at?" I asked him.

"Time passes in my lab, meaning time pauses in the outside world, while centuries pass inside here. We don't age, per se, but I have allowed different versions to leave, to gather supplies from the world beyond what you called my time bubble. That's why you see us at different times of our lives. They are part of me, but we don't share a mind... that would be ridiculous." Hanrion laughed, a high-pitched squeal through his oval mouth. It was deeply unsettling.

"If someone had the power to merge every timeline, how could we prevent it?" Suma asked Hanrion.

He led us past several versions of himself, each nose-deep into a tablet. They didn't even seem to notice our presence. We walked into a laboratory with computer screens plastered along one wall, and a case enclosed with an energy field.

"What I've done here is create multiple branches of myself, but it only works within proximity of this." He pressed a button and the wall to the left slid open, revealing a pulsing cylinder the height of the ten-foot ceiling.

"What is it?" Suma asked, stepping toward it.

"It's a nullifier, for lack of a better word. This prevents time slippage, and allows other dimensional versions of someone to exist in the same place. It's…"

"Dangerous," I finished.

"Yes. Dangerous. But necessary for me to continue my research. When my first experiment worked, I had to expand the reach of the nullifier. This took ten of me and five hundred years to perfect. Only then could I grow the facility more rapidly," he said proudly.

"What's your end goal?" Slate asked him.

Hanrion blinked, head cocked to the side slightly. His front two legs lifted, one after the other, and settled to the ground. The question seemed to stump him. "I… I want to understand time. To bend it, to travel along it like a piece of dust on the breeze. We've been thinking of time as linear for so long, but it's nothing like that. You, Dean Parker, have visited me before, and will be here an infinite number of times."

The thought made me uneasy. "You've already met me?" I asked.

He shook his head. "That's not how it works." I didn't ask him to explain any further.

"This…" Suma pointed at the nullifier. "Is this what Lom of Pleva has? Something like this?"

Hanrion pressed the button again, the doors closing now. "He would have needed to steal it from me, and I do not recall the name."

"But you said it yourself. He's somewhere in our future. If time is cyclical, or a loop, or whatever you're trying to say, couldn't he obtain the technology from you in your future?" Slate asked, making my brain hurt.

"But I am in a time pause. Unless..." Hanrion crossed the room, and I was still trying to get used to watching the man walk on four strikingly humanoid legs.

"Unless what?" Suma urged him on.

"Never mind. It's nearly impossible," Hanrion said.

"What is?" I asked.

"We could go forward and check. I have hesitated to do this, mostly because I fear it would create a paradox within my own mind. I can't see what happens to my research, for it will affect every detail of all of my versions hard at work here each day." Hanrion rested his hands on the desk in front of him, and I noticed he had just three fingers and a squat thumb on each.

"What are you saying? We can go into the future?" I asked.

He nodded. "I can send you forward."

"How will I return?"

"You'll be on a timer, with a tether to this place and time. Linked to the outside world's time, at least," he said.

I took a step back and glanced from Slate to Suma. They were difficult to read behind their facemasks in the dimly-lit laboratory. "What do you think?" I asked them, flipping off my translator.

Suma answered first. "I think if Lom's doing something, it's because of what we found in here. The mere fact that this guy can pause time and work alongside countless versions of himself is far beyond anything we'd ever imagined. With a nullifier, or the technology of one, someone with Lom's unlimited resources could expand on the technology, creating something that can back up his threats."

"Boss, this could be too dangerous. You should let me go. I'll scope it out. Send me a few years forward, and I'll see what's what. If Lom has visited Hanrion by then, we'll know," Slate suggested.

It was my job. My fingers tingled, and I wondered if that was the feeling all past Recasters had felt when they were about to change the universe. My gut had led us here today, and I was going to learn if Lom had this technology or not. I nodded, flipping on the translator. "I'll do it. Send me forward a decade for five minutes, then have me return to this present moment."

Hanrion smiled, a strange sight on his flat triangle-shaped head. His eyes sparkled as he pointed to the hall-way. "Come with me."

"You don't have to do this, boss," Slate said, grabbing my arm.

"Yes, I do. Pardon the pun, but we're running out of time." I followed Hanrion, trying to push the nervousness from my bones.

———

*T*he transport landed outside Dean's old house, and Jules quickly noticed how unkempt the grounds were. The grass was too long, the fields out back grown wild and unhar-vested. Auntie Natalia was obviously not doing well, and Jules reproached herself for not paying more attention to what was going on. They should have demanded she travel with them on *Light*, and then Jules recalled they had, but she'd refused to leave.

"This isn't good." Dean's voice was low. "I should

have been here with her."

It wasn't the time to agree with him. She exited the shuttle, and a dog barked and ran toward them. The second one was quickly behind, as Carey followed Charlie from the front porch.

Dean knelt, petting the family dogs as they went crazy on him, rubbing their scent all over his pants. "I've missed you two."

Carey barked, rolling onto his back, and it was Jules' turn to scratch his belly.

"Dean, is that you?" Auntie Natalia's voice was coarse, and Jules saw her rise from a rocking chair on the porch. The daylight was waning, the shadows from the house long, and she walked toward them, onto the few steps to the rocky pathway.

Dean rose, the dogs still rolling in the grass. Jules stayed behind as son went to mother. They didn't say a word: only stopped two feet apart, staring at one another, before embracing. Jules heard the tears form both of them, and snippets of the conversation.

"I couldn't find her. I failed you, Mom," Dean said.

Natalia's expression softened as he folded into the hug. She spoke quietly, calming the boy, and Jules felt tears forming in her own eyes. This family had been through so much; too much. They needed one another now, and Jules wished she wasn't invading this private moment.

"Jules, come over here," Auntie Natalia said, and she did, hesitantly. When she was near enough, Nat brought her into the hug, and she kissed Jules' wet cheek. "You did everything you could. Dean, your father would be proud of you."

That did it. Dean broke down. Jules couldn't imagine how difficult the last few months had been on the young man, all alone in the wake of his father's death. Magnus had been larger than life, and he'd cast his own long shadow over his family. Now Dean was here with his mother, the woman who'd raised him with firm rules and a soft heart, and he was that little boy again.

"I wanted to find her so badly," Dean whispered.

Natalia broke their contact and wiped Dean's tears with her finger. She looked tired, older, and thinner than she had, and Jules saw the same changes in her son.

"This has to end," Jules said before thinking.

"What does?" Dean asked.

She pointed, her indicator finger moving between them. "This whole thing. You aren't going to do Patty any good by not eating, not sleeping. She needs you both to be happy and healthy when you find her. You guys have each other, and the Parkers. Auntie, we left you alone to mourn, but that time's over. Now we're asking for your assistance."

Natalia stared at Jules, her face impassive for a moment. Jules prepared herself for an onslaught of lectures from her auntie that never came. Instead, she smiled, kissing Jules on the forehead. "I can see why he likes you so much."

"Mom…" Dean started for the house, the dogs chasing after him.

Nat waited, keeping Jules there for a moment. "Thank you for bringing him to me."

"You're welcome, but it's time to move forward. What do you have in the house? Anything to make dinner with?" Jules asked.

Natalia shook her head. "Not much. I haven't had an appetite."

Jules smiled, returning to the shuttle to grab a bag of supplies her mom had forced her to bring. "Then it's a good thing Mom sent this."

An hour later, the three of them were seated at the

kitchen table. Dean and Natalia tidied the house up while Jules cooked the spaghetti and meatballs. It was one of the few things she knew how to make, and she remembered helping Papa roll the balls when she was a little girl.

The dogs finished their dinners and flopped to the floor under the table, breathing softly. Being here was surreal after scouring space for seven months in search of Dean. This was comfortable, so different from being in their suite on *Light*. Jules could see the attraction to living on New Spero, away from it all. Could she ever have a life like this? With her Zan'ra gifts, she didn't see how it was possible. Even without them, would Jules be able to leave the adventure of space travel behind?

"This is so good," Dean said, slurping up a noodle.

"*Da*, it's delicious, Jules."

They spent the meal telling Dean's mother about the past months, and she listened intently, not saying much as she ate. Jules fed them seconds, and neither of them objected as she spooned extra meatballs onto their plates.

"What's next?" Natalia asked.

"I need to locate Dal'i. We're going to check the two new portal worlds," Jules told her.

"What do you mean, new worlds?"

"We all but forgot it occurred, but two portals surfaced on the Crystal Map last year. This hasn't happened since…"

"Since Jules sent the Theos on their way and fixed the entire system," Dean said, and Jules heard pride in his voice. He'd told her he loved her… did he still?

"And what do you expect to find?" Natalia asked.

"I don't know. It's either related to the Zan'ra or the Deities." Jules was sure of it.

"Are you taking Dean with you?" his mother asked.

Jules spun some noodles with her fork and glanced at

him. "Do you think I can convince him to stay behind?"

Natalia laughed at this and shook her head. "No. He's like his father, isn't he? All the trouble Magnus and Jules' dad got in together. You two aren't far off, are you?"

"I hadn't really thought of it that way," Dean said, wiping the last of the sauce on his plate with the crust of his garlic bread.

Natalia stood, starting to clear the dishes. She stopped, staring at Jules in the candlelight. "Thank you for reminding me what life can be."

Jules didn't know what to say. "We want you to come with us on *Light*."

Dean frowned at her. They'd planned on asking her in the morning, but now felt like the right time. While Natalia was full and happy.

"I'll think about it." It was as good an answer as they could hope for.

They talked for a while, sipping warm tea, and Natalia eventually excused herself, saying she needed sleep, and that she guessed that for the first night in memory, she thought it might find her easily.

Jules and Dean headed for the porch to enjoy a few moments of serenity while they listened to the dogs snoring beside them and the insects chirping in the fields.

———————

"*D*on't stray from the building. Stay within a few feet of your current location. When you return, do not tell me a thing," Hanrion instructed me.

"Are you sure? What if it's pertinent that you hear it?" I asked.

"Whatever it is, do not tell me."

I shrugged and peered at my two friends. They shared worried expressions. I almost sent them to advise Karo and Fontem of what we were doing, until I remembered that when we returned to the shore, no time would have passed. I didn't think I'd ever wrap my mind around this time-travel stuff.

"All I have to do is go into this chamber?" I asked, pointing ahead. The room was dark, pitch black, the walls made of something similar to charcoal-colored stone. I walked inside and turned around. The entire chamber was able to accommodate no more than five people, and I could touch both walls if I stretched my hands out.

"Don't move. You will be there soon." Hanrion shut the door, leaving me in total darkness. I took a deep breath inside my EVA, suddenly grateful I had one on. The logical part of my mind told me a spacesuit was useless against some devastating time shift, but I appreciated wearing it nonetheless.

The air around me shimmered, and I froze in position. I heard a clap, and the black walls around me were gone, vanished. It took a moment for me to understand what I was seeing. I wasn't in the same spot. I was in the middle of a crater where the complex used to be. I saw pieces of the metal walls adjacent to me, and I stepped over them, trying to comprehend why the entire place was destroyed.

"He did it," I whispered to myself. Lom of Pleva must have visited in this future. He probably stole the nullifier technology and disappeared, destroying Hanrion and the complex as well. Or he'd kept Hanrion alive, at least one version of the man, in order to build something capable of merging the timelines.

I climbed up the crater, the incline gradual and not overly steep. I found myself near the shoreline, but the lake had receded a good fifty meters from the rocky beach.

From here, I saw the entire region where the local scientist had set up camp, and it was a wasteland.

I felt the tug, saw the air shimmer, and just like that, I returned to the inside of the chamber. The door opened, revealing a concerned Slate.

"You okay, boss?" he asked, helping me out of the room.

"I'm fine. Hanrion…"

The four-legged man shook his head. "No. Do not tell me."

I was at a crossroads. I wanted to warn him that Lom eventually comes, destroys all this man has worked for. I wondered what would happen if I convinced Hanrion to relocate operations, to go into hiding, but he wouldn't do it. His fate was his own choice.

"Then tell me something. What is fueling the nullifier?" I asked.

Hanrion froze, glancing at the wall it sat behind. "There is a world with colorful stones. I found blue and purple-infused crystals, and found them the most conductive for the experiment," he said.

"No way," Suma said.

"Can't be," Slate added.

"The world where the Theos put the Iskios," I whispered. "Can you share the location with me?"

Hanrion nodded and passed me a tablet. "It's documented on here."

"Dean, if those rocks power it, then that's where Lom will build the nullifier," Suma suggested.

"Then we don't have a choice. We have to destroy it," Slate said.

I shook my head. "If what we're being told is true, that won't help. Lom is in another dimension. What happens here doesn't affect his timeline."

"There has to be a solution," Suma said, and I glanced at Hanrion.

I couldn't help but smile. "I might have an idea."

"Boss, I don't like it when you get that look," Slate said cautiously.

"Come on. Let's go. Hanrion, I need you to come with me," I said.

He staggered warily, mouth going wide. "I can't leave my experiments."

"I think you have enough versions of yourself to spare one."

"What do you need me to do?" he asked.

"Build another of these, a bigger version… on the crystal world," I told him, and all three gawked at me like I was the one who'd lost my mind.

EIGHT

Free me. The voice was different. Younger, possibly. Female, perhaps, but the desire to be removed from imprisonment was the same. Jules opened her eyes, gasping at the pressure inside her head. It subsided and she breathed normally, sitting up in the bed. The blankets had stars on them, and Jules remembered playing with Patty in here when they were little girls.

She'd slept in Patty's room and noticed Natalia hadn't changed a thing about it. Patty had lived aboard *Horizon* for the last few years, meaning the entire place felt like it was waiting for a little girl to come home. There were stuffed toy rabbits on a chair, with old books about princesses, unicorns, and magic wands.

Jules felt like she'd missed that part of life: the comforting make-believe world that every child experienced until their worlds were turned upside down and they were placed into a metaphorical box, being told who they were and what they could be by their parents and teachers, and later their employers. She'd never had it, not with her glowing eyes and mysterious powers.

Papa had tried to give her that life, to assure her that she could be anything, and he read to her every night: stories about justice, perseverance, adventure, and mistakes. She'd been on New Spero for one night, and suddenly, she felt too far from her parents, despite the fact that she'd been traveling alone for months.

Being in Patty's room was too real, and the girl's absence was palpable here. Jules had the crystal bracelet Professor Thompson once used against her, and she was going to use it on Patty when she found her, rendering O'ri's power over her useless. They needed a way to trap the duo, and for that, Jules needed Dal'i's help.

She slid out of the bed, her feet cold on the hardwood planks. Jules threw a robe on, which was too small, and sat at Patty's desk. There were a few books scattered over it, pens, a tablet; and a heart was drawn on her mirror with lipstick. Two letters were written inside the symmetrical shape, in the same red color. L + P.

How could they have missed this? L + P. Jules ran to the next room, dragging Dean from bed. He was shirtless, and she almost blushed seeing him like that, standing there rubbing his eyes. He was still too skinny, but Jules would make sure he ate better if she had to feed him herself. Carey was on the bed with him, and he hopped down, shaking off the night's sleep.

"L plus P."

"What are you talking about?" Dean asked.

"Come here." She ran to Patty's room, pointing at the mirror.

"So what?"

"L plus P. Lan'i plus Patty."

"We don't know that. Maybe it's something else. She was always thinking about some boy or another," Dean reminded her.

Jules opened the desk drawer, pulling on the clear handle, and sifted through it. Inside were more books, and she found a stack of papers, each with felt markers bleeding through the thin pages.

"These say the same thing. L plus P. And look..." Her

fingers trembled as she saw the child's crude drawing. It wasn't a great effort, and Patty had never been much of an artist, but it was clear what was in front of them.

"It can't be." Dean grabbed the sheet, staring at the paper as he held it up.

The figure was pale blue, with bright blond hair and sharp cyan for the eyes. "It's Lan'i."

"How is this possible?" Dean asked, but Jules didn't have an answer.

"She said he came to her in her dreams, on *Light*. Maybe he'd been doing it for some time," Jules suggested.

Dean dropped the paper and slumped to the bed. "She should have told us about this."

"We have to tell your mom," Jules said.

Dean shook his head, glancing at the doorway. "She's already been through enough. I don't think it'll do her any good. If anything, it'll be the opposite. She'll blame herself for not seeing the signs."

Jules sat beside him, the mattress sinking. "Like you're blaming yourself?"

"It's only natural. Hell, you probably are too."

"Of course I'm blaming myself. If I hadn't stopped the Collector, Lan'i wouldn't have been freed. Even if I did stop him, and if I'd agreed with Papa's gut instinct to leave him frozen in time and buried on Shimmal, we wouldn't be here now." Jules saw her reflection in the vanity mirror and almost laughed at her wild curly hair. A few years ago, she would have freaked out having Dean see her like this, but those things didn't matter anymore.

"Tell you what," Dean started. "Let's make a deal. You and I are done playing the blame game."

Jules took his offered hand and shook it. It was warm. "Deal." The smell of food wafted through the hallway, into the open door, and the dogs sniffed it at the same time as her. They took off toward the kitchen, and her stomach grumbled.

"Want something to eat?" he asked.

"I'll be right there."

Dean disappeared without another word, and she snatched up the kid's drawing of Lan'i. She folded it in fourths, that number feeling important, and slid it into her jeans pocket, which were draped over the rocking chair near the closet.

"*I*... don't think so."

I'd heard the tail end of Fontem's reply to my question before we'd left the shoreline. Karo seemed shocked to see us materialize behind them, and doubly perturbed as the pair stared at Hanrion.

Karo moved for a pulse pistol, but Slate waved him off. "He's with us," my commander said.

"What happened?" Fontem asked. "You weren't even gone a split second."

"I'd say it was a couple of hours. We saw what Hanrion here was working on, and we think he can help us with something," I said. "Suma will be leaving with some of the crew when we return."

Suma was the best suited to the job, even though I didn't really want to lose her from the bridge crew, and the science officer on *Light*. Hanrion suggested they could manufacture their own, much larger nullifier in less than a month, if they had the proper supplies. He'd brought the list with him, and Suma had assured me there was nothing on it we couldn't procure and transport through the portals.

A month. It was around the same time we'd be at Fontem's real collection, and the deadline felt like a real motivator. "Time to go," I said.

"Boss, you wouldn't happen to be carrying a backup jetpack, would you?" Slate asked, nodding toward Hanrion.

I hadn't thought of that. "Hanrion, we'll have to carry you between us. I'm sorry, this might be uncomfortable." My words translated, and our new friend seemed reluctant.

A couple of awkward hours later, we were safe on *Light,* the portal room growing dull.

Hanrion's eyes were wide as he followed Slate to the exit. "Let's show our guest some quarters, and Suma, gather a crew to help with the nullifier construction." Suma started off, urging Hanrion to come with her. He did so with a cursory glance at me.

"You really think this is a good idea? Destroying the crystal planet?" Fontem asked.

"Not just destroying the crystal planet. Obliterating every damned one of them in each timeline." I clapped him on the back. "I never liked that place. Too many bad memories." It was where Mary had been taken from me, and where the Zan'ra inside Jules had been hiding, staying concealed until the right moment. Watching that planet be abolished would be a pleasure. Not to mention, Lom would need it in his present to merge the timelines. If it wasn't there when he attempted to learn the technology, he'd fail.

We stood in the hallway, the guards remaining quiet behind us, and I saw the pulse of light creep under the doorway. Someone had just used the portal.

I waited there, letting the guards check on their tablets, using the camera feed. I peeked over a shoulder, seeing Jules on the screen. Two familiar faces were with her, and I let out a laugh.

I tugged my helmet off, dropping it to the floor, and the moment the door opened, I rushed over, grabbing Nat in a hug. I kissed her cheek and did the same to Dean, getting a less responsive reaction.

"Mr. Parker, I didn't realize we were that close," he said, laughing.

"Well, you were named after me. I think I can give you a hug every now and then. Especially when I haven't seen you in seven months." I held him by the shoulders, wanting to berate him, but from the look in his eyes, that was the last thing he needed. Instead, I said, "Nice to see you home."

"Dean, I hear you've been busy," Nat said. Her hair was shorter, like she'd shorn it off herself in an act of mourning.

"We had some business to deal with, but we're back for now. Jules, we're going to have a briefing in an hour. I'd like you to be there," I told her.

She looked tired, like she'd been through a lifetime since we'd seen each other last. "Can I shower first?"

"I'm heading that way. I'll walk you," I said, draping my arm over her shoulders. Nat and Dean walked behind us. "Karo, do you mind staying for this?" I asked the Theos, who was pacing eagerly behind with Fontem.

"Sure, Dean. I'm going to head to the cafeteria for some… food," Karo said.

Fontem took after him, and we continued toward our suites, the four of us piling into the elevator. Natalia had yet to spend the night on *Light,* no matter how many times we'd asked her, so it was nice to have her here. Magnus was dead and Patty gone, but at least some of their family was together.

When we arrived at the suite, I asked about the dogs, and Nat said a neighbor was watching them. They went into Dean's quarters, and lucky for the young man, he was tidy, neat like his mother.

When Jules and I were alone, I smiled at her, entering our unit. "You did it," I said quietly.

"I told you I would," she said, grinning at me.

"I never doubted you for a minute," I said truthfully. It was hot inside my EVA, and I stripped it off, leaving it on the floor of the entryway.

"Papa, you stink," Jules advised me.

"Thanks," I told her. I moved for the kitchen, noticing Mary wasn't in the suite. I needed some caffeine before I did anything. "You want a coffee?"

"I thought I was too young for it," she said.

"You're sixteen and a Gatekeeper. I think you can handle a shot of caffeine on occasion." I set to work, filling an old drip machine with water. I preferred it to the new-tech stuff everyone else was using.

Jules plopped down on a stool, and I noticed the redness seeping into her cheeks and spotted the tears forming. "What is it?"

She glanced up, meeting my gaze, and the tears poured. "I didn't think I'd ever see him again."

She'd been bottling so much up, something I was good at doing. The coffee brewed, and I moved to her side, taking the stool next to her. "You found him, and he's home. Not to mention, you convinced Nat to come aboard somehow. I'd say you've accomplished some important things."

"I don't need praise, Papa. I… I felt so weak. Dean was out there, all alone, and I was chasing after him. I should have been trying to find the other Zan'ra, or learning more about the Deities. That's what we need right now, not me following Dean around like a lovesick puppy dog." Jules averted her gaze, watching the steam rise from the coffee maker.

I hadn't been expecting that. "Do you remember the stories about your mother being taken by the Iskios?"

She nodded, wiping tears from her rosy cheeks.

"There we were, standing in that room under the crystal mountain, thinking we'd found the Theos, when it arrived. It took over your mother, and with the wave of a hand, it sent Slate and me back to New Spero.

"I spent months searching for her. I went all over the place, begging people for help, and when I finally found her near Sterona, I fought for her. *With* her… but I battled until I figured out how to save her… and you."

Jules had stopped crying, and she smiled at this. "I never thought of it like that."

"You and I are cut from the same cloth. I think he may be your Mary," I said, finding it a strange thing to be telling my sixteen-year-old.

"What if you'd failed, Papa? What if you'd found Mom and she won?" Jules asked.

"Then a lot of people would have died by the Vortex, and we wouldn't be sitting here," I told her.

"We need to find the Zan'ra. I know Lom of Pleva is important, but I think Fontem may be right. The Deities may be able to stop him," she said.

"I have another plan for that, but you'll have to wait until the briefing to hear it." I stood, kissing her on the top of the head before pouring two cups of coffee, adding a little cream to each, making hers like mine. She lifted the drink, cradling the cup in her hands, and took a small sip.

"Why can't you tell me now? What happened over the last couple of days?" she asked.

I thought about seeing Lom and decided not to tell her quite yet. "I'm speaking in forty minutes. And as you said, I stink and need a shower."

Jules nodded slowly, taking her cup to her room.

I stayed there, staring at the wall, aware I'd do anything to protect my family from Lom's threats.

---

*W*e were about to start the meeting when Mary arrived fresh from the bridge, with Sergo and Loweck at her side.

"Everything good?" she asked, giving me a light kiss on the lips.

I shrugged. "I wish I'd had a chance to talk to you first, but I didn't. We have a lot to do." I waited for the others to enter the meeting room, smiling at them, saying casual greetings. The whole time I was tense, with Mary matching my mood.

"What happened?" she whispered. She spotted Jules inside, sitting with Dean and Nat, and she waved at them. "This is nice to see."

"It is." I turned to Mary when the rest of the crew were inside, but spoke quietly so they couldn't hear. "I was stopped in the portal again."

"What?" she shouted. When everyone paused and stared toward us, I led her farther from the entrance.

"Lom of Pleva found a way to get to me," I told her. "I need you to hear this first, so you don't freak out in there."

"Did you tell Jules?" she asked.

"No."

"What happened? Are you okay?"

"I'm fine. He threatened me. Said he was coming for us… the usual," I told her.

"How did he do that?" Mary was strong, but I didn't want to tell her all the gory details, especially about his threats to my family. When I didn't instantly respond, she pressed a finger into my chest. "Spill it, Parker."

"He told me he tortured the older version of me. The one who'd been coming to warn me through the portals," I told her, and she deflated.

"Is that why you haven't seen him in a while?"

"I don't know. But if he can do this, who knows what else he's capable of? Since he's communicated with the Arnap, and apparently the Padlog…"

"The Padlog?"

Slate popped his head out the door. "Boss, they're getting a little antsy, and you two whispering over here isn't helping."

"We'll talk about this later," Mary said, taking the lead as she brushed an invisible seam from her uniform. She took a deep breath and entered the meeting room, composed as always.

I shut the door behind me and looked over the trusted crew inside. From left to right, I had Slate, Loweck, Suma, Sergo, Rivo, Fontem, Karo, Jules, Dean, and of course, Natalia. They were on the inside now, and the only one I had any reservations about was Sergo, not that I didn't trust him. But the words from Lom had me reeling. How confident was I about the Padlog thief? He'd screwed me over before, but he'd also done a lot to regain that trust. If the Padlog were working with Pleva, I had no doubt Sergo was unaware, but I needed to gauge his reaction to the news regardless.

"We have a big month ahead of us. I expect a lot from my crew, and also my allies, but this might be the most important quest of our lifetime. Someone seeks to destroy us. They want our Alliance gone. They don't just want control, they want to see the destruction of everything. Lom of Pleva must be stopped." I locked gazes with Jules, and saw determination burning in her eyes.

NINE

*J*ules hated Lom with a passion. She'd never met the man, since she'd been a baby when her father had dismissed him into another timeline, but she'd witnessed what his existence had done to Papa. Now, knowing he was working toward merging dimensions, she wished she could stop him herself. Could she find a way to travel into the future, to his exact reality?

Fontem speculated that the Deities could do this, and that might be her move. She'd been so distracted with her own thoughts, she sensed she'd missed something important.

"You saw him?" Loweck asked.

"Who? Who did you see?" Jules blurted out.

"Lom. He was in the portal. It was like the other times, where an older version of myself came with dire warnings, but it was Lom," Papa told her.

Shivers carried up her spine, and she balled her hands into fists.

"What did he want?" Sergo asked.

Jules noted how her father paused at his question, the way his eyebrow lifted. She could almost read his mind. Before he answered, Jules cut in. "We were attacked by Padlog ships."

Sergo's mouth fell open. "What? Where?"

"In Elion. We found Dean there, and Artimi managed to escape, but there were three of them. They destroyed the old station," she said.

"Wait, are you saying one of our Alliance partners attacked you?" Mary asked.

"Well, they might not have known it was me. I was in a foreign ship hired to bring me to Elion Station. I also saw one of their ships parked at the newer trade structure in the system. That's how I think they knew we were nearby."

"So they did know it was you?" her mom asked.

Jules felt all eyes on her. "I guess so. I can't be sure."

"What does this mean?" Slate asked. "Boss, you mentioned that Lom spoke of the Padlog."

Papa nodded along. "He muttered something about trusting a Padlog."

Sergo raised his arms. "Look, I can only assume what you're all thinking. Sergo would sell his soul for a buck. I have nothing to do with this. If I saw Lom, I'd shoot him in the fleshy bits of his face."

Jules watched the man, his big bug eyes wide. He buzzed uncomfortably.

"Sergo, lower your hands. I trust you," Papa said. Jules was glad, because she did too.

The Padlog pilot acted relieved and settled into his chair. "I have a lot of undesirable acquaintances that may be involved. Want me to do some digging?"

"Yes. Thank you. Find out what you're able, subtly if possible, and maybe we can trace it to the perpetrators. If we learn how he's communicating into the past, maybe we stop his plan. In the meantime, we're moving for Techeron, and we'll arrive in…" Her dad pointed to Rivo, who quickly answered.

"Three weeks, four days," Rivo told them.

"Suma will be leaving us for that duration, heading to

the crystal world with a new friend, Hanrion. They're working on a top-secret project, and with any luck, we'll at least have a backup plan, should we fail our other avenues." Papa smiled at Suma, who seemed nervous at the announcement.

"How is this going to work?" Sergo asked. "There's no active portal."

Suma answered him quickly. "We're bringing our portable Shandra ship."

Jules hadn't yet seen this ship, but the Gatekeepers were quite excited about the concept. They'd be able to travel to different worlds via a portal on the freighter, sending it to various planets with an android pilot.

"Has anyone tested that yet?" Rivo asked.

"It's tested and fully functional. We'll be able to travel there when the time is right," Papa replied.

"When we arrive at Techeron, I'll be heading in our Kraski ship, along with Fontem and Slate. We're hoping there really is a viable reason for this trek, despite not having all of the information." Papa glanced at the Terellion, who simply nodded, his lips pursed.

Jules didn't fully trust the man. At times, he seemed so helpful; at others, so distant. She suspected he had his own motivations, and doubted they were always in alignment with theirs. Still, he had come through for them, and if he said there was a means to stop Lom waiting within his secret stash, then they had to try.

"Jules, what can you tell us?" her dad asked, putting her on the spot. She didn't seem any closer to finding the other Zan'ra.

She saw all eyes on her and cleared her throat, suddenly self-conscious. When she'd been a little girl, everything had come so easily for her. Now people expected things of her, and the pressure was ever growing. "As you can see, Dean has rejoined us. He will not be leaving alone again," Jules said for his benefit. He'd promised her that, and she would hold him to it. "We haven't visited the two new worlds that showed up on the Crystal Map last year, and that's where we're heading tomorrow."

Dean took a drink of water and stuck his hand up just enough for her to stop, letting him add his two cents. "I wanted to apologize to everyone for my behavior."

His mother set a hand on the table. "You don't have to do this, son."

"Yes I do. I didn't stick around, and that was a jerk thing to do. Dad was dead, and my sister gone. I felt like I was responsible, that I should have been able to protect Patty from this guy, and when I didn't… without my dad to turn to… I lost it. I took that shuttle and vanished. I thought that if I could find her, I'd be able to explain what happened to Dad, and that she'd understand. That Patty would somehow return to us as herself, leaving this Zan'ra mess behind.

"The longer I was out there, the less sure I was of that, and there were so many nights I lay awake wanting to come home, to ask for help, every time I was about to, I saw Patty's eyes glowing purple. I heard her voice telling me and Jules to leave her alone. I selfishly pressed on, and I wanted you all to know how sorry I am for putting you through it."

He took his mom's hand, and Jules glanced at her parents. "Thank you, Dean. We understand, and that's the last time you need to apologize for it. Right, everyone?" Papa scanned the crowd, and they verbalized their forms of agreement.

"What do you expect to find on these worlds?" Karo asked her. "No new portals have appeared on the map since you…" He caught himself and reined the comment in. Not everyone knew Jules' role that day on the Theos homeworld.

Jules went on explaining her theory, which was nothing more than speculation. "I think they'll be Zan'ra-related. Or it might be about the Deities." Everyone in the room had been filled in about the ancient gods, and about the Zan'ra as well, so Jules didn't expand further.

"The Deity I've been… visiting spoke to me again," Jules told the group.

"What did it say?" Loweck asked.

"It told me to free it and the others. It said I'd be re-warded," she advised them.

"How many others are there?" Suma asked, but she didn't have an answer.

"Your guess is as good as mine."

"But you think you might find more of them on these new portal worlds," Slate said.

"Right. At the very least, there has to be a reason the portals regained their functionality. We'll find out soon enough," Jules said.

Papa had listened patiently up to this point, but he was still the only one standing. His hands rested on the top of his chair, which he was behind, watching them talk. "Fontem, you first warned us about the Deity's capability for destruction; then you suggested we free it to help with our Lom issue. Where's your head on the subject today?"

Fontem gulped, and Jules watched him closely. "I meant they have the power to create and destroy. They made races, Dean. The Deities appear to have made the Zan'ra, a race with unlimited powers, and from what we've seen, they can be very harmful."

Jules sank into her chair, knowing he was implying her actions that day across the wormhole.

"The Arnap deserved far worse," Natalia said, backing

her up.

"I agree. I would have made them suffer first," Slate said softly.

Papa shook his head. "This isn't about that, and let's agree that we all loved Magnus, okay? His crew died too. The Arnap are bad, and were consequently dealt justice."

Fontem sat forward, elbows on the table. "That's not my point. Regardless of Jules' reason for killing them, a Zan'ra was able to snuff out twenty thousand lives with the blink of an eye. Do you see why the Deities wanted to remove their mistake from existence?"

Jules cringed at his words, and her mom seemed to notice from across the table. She passed Jules a reassuring smile, and she somehow managed to return it.

"Jules is not a mistake," Dean said beside her.

"That's right, she's not, but Fontem's theory is sound. We can understand why they may have decided they'd created something dangerous. But…"

Mary finished. "The Four escaped."

"And locked them away?" Slate asked.

Jules had thought about that for a long time. Just who had trapped the Deities? Who'd destroyed the cities on Desolate, and placed the symbol of the four circles with the X?

"Four circles. The Four," she said, pushing back from the table a bit. Jules stood, moving for the digital board behind Karo, and drew the symbol.

"That's it," Papa said. "Why didn't we think about this?"

"We had too much on our plates," Slate said. "This is good, Jules. Now we have to assume the Zan'ra retaliated after evading capture."

Jules smiled at Uncle Zeke, appreciating how he'd said *the Zan'ra*, not indicating her.

"Keep an eye out for that symbol and be cautious on those two planets," Papa said, looking at Dean, then her. "If the Deities are indeed there, make notes."

"We know the drill. Observe, record, report." Dean said the three words the Academy had engrained into their minds for years.

Slate and Suma nodded proudly, since they'd been their professors on some important subjects for a few years.

"And, Jules, you have the…" Her dad clasped a hand around his left forearm, implying the crystal device Professor Thompson had used on her.

"I have it and will use it as needed," she assured him, imagining pulling O'ri's power from Patty.

Her mom updated them about recent Alliance updates, talking about New Spero, Earth, Haven, and Bazarn Five, and Jules listened, but only half-heard the conversation. She was too deep into thought about her revelation. Now that she saw the symbol for the Zan'ra, something felt different inside her. She was more connected to Desolate, the world with the Deity under the ocean's surface.

The meeting went on for another hour, everyone having a turn to discuss their roles and the work of the crew members around them. This was a time they could make suggestions or talk about issues, and Papa would listen, offering advice or telling them he'd consider their proposals.

Eventually, they were dismissed, and she lingered, staying with Dean and Natalia as the others left. Her parents waited behind, Mom shutting the door.

"Nat, it's good to see you. How are you?" she asked.

Natalia actually laughed. "This is strange, isn't it?"

"What is?" Papa asked.

"This. Us sitting here, months after Magnus died, talking about stopping a businessman from killing us. Jules and Dean, our kids, are chasing after gods and teenagers with superpowers. It's all… too much." Nat's laughter ceased, and Jules spotted the worry and stress slipping into her previous façade.

Her parents sat far across from them, and the table suddenly felt overwhelming in size. "Remember our first trip to Washington?" Papa asked, changing the subject.

Natalia nodded. "I'd never been to the States before that. Magnus was like a tourist, pointing out everything like it was supposed to be of significance to me."

"Do you remember how out of our element we were?" he asked. "At least I was. You and Magnus were tough, experienced in combat. Mary was a damned Air Force pilot, and then there was the thirty-something-year-old accountant from upstate New York, treading water, trying to stay rational in the boat dragging us along."

Jules smiled at him. She could hardly imagine the man in front of her scared and not in charge of anything. He was always so sure of himself.

"You seemed to do fine to me," Nat told him.

"I did, but only because I had you guys around. We were a team, remember?"

"It was a long time ago," Dean's mom said.

"That doesn't matter. We were a team then, when things sounded impossible. And what happened?"

Jules' mom answered when it was clear Natalia wasn't going to. "We won. We fought the Kraski, defeated the Deltra. We chased Leslie and Terrance out there, stopped the Bhlat, and kept going until we made it all these years later, with kids of our own, and starships to captain. We've created multi-world alliances and saved so many lives along the way. As a team."

"What are you trying to get at?" Natalia asked. It had been some time since she'd worked with Jules' parents on a mission, not since she'd accompanied Mary while Papa dealt with the Hunter on New Spero. Jules had been a little girl then.

"We need you on this one," Papa said.

"No you don't."

"Mom, give him a chance," Dean told her.

Natalia let out a cheekful of air. "You want the old Nat at your side, ready to pull the trigger and make the right calls, but that's not me any longer. I did it because of him. He demanded a lot of me, and I was there. The balance to a relationship."

Jules straightened at her word: *balance*. It was something her dad liked to talk about, the balance of the universe.

"Then recalibrate. Balance your son, balance your daughter. Balance *me*, for God's sake, but do it, because whatever we're about to fight is going to be bad. Ruthless and cunning. We need you in this fight, Nat." Papa's voice lowered, and his frown eased slightly. "*I* need you."

This was what she wanted to hear. It was evident instantly. She sat up, her face softening. "Fine. I'm in."

"Good. Lom's not going to know what hit him," her dad said, adding a wink.

———————

*T*he meeting went as well as it could have. It was obvious Sergo had nothing to do with the Padlog Lom had been referring to, but if there was one thing the tricky insectoid was good at, it was extracting data from nothing. I was confident he'd be able to find out who was feeding Lom information and taking orders from him.

It was late, but I was jacked up, nervous for so many reasons, but also excited to be nearing the end. I'd been worried about Lom since Jules was a baby. Sixteen years with the threat of him looming over my head, never quite leaving my train of thought.

Jules had gone to bed an hour ago, but when I glanced towards the hall, I saw her light was still on. She was exactly like me, probably anticipating our upcoming adventures the same as I was. Her path was different than mine, and she'd excel at it. She always did.

"You did a good job in there," I told Mary, walking behind her on the couch. I rubbed her shoulders, which were extremely tense, and she set her cup of tea down. Maggie was beside her on the couch, legs kicked out to the right. She snored lightly as I gave my wife a light massage.

"You too. We weren't wrong. We do need her. I remember our first meeting," Mary said. "You'd already spent some time with the pair, but I had no clue who they were. All I saw was a big, loud Scandinavian man, and a demure but powerful woman who wouldn't speak. They made quite the pair."

"Did you ever think they'd end up married, and that we would too?" I asked, moving around the couch to sit with her and the dog.

"Not right away. It was so surreal, seeing you, and hearing Bob had met you and your wife," Mary said.

"She wasn't really my…"

"You know what I mean. I get that Janine and Bob were fakes, spies or whatever, but it felt different then," she said. "Everything was so confusing, and there you were, this man taking charge. I was impressed with you. I won't say I was hearing wedding bells, but I did feel a little heart fluttering, maybe."

I laughed faintly, resting my head into the couch cushion. "It's hard to believe he's gone."

Her cool palm found my arm, and she nodded. "I

know."

"I don't blame Nat for hiding from everyone. I think I'd do the same thing," I told her.

"No you wouldn't. Not Dean Parker." Mary glanced over the couch, toward our daughter's room.

"She'll be fine. Jules is capable," I told her.

"If the Deities are freed, they might kill her," Mary said.

"Jules will know what to do. She always does," I said, with more confidence than I felt.

"I hope you're right. Want to go to bed?" Mary asked me.

"Sure. I'll be there in a few." I watched her leave, taking Maggie for one last bathroom trip. I headed to the fridge, unable to stop thinking about Magnus tonight. I opened the door, seeing his favorite beer still sitting there. We'd been planning on drinking them together. I'd managed to procure a case from Udoon Station, since it was the only thing that compared to the Padlogs' syrupy drink in his books.

I pulled one of the beverages out, popped the top of the plastic bottle, since it wasn't human-made, and took a sip. It was as awful as I remembered. Magnus' taste buds must have been broken. I sat down at the island, smiling as I drank the beer.

TEN

The Crystal Map was a convoluted tool, but one Jules was quite accustomed to using. She'd studied it for hours, then days, then weeks, when she'd first started her Portals class at the Academy. She knew the symbols for hundreds, maybe over a thousand, and could match almost that many to the planet's description. There were some she didn't remember, mostly due to the fact that they were yet to be explored and recorded by the Gatekeepers.

Some of them were far away, too distant to travel by ship, even with their current technology. Papa wouldn't let her go to any of those places, and for good reason. Sarlun was of the same mind, but claimed they would eventually investigate some of the locations. That there was so much out there that members of the Alliance had never seen fascinated Jules to no end. She used to dream of fairy-tale lands, with princes, swords, and strong queens leading thriving nations.

Now she suspected most of the planets were vacant, empty husks without life, but these portal planets were different. The portals had been placed there on purpose. The Theos had created many of them, emulating the technology they'd discovered in stones like the round one she'd found in the Nirzu valley, but some had already existed. Actually a lot did, like all of the Shandra that had appeared after she'd fixed the entire network on Karo's planet.

Those were older, ancient, from someone else's hand. They still didn't know who created them, not for sure, but Jules guessed it was the very same Deities. From what she could tell, there wasn't a lot they weren't capable of, which didn't explain how they'd allowed themselves to be trapped.

"Are you going to stare at that all morning, or are we going to leave?" Dean asked, nudging her with an elbow.

The map held so many pinpoints, and she decided they'd hit the closer of the two brand-new destinations. Without any reference on what was across, she was nervous to travel through, more nervous than she could recall when standing near a Shandra. She pointed to the icon, which was quite simple in its design. It was a single circle with a line through it. She thought there was something familiar about it, but it was a common shape, after all.

"Why that one, not the other?" Dean asked.

Jules shrugged, shoving the tablet into his chest. "Gut feeling." It wasn't, really, but she wanted him to be confident in her choice.

"Good enough for me."

They'd already said their goodbyes, and Jules was glad their parents had allowed them to leave by themselves. It was a far cry from a couple years ago, and while she appreciated the courtesy, she almost wished Papa and her mom were outside, waving goodbye to them.

"Are you ready?" she asked, and he nodded, rapping his gloved knuckles on his helmet. She did the same, smiling at him, and activated the portal.

For a moment, she expected Lom to stop her in the portal's netherworld, but nothing of the sort occurred, and they arrived inside a stone-walled room. The portal stones cooled quickly, and they were different than most of the crystals powering the Shandra. These were rounded, where the others had hard lines and flat surfaces. These were older; Jules could feel it.

Out of habit, she'd shot a sphere around her and Dean, lifting them from the ground. It surprised Dean, and he tripped on his feet, sprawling into her. "Can you at least warn me when you're about to do that?" he asked, frowning through the facemask.

"Sorry." She let it go, and their feet dropped a foot to the room's rocky floor.

"Where's the exit?" Dean asked, using a light on his arm to scour the dark stone walls. The room was eerily quiet, their voices carrying through earpieces.

"I don't know." Jules stepped forward, finding the room didn't have a door. "I think we can just walk out."

"This feels strange. It's not like the portals we've used," he told her, and she nodded in agreement.

She was almost in a trance, her footsteps tender as she moved for the exit. The ground was on a slight incline, and after a few minutes, she saw a sliver of light ahead. There was something familiar here, like she'd visited it before. "Dean, I pressed the proper symbol, right?"

"You did. I watched. Why?"

"Because I swear I've been here." Her voice was a whisper, and Jules continued forward.

"No way. Wait, is this like you at Menocury L05?" Dean asked.

"I don't think so."

"That was scary. You were almost possessed or something," he told her with a slight waver to his voice. She remembered it all so distinctly.

"Wait, Dean." She lifted an arm, and he stopped beside her. The tunnel had begun to shrink, driving them closer as they neared the opening to the underground passageway.

"What is it?"

Jules stared at him, seeing her green eyes glowing in his facemask. "That's it. I projected when I was there. I touched the stone, and I saw Regnig, I saw Mom… I saw Papa as he was trying to stop Frasier."

"What are you talking about?" he asked.

"The stones… that's how Dal'i came to see me!" Her heart thrummed, and she wanted to turn around, to head to the Nirzu's new planet, where they'd uprooted the ancient round portal stone and brought it with them.

"I don't understand," he admitted.

"I think I can reach her, Dean!" She wanted to kiss him but settled for resting her helmet against his.

"Patty?" he asked.

"Maybe. I may try Dal'i first, since I know she'll listen. She can help us, I'm sure of it." For the first time in months, Jules thought she was on the right track.

"Let's return, then. Go to the Nirzu…"

"Not yet. This place is important; otherwise, we wouldn't be here. Why would they open up after all this time, right when we're dealing with the Zan'ra and Deities?" she asked, but he didn't have an answer.

Dean kept walking, taking the lead now. He pulled his pulse rifle, and Jules fed stored energy through her arm to her fingers, ready for anything as they reached the opening.

Whatever she'd been anticipating seeing, it wasn't this. They stood close, peering through a circular hole into a valley. Things like stubby palm trees grew everywhere, the bright blue sky was cloudless, and giant flowers clung to the ground in random patterns throughout the region.

"It's beautiful," Jules whispered.

Dean pulled something from his pack and released it, sending the drone high into the air. "Let's see what's going on here."

They climbed from the gap, Jules scanning the area for any threats. She heard nothing but the trilling of a million insects. Her suit was cooling her skin, telling her it was hot outside, and she glanced in the distance to see wavy heat lines. They were slightly elevated here, and she spotted a lake a couple of kilometers from their position.

"Not much to see." Dean flipped his tablet around, showing her the drone's camera feed. It hovered over the landscape, past the lake and through the valley.

"Take it above the ridge." She pointed to the left, and he used the controls to do just that. A minute later, they watched the feed as it showed them another valley, this one much the same.

"I don't see any signs of civilization, but we'll send another couple of drones up, let them advise us when they spot anything useful." Dean pulled another two from the pack and sent them away.

Jules started to walk in the direction of the lake, and Dean grabbed her arm gently. "Where are you going?"

"I'm not staying here. We have things to do, Dean, and waiting around isn't one of them," she told him.

"We're supposed to observe, record, report. Remember?"

"I know the protocol, but we're a little past that, aren't we? I need to find out why this world opened up to us and what's hiding here." Jules continued on, using her abilities to lighten her heavy pack. "What's the gravity at?"

Dean took a few steps, nodding to her. "You're right. It's a little stronger than we're used to, by five percent."

Each world they'd lived on was slightly different, but Earth, New Spero, and Haven were almost identical in nature. This was a little different, but manageable.

"Looks like the air is breathable, but I recommend we

leave the suits on," Dean told her, and Jules didn't argue. It would be safer that way, because they had no idea what was here. There were cases of Gatekeepers thinking they were protected, removing their helmets and dying from a simple bug bite.

"Come on. Let's move." Jules waited for him, and they walked over the rocky ground, entering a grassy field a few minutes later. The flowers were even larger than she'd imagined; huge petals spread open in the hot summery air. She neared one, staying far enough away that it couldn't grab her if it was sentient. It reminded her of Patty, dancing in the grass, darting from their group on the day she was expelled from the Academy.

If only Jules had been able to prevent that moment, maybe the girl's future would have been set down a different path. The idea had her contemplating Fontem's timeline theory, and it made a little more sense. Each decision would set her and the people around her into an alternate future. Jules needed to make the correct choices to keep everyone alive. It was a lot of pressure, but somehow it felt like hers to bear, and she was ready for it.

She stared at the stigma of the flower, seeing the drops of sweet dew on it.

"Stopping to smell the roses?" Dean asked, coming beside her.

"I guess so. This place seems so peaceful."

"Where there's quiet and calm, there's usually noise and chaos around the corner," Dean said, and she wondered if he was quoting something he'd read.

"The balance, right?" she asked.

"Something like that. I remember Dad saying it to me once, and he was correct. Any time my life has become too comfortable, something happens. Isn't that the way?" He turned from her, continuing on.

They reached the lake an hour later, the terrain more difficult to traverse than she'd assumed. She could have used her sphere to carry them, but Dean had asked to walk this part of the trip, and Jules was enjoying the time outdoors, even if she couldn't feel the heat against her cheeks or the breeze on her forehead. It beat stressing about finding Dean and Patty.

Dean squatted at the water's edge, the pebbles crunching under his boots. His gloved finger dipped into the lake, and he stood up, staring across the expanse. "Are you sensing anything?"

"It doesn't really work like that," Jules told him.

"Where to?"

She scanned their surroundings. The palms cast shadows over them now, and she watched the leaves sway over the lightly rippling lake surface. "I don't know," she admitted. The truth was, she was hoping her abilities picked up on something. Grabbed hold of a notion, or that they'd see a sign of the Zan'ra. So far, there was nothing of the sort.

"Let's keep going around the lake. If we don't see anything, we'll watch the drone feeds and find out what else is on this continent, okay?" Jules suggested, and Dean nodded amiably.

Their boots pressed imprints in the shoreline, and Dean led her to sturdier ground as they went. They talked about his last few months, and the trouble he'd continually found himself in. She told him of the trail he'd sprinkled behind him, and how she thought she was on his track so many times.

A couple of hours later, they were on the opposite edge of the lake, with nothing but a strange rock formation ahead of them, surrounded by more of the palms and a field of bright purple and pink flowers.

"Do you hear that?" Dean asked.

Jules shook her head. "I don't hear anything."

"Exactly. The insects. They stopped chirping," he told her, and she realized he was right. Their song had become part of the backdrop, and now it was gone, the entire region deathly silent.

"This isn't good," she whispered, spinning slowly on a heel.

Dean's gun was in his palm, and they moved toward the rock outcropping. The stones were rounded, light gray, and twice as tall as they were.

"I don't spot anything coming," Dean said. He started to climb onto the rocks, his footing slipping near the top of the first one. She helped catch him with her abilities, and he smiled sheepishly. "Thanks."

"What do you see?" she asked.

"Not much. More trees…" He stopped, pointing in the opposite direction of the sun. "Wait, the treetops are moving."

Jules got a sinking feeling in her stomach, and the ground began to shake, a slight tremor beneath her boots. "Dean, get off those."

"Something's out there," he said quietly.

"Dean…" Her hand was pressed to one of the stones, and she saw it had begun cracking. It wasn't a rock.

He fell from above, landing on the ground with a thud, and she staggered from the gray stone.

"It's an egg," Dean said.

Whatever had made those eggs had to be huge, and judging from the booming incoming steps, it was heading in their direction.

———

"*H*ave you thought this through? Is destroying the crystal planet the best option?" Sarlun asked. His projection wavered over my office floor.

"I can't say it's the best option, but if he's using it to build a giant nullifier in the future, I can erase all timelines of that planet, rendering him helpless," I said.

Sarlun rubbed his temples. "There are so many unknowns, like how this could reverberate throughout our and the other timelines."

"Do you have another solution?" I asked him.

The head of the Gatekeepers was getting older, and he'd become even less impulsive as he aged—not that he was ever a risk taker. "We could try to wake these Deities."

"And let them kill Jules?" I asked.

"We can't say for sure that would happen. Fontem thinks…"

"Fontem is in it for himself," I blurted out.

Sarlun paused, his snout twitching to the side. "Is that what you think?"

I nodded a few times. "He's never been straight with us. His comments are wishy-washy. You want to talk about secrets, Fontem has a few buried in his closet, maybe some under the floorboards too."

"I thought you liked the Terellion," Sarlun said.

I leaned onto the desk, grabbing my cup of coffee. "Sure. I do like him. But why is his hand of cards so close to his chest?"

"Maybe he doesn't think we're ready for what he has to tell us. Fontem is an intelligent being with loads of experience, and I imagine a lot of it would be a little heavy for our brains," Sarlun said.

He was making some sense, but there were too many what-ifs surrounding the man.

"Dean, he's leading you to his real collection, his treasure trove. Would he do that if he didn't want to be a part of this team?" Sarlun asked.

I considered the question before speaking. "I don't think he'd show us if he didn't have a selfish motivation."

"And what is that, exactly? He's worked tirelessly with Regnig, helped you learn more about the Zan'ra, and now you're spending months to seek out his hidden devices. You must trust him to an extent."

"I do, but I also think Fontem is doing this because it aligns with what he wants," I told him.

"And what is that? You still haven't told me." Sarlun was growing exasperated, and that hadn't been my intention.

"His wife. The stories say he was obsessed with reuniting with her. Maybe that's what he's doing. Fontem seeks a way to find her again," I said.

"How? You're suggesting he'll bribe a god with the chance to see his wife again?" Sarlun saying it out loud made me laugh.

"I don't know what I'm saying, but I have to be cautious with him. I trust my gut, and it's solid on this one, Sarlun." I relaxed a bit, and his expression softened.

"Okay, that I can trust too. I hope you make sure Suma is fine out there on this fool's errand. Messing with space and time is an extremely easy way to end up dead. If anything happens to her..." Sarlun didn't finish the comment, though it felt like a veiled threat.

"She's going to be fine. It's Suma. If anyone can build a device to pause time and merge dimensions around a planet, it's her. And this Hanrion may be unstable, but he's clearly brilliant. You should have seen that place," I told him, remembering the dozens of versions of the same man walking around, working on their tasks. I definitely didn't want other Deans out there representing my face.

Slate had assumed that was what happened when my clone took the Delineator from my hidden stash, but we'd never obtained proof of another me. Maybe he'd used it to leave again. Somehow, thinking there was an older me watching my back was comforting, if not confusing.

"When do you arrive at Techeron?" Sarlun asked, even though I knew he was aware of our ETA.

"Three weeks or so," I told him. I wanted to fast-forward the next while, but at least this gave Jules some time to find the others.

"I can see your cogs spinning. What is it?" Sarlun asked.

"Is it all connected?"

"Jules and the others with what… Lom?"

"It seems impossible they can be interlaced, but it feels like everything is. I can't help but think it means something." A headache started to creep into my temples.

"It's natural to connect the unexplained in an effort to feel in control of the outcome, but even so, it's highly unlikely. Perhaps Fontem is correct, though. Maybe you can use the Deity to help rid the universe of Lom. He's breaking every fundamental law of physics, and we risk destroying everything if he succeeds," Sarlun said.

"Who's to say these beings will hear us out?"

"You can't know until you ask," he said, giving me a smile.

"It's beginning to feel like we might not have a choice. Okay, I'd better sign off and get to the bridge. The crew is growing restless, and I need to ensure their spirits are high," I told him.

Sarlun's projection shimmered again as he stood. "Be careful, Dean Parker. I've known you a long time, and you have an innate ability to make the correct decisions, but I fear Lom of Pleva brings out the worst in you. He makes you impulsive, and threatening your family is the one thing he does purposefully. That's why he continues to do it. You need to harness your emotions, think this through logically, and ultimately, you will make the right moves when it's time," Sarlun said.

Sage wisdom if I'd ever heard it. "Thank you. You've been a good friend and mentor, Sarlun," I said, and with that, our call was over.

ELEVEN

Dean was on his feet an instant later, pulse rifle aiming toward the incoming beast. They couldn't spot it through the thick vegetation, but it was there, rushing forward with chilling ferocity. The egg near them continued to crack, lines running horizontally across the exterior, and Jules peeked at it to see a snub-like beak protrude. A section of the shell fell to the ground, and she was greeted by three gaping white eyes with small dots for pupils.

Instead of hesitating, she encircled herself and Dean with her sphere, and lifted them in the air. She stayed there, hovering ten feet above the eggs. Another started to wobble, meaning a second was now about to hatch.

"There it is," Dean said from her right. He still aimed the gun, even though they were inside her shield.

It emerged from the cover of the stubby palm trees, shrieking as it saw someone near its eggs. The thing looked like an alien version of a dinosaur. It relied on two immense legs as its thrashing tail clubbed a tree, cracking it in half. Spikes lined its back, all the way to the front of its head, and it paused, shrieking violently. Its arms were powerful, and she was sure she saw a thumb there, making it an even more dangerous creature.

Big teeth protruded from a long jaw, and they were yellow, flesh-covered, and overlapping one another.

"Jules, there's more." Dean pointed to the left, and she saw them. At least ten of the giant monsters walked to the outcropping, silently watching the invaders with interest.

"Then we're going to leave," she said, moving them backwards through the air. Jules wavered, the shield flickering, but it held.

"What was that?" Dean asked, eyes wide in horror. "Are you losing the powers?"

She shook her head but couldn't explain the temporary fluctuation. "I think it's okay…"

The creatures grew nearer, walking with heavy treads, the rest of the eggs crumbling under the vibrations. An egg fell to its side, the gray-speckled shell splitting in half. A baby tumbled out, flailing its skinny tail. Jules guessed the thing already weighed more than she did.

Her head ached suddenly. One moment she felt strong and capable, the very next she was in pain, and she glanced at Dean, feeling the trickle of blood running over her lip. It was inside her EVA helmet, and she wasn't able to wipe it off.

"Jules, what is it?" Dean asked, but his voice was far away, a distant echo in the recesses of her mind.

She saw the figure, a giant shadow waving in the breeze, as if it was tethered at its feet. She glanced down, recognizing the circle symbol etched into the coffin it occupied. *Free me, Ja'ri. You know you must. It is the only way.* The voice was distinctly female: strong and raspy, but a woman's.

"Jules, what's happening?" Dean shook her, and she broke from the daydream, the shadow behind her eyelids dissipating. She returned to her body, and the sphere disappeared. They were thirty meters in the air, and Dean windmilled his arms as gravity took hold, but Jules managed to reactivate the sphere just in time, catching herself.

Dean continued to fall toward the shells, and the monsters raced for his plunging form.

Jules shouted, sending a tendril through the sphere, and lashed it to his ankle. He dangled there, slightly out of reach for the aliens, who jumped and clawed toward him. One landed a blow, battering Dean to the side, but she lifted him up to avoid another strike.

She moved now, out from under a spell, and had to rein herself in as fury battled inside her. These creatures weren't going to harm Dean. She recalled the Sprites that had taken her mother and Dean last year, and the bloodshed in the aftermath. She couldn't let that happen again. These creatures were trying to protect their young, and she and Dean were the invaders.

Jules calmed, pulling Dean into her sphere as they raced over the palm-like trees, heading farther into the valley.

"What the hell was that?" Dean asked, panting for breath between words.

"There's a Deity here," she said.

"Are you sure?"

"One hundred percent. It showed itself to me. Called me Ja'ri." She paused, waiting for a reply from Dean. She expected he'd order her to return to the portal, to observe, record, then report, but he surprised her.

"Then let's go find it. Maybe you can ask it some questions," Dean suggested.

All those times visiting Desolate, and she'd attempted to query the underwater god, but he'd been quiet for most of her trips. Then, when he'd actually spoken to her the day of the lightning storm, she'd been unable to pull any useful information out of him.

"He said I'd be rewarded if I helped," she told Dean.

"What does that mean?"

They floated lower than she'd normally go, on the off chance the Deity pulled her from concentration again. "Your guess is as good as mine, I'm afraid. Fontem thinks we might be able to ask a favor of them. That we can stop Lom of Pleva," she said.

"I just want to find Patty," Dean said.

"If Lom does what he's attempting, there will be no future for her," Jules tried to explain. "For any of us."

"I know, but… you *will* help me, right? You promised." Dean squinted behind his mask, and Jules nodded in reply.

"I will."

"Where's this Deity you saw?" Dean asked.

The planet was immense, and there was a lot of surface to cover, but Jules assumed the situation would be similar to Desolate. She knew how far it was, relatively, and she tried to picture the landscape the god had shown her a few minutes earlier. She'd heard the sound of rushing water and observed a massive tree behind the shadow.

"Dean, check your drones for a waterfall near a huge tree. Not a palm like the others. This one looked more like an oak tree with black leaves," she told him, and he slipped the tablet from his pack, activating it a second later.

"I'm on it."

How many Deities were there? The circle on the coffin… that had to mean something. Did the underwater one have that same mark? She closed her eyes, trying to picture it, and they sprang open. It did have the mark, she was certain. It was faint, maybe burned into the wood, but it had been there.

She puzzled over it as they moved across the terrain, and she spotted more of the local creatures below, drinking from a peaceful lake in a glade.

"Circles," she muttered. "What does it mean?"

"Jules, what are you going on about?" Dean asked, not

tearing his gaze from his tablet.

"The Deities are in coffins. Presumably, the Four placed them in those, sealing them from the outside world. I have to guess the Zan'ra were unable to kill the gods, so they trapped them instead," she said, feeling like she was still missing something.

"Four… didn't you say there were four circles on Desolate's symbol?" Dean asked.

"That's it!" she shouted, drawing his attention from the video feeds.

"What's it?"

"The four circles. There will be four sealed Deities, one for each of us. That symbol, it's been found by Regnig and Fontem on a few things, passing references to the Zan'ra. We're the four circles. The Four," she said, as if that really explained anything.

"So there are four of these things? And you're saying the second is here?" he asked.

"At the tree with the black leaves…" She glanced toward the horizon and was glad there was still a lot of daylight remaining.

"Where are the other two?" Dean asked.

"I have to assume the Golnex system has one, since your sister and Lan'i were spotted there searching the mountains, and that leaves the fourth on the next newly-discovered portal world," Jules said.

"Then…"

"Maybe they're doing their rounds. We might be able to find them on the next world, if we time it right," Jules said.

"Or they've already been there. Or here."

"Patty didn't know about the new spots on the Crystal Map, so maybe not."

Dean shook his head, peering up from the tablet. "But

we have to assume this Lan'i guy has knowledge of their locations."

"Unless they didn't share it with one another. I don't think Ja'ri and Dal'i were tight with them. I get the feeling there were two sides of the Four, alliances if you will. Pairs against one another. O'ri and Lan'i on one side, me and the orange one on the other."

"Ja'ri," Dean said.

"Yes?"

"Ja'ri, not Jules. You're referring to her as yourself, but you're not a Zan'ra," he told her.

"I'm beginning to question that," Jules replied.

"Don't be ridiculous."

"You've seen what I've done, what I'm capable of. These Deities were right to destroy us. The Four should never have escaped," Jules told him, sure of her words.

"But they did, and somehow you were infused by the long-hibernating Zan'ra, just like my sister has been infused by O'ri. You realize if they didn't exist, or if the Deities had managed to stop them, you'd be a regular girl right now," he said.

She almost laughed as they floated in a green sphere above the palm trees on an alien world. There was nothing normal about what they were doing, and there weren't many normal things about Jules herself either.

"Is that what you'd prefer?" she asked him, feeling the glow from her eyes intensifying.

"Jules, that's not what I'm saying," Dean told her.

This was as good a time to talk about those three words he'd told her seven months ago. There was nowhere for him to run to, no way to evade her questions.

"If you had the choice, would you trade the powers? Would you expel the Zan'ra?" Dean asked her before she could mention anything else.

She'd considered that very question in her own mind countless times, but having Dean ask it made her angry. She wanted the older boy to accept her for who she was, not wish for someone different.

"Are you mad?" he asked softly.

"What makes you say that?"

"First off, your arms are crossed, you're tapping your foot and you're glaring at the trees." He laughed, turning her to face him inside the sphere. They continued moving slowly over the treetops, and he opened his mouth to say something else when she saw the image over the tablet screen.

"That's where she is!" Jules shouted, pointed at it.

"She? The Deity is a woman?"

"That shouldn't surprise you so much," she told him.

"I guess I just thought of them as sexless. What's the point of gender if you're a god?"

It was a good question, one she didn't have an answer for. "Where is that?"

Dean used the device, mapping out the location of the tree with the waterfall roaring in the backdrop. A few seconds later, they had it marked, and it was twenty kilometers away. She increased their speed, shooting quickly over the treetops, above a ridge, over another pristine lake, and slowed as they neared their destination.

The tree was extraordinary, the trunk a good five feet wide, with thick white bark. Knots protruded from the base, forming a perfect circle, a symbol for the Zan'ra. This was it.

Jules lowered them, and when their boots touched on the soft moss-covered ground, she flicked the energy bubble off. Dean took a tentative step toward the tree, and she followed beside him, staring toward the crown. Thick branches blotted out the sunlight, the long, vein-covered black leaves danced in the breeze, making a comforting rustling noise. It reminded her of the oak tree back home on Earth, the one she loved to read a good book under on a hot summer day.

This was a far cry from the angry ocean on Desolate, a fitting burial site for a god. The waterfall roared from the left, liquid feeding from higher along the mountainside into the lake behind the tree. This water had fed the tree and kept these great roots strong over the years.

"How old do you think it is?" Dean asked.

"Very ancient," she answered.

Dean strolled forward, reaching a hand for the trunk, when Jules saw the other girl sauntering up from the lake. She was diminutive: no more than four feet tall, and her hair was cut short, wet and plastered to her head. Her face was round, pleasant, but it was the eyes that made Jules smile.

"Dal'i," Jules said, startling Dean, who stumbled from the half-naked girl approaching them. Her eyes burned a bright orange, and she grinned in return.

"Hello, Ja'ri. I've been waiting for you," the other Zan'ra said.

---

*T*he ship was quiet at the off hour, and I briefly chatted to the portal guards before entering *Light*'s Shandra room. The symbols glowed to life, and I waited near the entrance as the doors closed behind me. The mere fact that an entire network of portals existed was mind-boggling. I remembered when Slate and I had first used the one on New Spero, finding Sterona and Suma when she was younger than Jules was now, then using the portal again to kidnap the Empress on the Bhlat homeworld. Leonard had followed me, and I'd been so angry. Turned out I couldn't have done it without him, and I thought there was a lesson in there somewhere.

I continually tried to do things on my own, and so did Jules, but at the end of the day, we were at our best when surrounded by the people we cared about. I was better with Mary, or Slate, or… I almost thought *Magnus*, but repressed the memory of the man. Now wasn't the time to become caught up in an emotional rollercoaster. He was gone. I was here.

I peered at the glowing green crystals beneath the glass sheet, and walked toward them over the smooth black-tiled floor. The entire Shandra network was awe-inspiring, and I stood at the table wondering how it was that an older version of myself was able to track me mid-transfer.

The mere fact that there was a world between worlds was confusing enough. What was that place? Did it exist? Was it some other dimension or a purgatory of sorts? I tried to imagine how old I'd been. I hadn't seen that man in years, but he'd been slightly wrinkled, hair graying, not unlike my own now. I had aged since then. Was it only five years off my current timeline? Ten?

Somehow Lom knew about it and had tortured the details from me in some future I'd never see. Or had he lied about that?

I wanted to confront him, to face Lom of Pleva inside the portal's whitewashed world, but I had no idea if he'd try to find me again. Mary had wanted me to stay away from using the network until we'd figured this all out, but I couldn't. Not with his threats hanging over my head.

I felt the noose tightening around my neck and hoped my stool would hold me up for a while longer.

The gun was holstered at my hip, and I chose the

symbol for Earth first.

"Come on, Lom. I have some questions for you," I said quietly, pressing the icon.

I arrived under Giza in Egypt and saw the guard peer into the room. "Sorry, wrong destination," I told her.

She nodded, recognizing me, and I found New Spero's icon, bringing it to life.

Once again, I traveled through without issue, ending inside the mountain's Shandra room, the symbols glowing hotly in the stone walls around me. "Damn it," I said, wiping my sweaty palms over my pants. I was dressed casually in a long-sleeved plaid shirt and dark jeans, not wanting this to be official business. Mary would kill me if she knew what I was trying to accomplish.

I thought about staying and going to see Leonard. It had been a while since we'd talked, but I was invested now. I wanted to see Lom.

I found the symbol for Haven. I'd do this all night if I had to. If Lom had been able to track me before, I suspected he was able to do so again. I activated it, white light filling my eyes, and when I blinked, it was still there. I was in the strange region between worlds.

"Show yourself!" I shouted.

Silence.

"Lom, I know you're here. I want to talk!"

More silence.

"Maybe we can strike a bargain," I said. Quite often, peaceful solutions could be found in times of war, and I'd managed to do it in the past, but there were also instances where fighting was unavoidable. Jules had showed me that when she'd destroyed the Arnap. I needed to be more like her in that way.

I heard his laughter, the booming, almost mechanical sounds as his cybernetics kicked in. He floated toward me like before, but faster this time. He was probably getting stronger here, attaining more control. That was good information. If he could master this world, it meant I could too.

When he was near enough to converse without shouting, I moved, willing myself forward. It was the first time I'd done so, and the space around me warped as I floated closer to him.

His flesh eye opened slightly wider, and a half grin met his non-metal part of his face. "Dean Parker. How did you know I'd come?"

I shrugged. "Seems like you'd be watching. It's what you do."

He was even more imposing today, as if he'd grown another two feet, and I suspected it was an illusion of this place. Something he'd done to appear stronger, to gain the upper hand.

He didn't speak, motioning toward me, as if urging me to go first.

"A bargain. What is it you really want, Lom? Perhaps there's another alternative," I told him, feigning a little desperation. It wasn't difficult to accomplish.

He laughed again, the sound equally disturbing. "At times, you seem to understand me, and at others, you fail miserably."

"There's always a concession to be had. What do you want?" I asked.

His smile dropped. "I want you dead."

"Out of all the people you've had altercations with, what about me has set you so over the edge?"

"It wasn't supposed to happen like this. Earth was ours."

"The Kraski? I know you sold them the hybrid technology, and the idea, but what was in it for you?" I pressed him. This was good. What I wanted. To get him talking.

"There have been a lot of threats over the millennia, Parker. Most recently, the Arnap, the Kraski, the Bhlat, but countless before them. Money is made in times of war, not in peace. When you came along, waving this idiotic white flag, you somehow managed to thwart everyone, and not only did you prevent the Kraski, then the Bhlat from owning you, but you ended up working with them. The Alliance of Worlds. You can understand how problematic that is for someone like me."

"You were gone before we formed an alliance. It's not about that, is it?" I asked, but it reiterated he was being fed information from someone here in my timeline. We'd already assumed that, though.

"You want to know what I'll do?" he asked, his frown vanishing.

"What?"

"I'll move on right now, if you sacrifice yourself," he said softly.

Goosebumps covered my arms under the shirt sleeves. "Is that so?"

"Yes." He drifted closer, the space around him dark and ominous over the white backdrop. He was huge, and I had to convince myself to stand firm. I knew at that instant the pulse pistol at my hip would do no good here. If it was possible to be killed, he'd have done it already.

"What does that entail?" I asked.

He sneered. "You go to Udoon Station. Alone. Meet my contact, Viliar."

"Then what?"

"You come to me, and you die," Lom said.

"And you'll stop messing around with all this time merging, end-of-existence crap?" I asked, unable to hide the tremor from my voice.

"Dean Parker, I swear I will stop once I have your head on a platter," he said.

"I'll think about it," I told him, turning away.

"Don't think too long." I heard his voice as the brightness filled my eyes, and I blinked them clear, finding I was inside Haven's portal room.

TWELVE

The fire roared, snapping and cracking as the green wood sizzled under the extreme heat. Dal'i's eyes were bright orange, and Jules thought the fire's reflection amplified their intensity.

"Tell me again," Dean said, and the girl shrugged in such a universal gesture. His helmet was on the ground beside hers, once Dal'i had convinced them nothing here would harm the human body.

"Look, I've already told you what I can," she said, using English.

"That you have no idea where the other two are, but that Jules had the ability to track the Four," Dean said, his tone clearly disbelieving.

"I don't know how to do that, Dal'i. You're going to have to teach me to project myself, and whatever else you can recall," Jules told her.

The Zan'ra laughed at this, as if Jules had made a funny joke. "Are you truly not in there, Ja'ri?"

Jules shook her head, tapping her temple with a finger. "This is all Jules Parker. I wish I could remember some of it, but I don't think that's how it works."

"It might be better this way," Dal'i said quietly.

"Why's that?" Dean asked. The fire crackled, and a piece of wood flew toward Dal'i. It stopped in midair, and she smiled at it as it burned to ashes a foot from her face.

"Because the Four had to do some terrible things to survive. How far would you go to preserve your race, Dean?" she asked him, her grin predatory.

"I guess I'd do whatever was necessary. That's our instinct, right?" Dean changed the subject. "Tell me about O'ri."

Jules glanced to the sky, seeing nothing but distant stars in the black backdrop.

"O'ri wouldn't stay hidden. He was such a fool. At one point, he vanished, and then I heard about some race called the Stor. Apparently, one of them found his essence, much like Jules here discovered Ja'ri. The young man grew powerful, tapping into the strengths of the Zan'ra. He helped raise the people to new levels, healing them, fending off invaders at one point, and then"—Dal'i snapped her fingers loudly—"he disappeared. He was gone for a hundred years, or so the tale goes, but his fame only grew among the people in that time. They built statues for him, using purple emeralds as his eyes."

"But he hurt them when he went home," Jules whispered.

Dal'i nodded, poking at the fire with a stick of orange energy. "We have no record during those years, because I never saw him. Neither did Lan'i. But it had to be bad, evil. When he once again returned to the Stor, they heralded him as a god, a hero, but he enslaved them. Eventually, I took it upon myself to stop him."

"You sealed him away?" Jules asked.

"I had a little help," she admitted.

"The Deities?"

"Good guess. I let mine out. Tricked her, really. They have such a singular focus on destroying the Zan'ra that it was simple enough. I left her tethered to the coffin, and she removed the essence from the boy that O'ri had been restored into," Dal'i said.

Jules stared at her, scared but excited. "Are you saying that these gods can split me from Ja'ri? I could be... human again?"

"If you don't mind living unresponsive for the rest of your miserable life," the girl said. "The kid was catatonic, and lasted just a few years under someone's care."

"How did he die?" Dean asked, but Jules had a good idea.

"Self-inflicted," she said quietly, and Dal'i nodded.

Jules was tired, but she had too many questions for the Zan'ra. It was surreal being with someone else like her, and while the initial rush of adrenaline had subsided, her curiosity was still growing.

"I just want to get my sister back in one piece," Dean told her.

"It may be possible, but we'd need to offer something to the Deities that they couldn't refuse," Dal'i said.

"What about Lan'i? Is he evil?" Jules asked. She did recall him trying to strangle her father, but she might have done the same thing if their roles had been reversed. Self-preservation was an extremely powerful instinct.

"Lan'i means well, but he's always been impetuous," Dal'i said. "He wants nothing more than to keep the gods buried, and he's making his rounds with O'ri to ensure this. They've been here, but there is one more location they haven't gone to yet."

"Desolate," Jules said.

"Is that what you call it? That seems fair, though the name of that world was once Uleera. Our home," Dal'i said, breaking her eye contact with Jules. She stared into the flickering flames in silence.

"What? Desolate... I mean, Uleera is the home of the

Zan'ra?" Jules asked. The hair on her arms stood up, and she glanced around, suddenly feeling vulnerable. The tree swayed proudly a few meters from them, and the background noise of the waterfall continued, though she barely noticed it now. Her gaze drifted to the base of the tree, where a coffin was buried ten meters below, the roots likely grown through the box, clutching it firmly in place.

"It was."

"How is it you are still you? If O'ri and I were lost, how did you remain Dal'i?" Jules asked.

Dal'i peered up again, the orange in her eyes even brighter. "It hasn't been easy. Ja'ri couldn't handle eternal life, and you know about O'ri. Lan'i and I were the only two out here for a very long time," she said.

"Do you trust Lan'i?" Dean asked.

"I have no choice. We're all in this together," Dal'i replied.

"Why didn't you two stay close if you were so tight?" Dean fiddled with a pebble, rolling it over his knuckles.

"We tried, for a while. But spending thousands of years with someone you disagree with isn't an easy task."

Jules tried to understand her explanation, but one thing Dal'i kept deflecting was her queries about the Deities. She needed to expand on this. "The Deities destroyed us? On Desolate?"

"That's correct." Dal'i peered over her shoulder, as if making sure this ancient god was safely buried beneath the tree.

Jules thought about all the bones of her people… No, not *her* people. The Zan'ra. She was human; the powers inside her belonged to one of the Four. She was still Jules, daughter of Dean and Mary Parker. Sister to Hugo. The idea that those people died because a group of gods changed their minds about their creations was sickening.

"Why did they make the Zan'ra, then destroy them?"

"Not all of us had the abilities. Only a few, actually."

This was news to Jules, and she contemplated it. "How small a percentage?"

"Maybe one in a thousand had some form of power like us," Dal'i said.

Dean dropped the pebble and reached to pick it up again. "Then why did they destroy everyone?"

"The power was possible in any child. There would be three generations of normal Zan'ra, with no sign of the essence in any of their lineage, and a couple could conceive a child born with the abilities. They didn't want to risk it." Dal'i took this devastation with ease, but Jules supposed she'd had eons to ponder and accept their reasoning.

"What are the four circles? The Four, right?" She pointed toward the tree, where the circle was etching into the bark. "It's on the coffin too, on Desolate."

"You've been there?"

"I have. I've spoken to him," Jules advised her.

For the first time, Dal'i acted shocked. Nothing seemed to bother this girl, but something about this news struck a chord. "What do you mean, you spoke with him?" She stood, and even upright, she was almost eye-level with Jules.

"I wouldn't say it was a great conversation. One day I fell into the ocean, and he talked further. Told me to free *them*, and that I knew what that meant. It was more frightful than her." Jules pointed to the tree trunk.

The orange in the Zan'ra's eyes dimmed momentarily. "We cannot speak to them, not through our seals."

"I can."

The girl shook her head, eyes frantic. "This is bad. If they're able to talk to you, then it's worse than I thought. We have to reseal them. It will take all of the Four, and that won't be simple to orchestrate." Dal'i paused, tapping her chin slowly. "What did she say?"

"She came to me as a shadow vision, telling me I must free her. That it was the only way," Jules said.

"Jules, we might need to free them," Dean said. "Your dad said with Lom of…" Dean was lifted from the over-turned tree he was perched on, orange tendrils of energy snaking around him. She floated along, moving toward the center of the mountainside lake.

"What did you say?" Dal'i's voice was deep, booming and it echoed in the quiet night.

Jules threw her sphere up quickly, racing to his aid. "Stop it!"

Dal'i didn't listen. She pulled the burning ropes tighter, and Dean let out a shout.

"We must never free the Deities. It will mean our death. The Four will be gone, all signs of the Zan'ra re-moved forever. We cannot allow this," Dal'i said, and Jules moved beside her.

"Let's discuss what our situation is. Maybe you can help," Jules said.

Dal'i glanced at her. She was floating, but not in a bub-ble. "Promise me you won't do anything to release them from their binds."

Jules shook her head. "I'll do anything to stop Lom of Pleva from harming our universe. Release Dean, and I'll fill you in on our plan. If he's successful, none of this will mat-ter. A million versions of you will fuse together, rendering you mad in an instant. We can't let this happen. I won't."

Dean gasped as she let him go. He began to plunge toward the icy water, and Jules shot below him, encircling him in her sphere. He stood, clutching at his chest where the tethers had burned his EVA slightly.

"Tell me of this Lom." Dal'i headed back to the fire,

and Jules glanced at Dean.

"You okay?"

"You still have the bracelet," Dean told her, tapping her forearm. The device from Professor Thompson was strapped under her sleeve, but she didn't want to use it to steal the girl's powers. Her essence, as Dal'i called it. She wanted to befriend the girl, because that was her one way to see this through and bring Patty home.

"Come on. Let's finish this conversation." Jules brought them to the warmth of the flames, and as she started to tell the other about Lom, she saw the shadow rising from the tree's trunk.

———————

"Boss, this was foolish," Slate told me.

"I have to agree with Zeke," Mary said. "How could you put yourself at risk like this?"

Sergo buzzed across the table, and Loweck drummed her fingers on the surface. Suma was noticeably absent, having been sent to the crystal world where Jules' Zan'ra essence had been hiding out for thousands of years. I had no idea if our plan would work there, but it was worth the effort.

"What? I had to see if he was watching me, and he was. I proved he's able to track me," I assured them, but it wouldn't make a difference. I'd stuck my neck out tonight, and it could have ended poorly.

"What did you really get out of this?" Slate asked. He was pacing behind me, arms crossed over his broad chest.

"I found out he has operatives at Udoon Station," I said.

"Great. The same place where we trapped him the first

time. Don't you think that's a little convenient, Dean?" Slate asked.

"And who the hell is Viliar?" Mary asked.

"Not one of the Padlog—at least, not that I know, but I do have some information," Sergo said. "The Supreme has done his own digging, and one of the factions has been overheard being sympathetic to PlevaCorp. There's even evidence of this group meeting with some of his corporation's ships in the Deeli system. He questioned them, and they said they were just trading goods, but he noticed they were very skittish."

"Good work, Sergo," I told him, making his antennae wave slightly. "Do you have someone's name? I'd like to have a chat with him."

"Her name is Foral, and she's a mean one. She's listed as a mining hauler, but we all knew her as a space pirate and curator of specialty goods. I may have... *traded* with her once or twice. In my youthful years," he added.

"Would you be able to set something up?" Mary asked him.

Loweck looked dubious. "Won't she find out you're working on *Light* for the Alliance?"

"She'll believe any story I tell her. How about I mention the Inlorian bars I ... 'borrowed' from Inlor all those years ago. Remember that?" Sergo asked, and I laughed.

"You were so close to being killed that day. Don't you remember?" I threw that back at him, and he waved his hand in a dismissive gesture.

"I wasn't worried," he said.

I decided to let him have his delusions of grandeur, since I'd saved his life by mere seconds. "Okay, contact her, set up a meeting. Say you managed to recover your chest of goods, and you need to offload them because you're too hot," I suggested.

"Done. Where do you want to meet her?" Sergo asked.

"How about Bazarn?" Rivo asked, spinning around in her chair. She'd been so quiet, facing the wall, that I'd forgotten she was even there.

"Why Bazarn?" Mary asked.

"Because I hold power there, and we can trap them and use my interrogation room," Rivo said.

"You have an interrogation room?" Loweck asked, eyebrow raised. Her orange hair fell over her brow, and she brushed it back. "That's so cool."

Rivo smiled. "Dad had a few enemies, as you know, and occasionally, he needed to... pry some information from spies. You'd be amazed at what these stuffy business types will tell you with a few simple threats."

I cleared my throat, shaking my head slowly. "While I don't condone torture on the whole, I agree this is a good plan. Bazarn. If she can make it in week, let's do that. We'll use the portals and figure out how Lom is contacting this Foral. Everyone good?"

"Dean, you still didn't tell us what Lom demanded," Mary told me in front of the group. I'd intended to bring it up in private with her alone, and maybe Slate.

"Yeah, what did the old tin man want?" Slate asked, probably trying to add some levity to the grave scenario. It didn't work.

"He said to turn myself in to this Viliar at Udoon," I informed them, glancing at Mary, who remained stoic.

"To what end?" Loweck asked.

"He said I'd be able to travel to his time, and he'd stop messing with things here." I stood, sending my rolling chair a couple of feet, and Mary's hand flew to her mouth in an over-dramatic response.

"You can't be thinking about it," she said.

"I haven't had time, but the reality is, I would if I

believed him."

"Boss, tell me you don't believe him," Slate said.

"No. Not for a second. He'll stop at nothing to destroy us, even if he has to bend space and time to accomplish it. Which is why I need something from Fontem's cache."

"What is it?" Sergo asked, but I couldn't say, not yet.

"All in due time," I advised them. "Meeting is adjourned."

The others started to file out, and Sergo stopped at the doorway. "Uhm, Captain… Can I ask a favor?"

"Sure, what do you need? I asked the bug-man.

"Can we keep the name of our contact from Walo?" he asked.

I had a feeling I knew where this was headed. "Why?"

"Well, those lonely nights in the cold dead dark of space can be tough. It was only once, but I think Foral might still have feelings for me. I mean, I'm good at buzzing an antenna, if you know what I'm saying." Sergo's mandibles opened and closed a few times, and I pushed past him.

"I can't make any promises." I walked through the corridor, following after Mary and Slate.

Sergo shouted down the hall after us. "It was way before Walo. She's just… the jealous type."

Slate craned his neck and smiled. "If you think you're in trouble with Lom, imagine being Sergo when Walo finds out about this."

THIRTEEN

The shadow wavered by the tree, and Jules braced herself for the Deity to push words into her mind, only it didn't. The cloud dissipated, leaving them alone. It didn't look like the others had noticed.

"It was quite the feat, fixing the Shandra," Dal'i told her. Dean lay a short distance away, gently breathing as he slept. It was late, but Jules had too much catching up to do to sleep yet.

"What were they like before the Theos?" Jules asked, nervously glancing at the tree again.

"They were used a long time ago. Commonplace among most races. They inspired commerce and community, but also created tensions and war. Eventually, they were shut down," the girl said. It was hard to think of her as anything but, since she was so small and youthful in appearance. Jules was the real girl here, having lived for a short sixteen years: a sliver of time in comparison to the other Zan'ra sitting opposite her.

"Then the Theos came along and added more of them, using the same technology, and once they messed the balance up by destroying the Iskios, they were faltering, dying off. They decided to place themselves in the stones, offering their lives to fuel the portals. It was quite the feat, one I never expected to see in my lifetime.

"And when the Vortex arrived, and they were banished for good, the Theos once again had no choice but to depart from the stones," Dal'i said.

"The Vortex. That was my mother. My father stopped it, sending it to another dimension," Jules told her.

"You're joking, right?" Dal'i's mouth twisted into a sardonic smile. "You have quite the imagination."

"No, it's true. I was born shortly after. My mom was pregnant with me, and we assumed I was Iskios, because of my green eyes. Turns out Ja'ri was waiting there for a host. She entered my mother, but was probably pushed aside by the Iskios, so she came into the womb. At least, that's how I picture it now," Jules said.

"You have got to be kidding me. That's amazing. And your dad saved you two?" Dal'i asked.

"He did. He saves a lot of people. He's a great man," Jules said, suddenly shy for some reason.

"Sounds like I have a lot to learn. Perhaps tomorrow we can continue," she said.

"You need sleep?" Jules asked.

"Don't you?"

"Sure, but I thought…"

"We remain flesh and blood. You and I aren't that far off, even if you *are* human." Dal'i had no pack and lay on the ground without a blanket. Jules had an extra rolled up in her pack and passed it over.

"Where will we go?" Jules asked, moving closer to Dean.

"To the next Deity. See if he's feeling talkative," Dal'i told her.

Jules closed her eyes, envisioning a shadow moving behind her lids, and she fell asleep to the sound of the rushing waterfall and the crackling of their fire.

I was uncomfortable with our new guest being on board *Light,* but I opted to defer to Jules' decision. If she was confident that Dal'i was on her side, I had to support it.

Almost a week had passed since Jules and Dean had arrived with the other Zan'ra and so far, I'd rarely seen Jules without her new ally at her side.

"Good morning, honey," Mary said, stretching and adding a deep yawn. She wore a fuzzy white robe and came to the island, pulling up a stool beside me. "Couldn't sleep?"

"Not really." I'd been up for a couple of hours already and had taken Maggie for a walk around the ship to clear my mind. We were less than two weeks from Techeron, and I was still waiting for Jules to extract information from Dal'i, who'd been less than willing to speak with anyone but my daughter.

Jules had been keeping quiet too, which was a little worrisome, but she told me she was fine, and that they were working on a plan. She'd assured me she'd fill me in when it was drawn up, so I left them to it.

I walked to the kitchen, pouring Mary a cup of coffee, and slid it across the countertop to her. She peered down the hallway and leaned in, whispering. "We asked her to stay here in our suite, Dean. Is that what's bothering you?"

Dal'i had stayed in Hugo's room since they'd arrived, and other than the glowing eyes, she seemed like another teenage girl.

"No. It's not that. Too many unknowns. Seeing Jules with another of the Zan'ra... It feels a little permanent," I said, not certain what I even meant.

Mary nodded anyway, sipping her coffee. "I get it. How

do you think Dean's doing?"

"Fine. At least they let him in on their conversations. That must have taken some convincing on Jules' part." I smiled, imaging Jules giving the other girl an ultimatum.

"They're leaving today, right after you," Mary told me.

"I know. Do you really think Patty will be there?"

"Let's hope so. Jules has the bracelet, meaning she should be able to neutralize the essence, or whatever they're calling it." Mary sipped her coffee, and I stood. I was restless.

"I'm going to try to return today, if possible," I said. "Interrogating one of Lom's Padlog contacts doesn't seem fun, but hopefully, we'll bring some solid details home with us."

"Then we'll be near Techeron soon. Fontem better not be leading us on a wild goose chase," she said.

"With that guy, I wouldn't be surprised." I cleaned up my dishes and passed by Mary, leaning in close enough to peck her on the cheek. "It'll all be over soon, and we can return to some sense of normalcy."

Mary averted her gaze, staring into her coffee. "That's the plan."

An hour later, I wandered over to deck two, finding our entourage ready to go. Slate leaned against the wall, wearing dark gray pants and a long-sleeved black shirt. Loweck was beside him, her green hair and orange skin a trademark of her distant race. It was a good thing no one stood out on Bazarn, not with the constant thrum of visiting aliens. She had on a gray jumpsuit and smiled as I neared them.

"Why do you look so happy?" I asked her.

Loweck glanced at Slate. "I've been cooped up here for too long. It's about time I was asked to do something important and serious."

"I fully trust you to put Foral in her place if she gets out of line," I told her, and she beamed at her husband.

I walked over to the petite Molariun woman and set a hand on her shoulder. "Rivo, thanks again for hosting this. I'm glad to have you joining us."

Rivo wore her business attire, a white pantsuit, and she seemed so much older than the girl I'd rescued from Lom's robopirates years ago. "It'll be good for me to peek my head into the Alnod Industries offices again, to remind the subordinates I still run the show." She winked at me, and Sergo buzzed near the door.

His antennae flickered nervously on the top of his head. "What's the matter, Sergo?" I asked.

"Walo." He pointed at the corridor, where the Supreme's granddaughter stalked toward us.

Her wasp-like face was set in a deep frown. "Foral... you were with Foral?"

I stepped away, not wanting to be in the middle of a relationship dispute. They moved farther down the hall, but we could hear their arguing as if they were right beside us.

"So..." I turned to the group. "Foral is supposed to be meeting Sergo at the promenade in an hour. We're going to be close by, and when he leads her toward Kennio Lounge, we intercept, toss her in the shuttle, and head to Alnod Industries."

Slate nodded along, resting his pulse rifle on his shoulder. Loweck reached into a brown pack and pulled five small disks from inside. She passed one to me, then to each of the others. "Stick these in your pockets. If anything goes wrong, we can track one another on our wrist tablets."

I lifted my arm, tapping the screen, and saw the blinking lights as they synced with the programming of my localized map. "I hope we don't need these."

"Better safe than sorry," Slate said, using the old adage.

Sergo walked over, his shoulders slumped. "Walo wants to come." His voice was quiet, pleading.

Walo bristled behind him, arms crossed. "Captain, do you mind if I tag along? I wouldn't want his… stinger falling off without me around."

I stifled a laugh and nodded. "Sure, Walo. You can join us. Everyone ready?"

We entered the portal room, and before we left, my thoughts drifted to Jules. I'd said my goodbyes, and considering they were about to head to the next world holding a Deity, where they expected to meet Patty and the other Zan'ra boy, she'd been oddly calm about it.

When we were in position around the table, Rivo activated the portal, sending us to Bazarn Five. We transported instantly, and I was glad Lom hadn't chosen to drop by for an uninvited visit in the void. I didn't want to waste time on that today, not when we were growing closer to solving this puzzle.

Bazarn's Shandra room was as ornate as ever, a regal entryway to the most luxurious vacation planet. I'd been through a lot on this world. Lom had attacked while I'd first met Rivo's father, Garo. I'd met Regnig here, deep underground, and Jules had realized how powerful she was as someone attempted to blow up the Peaks of Duup resort after Garo's funeral.

"Dean, you okay?" Slate asked as we walked toward the exit.

"I'm fine. Just thinking about Bazarn. Lots of memories." The guards were the same race as they'd always been, huge and growling.

They weren't the same ones I'd grown to befriend. Those two had moved to Magnus' ship *Horizon*, meaning they'd been killed along with the rest of the crew seven months ago.

This duo let us pass the moment they spotted Rivo behind Slate. She was essentially royalty here, and we entered the next room, a quiet foyer leading outside by a wide set of stairs.

We exited, ending at the promenade, and it was clear that commerce was in full swing on Bazarn Five once again. People of all shapes and sizes lingered about, walking in groups, talking amongst one another as they sought transport to the resort of their choice. It was a nice sight, but for now I was on alert, scanning the area for signs of any Padlog.

Sergo leaned in, talking over the crowd. "We're going to move into position. It wouldn't do us any good to be seen here with you, because if I know Foral, she's watching."

I nodded, sending the two Padlog on their way. Slate went ahead, cutting a trail for the rest of us through the crowd of people. I was wearing casual clothing, and had strapped a pulse pistol around my hip. While it wasn't stiflingly hot out, the pressure of bodies around us caused me to sweat, and I finally breathed easier as we neared the edge of the promenade.

"It's busy today," I told Rivo.

"Good news for the economy, but I'm not seeing my shuttle anywhere." She scanned the parking lot, and I saw nothing marking her private Alnod Industries transportation.

The smells of various food markets wafted through the air, and I heard at least four different music types from vendors outside the promenade. The restaurants were busy, and I glanced at one across from us with people on a rooftop patio, enjoying the sun. The place had a carnival feel, reminding me of Pier Thirty-nine at San Francisco. If we were on Earth, it would have been full of blinking lights, freshly popped corn, and cotton candy.

Someone bumped into me, nearly knocking me over, and before I could turn to the offender, I spotted Sergo pacing toward us. His gaze locked with mine, and he gave a slight shake of his head. He was afraid.

"Something's wrong," I whispered to Slate, but he was looking in the other direction. I tapped him on the shoulder. "Slate, Sergo's coming." I pointed, and he saw the gun the same moment as I did. Slate shoved me out of the way as the blast raced past us, striking a parked hoverbike.

A shuttle lowered directly behind us, causing a group of tourists to scatter, and the door opened, revealing an armed Padlog. Slate moved to track his pulse rifle, but the enemy shook his head as five armed attackers circled around our team. They shoved Sergo and Walo between us, and a Padlog woman with the face of a spider walked forward.

"Drop the weapons," she said, her fangs waving slightly.

"Boss, what do you want to do?" Slate asked, still gripping his gun. Loweck was tense beside him, and I knew it was eating her alive to not attack them. I didn't doubt she could disarm a few of the enemy before being overthrown, but now wasn't the time for heroics.

"Foral, I presume?" I asked, stepping toward her.

She spun her long gun around, jabbing it into my stomach. I keeled over, gasping for breath, and heard Slate struggle with someone. I reached for my pistol and was knocked to the ground as Foral clubbed the back of my head. I hit the concrete, and everything went black.

FOURTEEN

*B*oria was dead. Jules stepped from the cavern where the Shandra remained hidden, and balked at the gray-brown landscape. A strong wind carried over the emptiness, bringing a chill, a bitter sensation through her bones.

"What is this place?" Dean asked, and she saw the reflection of the desolate land through his helmet's facemask.

"This is Boria, but it's a far cry from the world I remember." Dal'i walked up and out of the crevasse, leading them to higher ground. She stopped as soon as they were on the flat earth and slowly took in the setting.

"What was it like before?" Dean asked.

"Lively. There were no people to interfere with nature, but the land was full of animals. The ecosystem was healthy and hearty. The trees rose high into the sky, the grass was deep and dark. Can it be that I've been away this long?" Dal'i wasn't in a sphere or an EVA, but she had no problem breathing, so Jules removed her own protective energy barrier, taking the advice the Zan'ra had offered in the past week. She'd been training Jules to do simple tasks, wondrous things Jules had never thought even a Zan'ra could accomplish.

At times, the orange-eyed girl seemed like a peer, another teenager with nothing but boys and clothing to think about, but now she was ancient, her voice different, her posture bearing the weight of millennia. Would Jules live forever? Would she want to?

Dal'i turned toward Jules, eyes streaming with tears, and Jules grasped her hand, keeping hold of it. "Ja'ri, what have I been doing? Clinging to some archaic hope that we could correct what was once wronged? I've wasted so many years. The others were right to seal themselves away. O'ri never expected to return to life. The Deities know Ja'ri wanted to stay preserved forever."

"Why?" Jules asked her. "Why did Ja'ri do it?"

Dal'i met Jules' stare, her eyes burning hot orange. "You don't want to know. We all have secrets we live with, terrible things we've done. The Deities may have been right."

Jules shivered. The Zan'ra girl suddenly sounded like an elderly woman. "I deserve the truth."

"You want to hear what Ja'ri did? The races she devoured? The planets she destroyed in an effort to stop the Deities? Is that something you can handle?" Dal'i shouted, and Jules fell back like she'd been slapped. Dean caught her, his arms supportive and strong.

He whispered in her ear. "Ja'ri's not you, Ju. You're not the same."

But she was. Jules had destroyed the Sprites. She'd done the same to the Arnap. *The races she devoured.* Perhaps she *was* Ja'ri, only reborn.

"What about this place? What happened to it?" Dean asked, pointing to the immense clay-like ground ahead of them.

"I don't know. Maybe the Deity trapped here is leaking, sending poison throughout. I closed off this world a long time ago so that none could visit it. I couldn't risk anyone stumbling upon the god."

"And Desolate… I mean, Uleera?" Jules used the name

Dal'i had given her for the Zan'ra homeworld.

"It's not supposed to be open either. How did you access it?" Dal'i asked.

Jules hadn't thought of it. She'd been compelled to visit, but the truth was, she'd never attempted to bring anyone else there. "I'm not sure."

"Come. Let's find our buried enemy and wait for the others. I sense them closing in," Dal'i said. She'd tried to show Jules how to use her projection abilities. It also allowed her to track someone, at least by a feeling, if not by empirical data. So far, Jules had been unable to feel anything from Patty and Lan'i, even if Dal'i claimed to.

Jules threw her sphere up, circling it around Dean. It had taken a lot of persuading for Dal'i to permit Dean to join them, but in the end, she'd agreed he couldn't mess anything up. She glanced at the pair of them with something close to contempt as she rose from the ground, no energy visible around her, and Dal'i raced forward faster than Jules thought possible.

She chased after the girl, the landscape below rushing by in a brown blur.

"I don't like it here," Dean grumbled.

"Neither do I," Jules assured him, moving higher into the sky, tracing after the Zan'ra's movements ahead of her. The ground arced over the horizon, with no landmarks to go by.

"I don't see any water," Dean said.

She scoured below, slowing slightly to see the view. It was nothing but an expanse of rock and beige dirt. She continued on, and in a few minutes she began to see the start of a peak in the distance. As they grew closer the mountain became larger, until Jules was sure the thing had to reach through the atmosphere.

"We're going up there?" Dean asked. The clouds hung

around the midway point of the peaks, four jagged points connecting near the base. The Four.

She lifted them through the thin clouds, dampness dripping from her sphere as they broke through, moving for the top of the mountains. Dal'i was already there when Jules arrived, standing on the precipice of the rocky top.

Jules landed them on the flat top, which was only a few meters wide, and stood near the middle, a wave of vertigo threatening her vision. Dean remained still, staring over Dal'i's shoulder, and Jules caught the view he was quieted by. The planet curved here from this high vantage point, making the view of Boria a pleasant one, despite the boring and mundane landscape. From here, Jules felt what it must mean to be a god, to mold worlds and people, to change futures.

"Where's the Deity?" Dean asked, breaking the silence.

Dal'i stepped to the edge of the platform, pointing down. Jules hesitantly moved there, peering over the side to see the coffin fifty meters below, four chains mounting it to each of the four mountain peaks.

"Isn't this a little dramatic?" Jules asked.

"This was O'ri's work." Dal'i looked to the sky. "The others are near. The Four will be together again."

Jules stared at her, then peered at the clouds. She was nervous to hear that Patty and the other boy were coming, but that had been the plan all along. It didn't change the fact that she wasn't ready to face off against them.

Jules pointed at the coffin over the cliff and focused on it. "O'ri did this one?"

She nodded. "Mine is beneath the tree. You placed one under the water on Uleera."

"And Lan'l's is the one I heard about in the Golnex system?" Jules guessed.

"That's right. One for each of us. O'ri was the most

dramatic, though I've always appreciated your work too." Dal'i grinned for the first time since they'd arrived on Boria.

The chains held the long box up, but the heavy wind shook it from side to side, rattling the metallic bonds. "Can you speak with it?" Dean asked.

Jules closed her eyes, willing it to talk with her. *Hello, Deity. I am Jules, but you may recognize me as Ja'ri. I'd like to speak with you.* The other Zan'ra wanted nothing more than to keep them imprisoned, but Jules was sensing an alteration from Dal'i over the last week. Being around people again seemed to be changing her.

"Anything?" Dal'i asked, but Jules told her there was nothing.

They sat on the rocky mountaintop, staring over the world like guardians of a dead planet.

Jules decided to investigate, to take matters into her own hands, and she tapped Dean on the shoulder, gaining his attention. "I'll be right back."

He glanced toward the edge and nodded his understanding. "Be careful."

"I will." She hovered, moving toward the opening between the mountain peaks, and lowered toward the hanging coffin. Was the Deity sleeping inside? Was it aware, awake, slowly going mad by the thousands upon thousands of years being contained?

At last, you've come.

The voice was powerful, low and deep. Jules floated above the wooden case, peering at it from her perch. "I'm here."

Do the others know? it asked.

"The other Deities?"

Your true self. Do they know?

"I don't understand," she said.

It laughed, a booming sound in her eardrums. She felt the blood falling from her nose and ears again, but didn't react. *Free me. I will explain. You are special.*

"You want to kill the Zan'ra. What will happen if I do free you?" Jules asked.

You will not be harmed. We will strip them of their powers. We make the same agreement we made before.

Jules reeled at the words. "You offered this to them before they sealed you away?"

We offered it before they killed their own. The Four dealt destruction to the Zan'ra. They must be stopped.

The Four? "You're saying the Four killed their own people?" Jules was appalled and glanced up. She was still alone here.

Child… remember…

A gust shook the coffin, and something poured from the wood, an inky black mist entering Jules' sphere. She inhaled, and it filled her.

Ja'ri smiled at her work. The Zan'ra were gone. At first, they'd listened to Lan'i's suggestion of creating burial shrouds near the Shandra, but eventually, the others saw her side and stopped helping him. She stared toward the lake far from the city, knowing Lan'i was occupied, moving the bodies of their people. He was weak. They were all weak.

Ja'ri was the only one who could lead, who could prevent their deaths. The Four would become one, when she was finished sealing the damned Deities away. For that, she needed their strength.

The city still burned, and she could smell the singed flesh of her people.

She smiled, elation filling her bones, and she clapped her hands, bringing her to the ocean. The others arrived seconds later, staring at the box. It shook and rattled the chains binding it, but the god was trapped.

Ja'ri lifted it with nothing but her thoughts, and plunged the coffin into the raging whitecaps. A storm brewed, a last-ditch effort of self-preservation from the Deity, but it was pointless. He was done.

Jules' eyes snapped open, and she panted, disgust filling her. "That isn't me!" she shouted, wanting to shoot the essence of the evil Zan'ra from her body.

I know.

"Then why do they all think of me as Ja'ri?" Jules asked.

A shadow emerged from the coffin, filling the air in front of her. It took a form with two strong arms, two strong legs, an elongated head, and something similar to fins jutting from its neck. *We had one last gift, left on Lainna.*

"Lainna? I don't recall where that is," Jules admitted, and the shadow flashed, an image subsequently burned into her mind. Colorful shards, crystals and gemstones. "The crystal world. That's where my mom was possessed by the Iskios."

I know nothing of that trivial point in our timeline. We guided you there to free us.

Jules trembled, listening to the words. "Are you saying… I'm not a Zan'ra?"

In a sense. You were made to give the impression of the one they call Ja'ri. They would trust you, show you our resting places. You are to free us.

Jules couldn't believe her ears. It was too much to take. After what they'd been through, she'd just learned she wasn't some terrible Iskios creation. Then she'd been part of something, a Zan'ra; at long last she'd discovered she belonged. Now she'd learned they were evil, and she wasn't one of them after all.

"If I'm not Zan'ra, what am I?" she asked.

The shadow grew, filling the void between the mountains. It laughed, as if she'd told the universe's funniest joke. *You are one of us.*

Blasts of orange, purple, and blue cascaded from above her, striking the shadow. It shrieked, hissing and evaporating into the coffin. Dal'i arrived beside her, still firing a wave of energy at the wooden casket. More purple and blue shot from overhead, and Jules saw the forms of the missing Zan'ra.

"Patty!" she shouted.

"Come. We have much to discuss," Dal'i said, urging Jules to follow.

They landed on the flat peak, and Patty settled to the ground near her brother. "Dean!" she said, wrapping her arms around him.

Dean hesitated for a moment, as if this were a dream, but eventually picked her up, spinning around in a circle. "Patty, you're here."

She looked older, her lighter hair long and pulled into a top bun. She wore a dark uniform with silver accents. Lan'i's outfit matched, and he ran over, excitedly greeting Dal'i.

Jules ran over to Patty, taking her hands. "Are you in there? Is it you?" she asked.

Patty rolled her eyes. "God, you're always so dramatic. Of course it's me."

Dean spoke, keeping his voice low. "How could you do this?"

"What? Lan'i told me about the gods breaking free, and how he couldn't seal them away without my help. I helped. No biggie," she said.

Dean's arms flew in the air. "No biggie! You disappeared for seven months and never sent a damned message to Mom or me? No biggie?" He was shouting, and Jules set a hand on his shoulder.

"Mom and Dad are busy, and you're having fun with Jules on *Light*. I didn't think you'd care that much," Patty said, acting like the spoiled selfish kid she was.

Dean looked ready to explode, so Jules stepped between them. She still hadn't had time to process what the Deity had just told her, but she could later. Now she had some news to deliver. "Patty... your dad..."

"What about him?" she asked, eyes big and glowing purple.

"He's dead."

* * *

My head pounded fiercely, and I blinked my eyes five times to clear some of the cobwebs. The room was bright, too light for my current headache. I glanced around, seeing I was alone in the cell.

We'd been ambushed, indicating someone had known we were coming. How? I trusted everyone with me, but that didn't mean one of my lesser crew members couldn't have been bought. How far did Lom's reach extend from the future? I had to deal with him sooner rather than later.

I almost smiled at my train of thought. I was locked in a cell, being held captive by Foral, and here I was, planning my attack on Lom in some future timeline.

My personal tablet was still on my wrist, and I lifted it, checking to see where the others were being kept. The other four icons blinked a short distance away, telling me they were in a room together. Walo wasn't tagged, since we hadn't been expecting to bring her along.

Footsteps carried from outside the cell, and I flicked the device off, not wanting to draw attention to it. I ran a hand over my chin, feeling only a slight amount of stubble. I couldn't have been out long, suggesting we were likely still on Bazarn. That was a good sign.

My cell was white-walled, the paint stained with brown markings in a few spots. I wondered if it was dried blood.

"Dean Parker." The female voice was sharp, and the metal door slid to the side, revealing the spider-like Padlog. Her hands were fuzzy, her eyes round and multi-faceted.

"Foral, I presume?" I asked, standing and stretching my back and legs.

There was a big Padlog behind her, armed to the teeth, which reminded me I didn't have anything close to the upper hand right now.

"Come with me," she said, waving for me to exit the cell. I obeyed slowly, and she lingered nearby, assessing me. "You're much less impressive than I was led to expect."

"Thanks," I replied. "Does that mean you'll let me go?"

She smiled, a strange sight on her alien face. "I don't think so, Parker."

She spun on a heel, and I moved behind her through the corridor. The lights flickered, and I guessed we were in an underground facility. The ceilings were short, and we ducked our heads as we passed into a larger room. She pointed to a chair across the room. "Sit."

I nodded, moving for the metal seat, but not before peering around the space, looking for something to help me out of this mess. It was empty, save a desk with no drawers, and a few pieces of paper strewn about. Water dripped from the corner of the ceiling, forming a brown sludge pile that rolled toward the front of the uneven room.

"I said sit."

I sat. Foral stayed standing, arms crossed, and the guard stepped into the room, holding a gun that probably weighed more than I did.

"What were you hoping to find out here?" she asked me.

"I was hoping to get a little R and R. You know… gamble in the Cloud Casino, drink some nectar, find a beach." I grinned.

"Parker, don't mess with me. At least one part of the rumor is true," she said.

"What, that I'm devilishly handsome?" I asked as she crossed the space slowly, like a predatory spider.

Her hand sprang out, slapping my cheek. My head flew to the side, blood welling on my lips.

"That you're a fool, and your mouth is bigger than your brain," Foral said.

I kept my eyes down and wiped the blood away. "I'm glad your reconnaissance was right for once."

"For once?" she asked.

"I know exactly what you've been doing. Lom let it slip. You think you guys are so smart, taking money from a ghost, but it'll catch up to you. Not to mention the Alliance has been given your name and description, as well as your ship's ID tags," I told her, half lying. Some of that was true.

"I don't think…"

"Also the Supreme. See, when he heard that one of his own had betrayed him, as well as the Alliance he'd worked so hard to join, he went berserk. Directed his private guards and bounty hunters to find you and bring you to justice." That part was accurate. I'd made the call myself.

"You don't expect me to believe that." Foral looked dubious, but I simply shrugged.

"That's for you to find out. I hope PlevaCorp has paid you well enough for you to go into hiding for the rest of your life." From the expression that passed over her face, I had her. "Of course, there is another option."

"Letting you go?" She laughed, her pincers clicking together.

"How does he communicate with you?" I asked.

She nervously glanced at the guard, her expression telling me she'd lost power. I'd shifted the interrogation.

"How?" I stood, and the guard raised the gun, aiming it at me.

"It was a lot of credits, Parker. You'd have done the same thing," she said softly.

"I don't presume to understand your situation. Perhaps I would have, in your shoes, but I'd also know when my time was up, and when I needed to barter for my life. You need to do that this instant," I told her.

"The message came from an executive at PlevaCorp," she said. "We met, and they gave me the credits."

"What were the instructions?" I asked, stepping closer to her.

"There was a list. From following your daughter to tracking *Light*. We have operatives on Haven, and elsewhere too," she said. "You have to take me off the kill list. The Supreme will never let me live otherwise, and my crew didn't have a choice. They work for me, but they don't deserve this."

"Tell me everything," I said, and she nodded.

The first gun blast sounded from down the hall, and my eyes shot wide. The guard in the room with us turned, stepping into the corridor. A second later, he was firing at an unseen enemy, and I saw him drop, a pulse striking his skull. It sizzled and smoked, and Foral was on me, grabbing my neck from behind and pulling a knife. She staggered toward the doorway, calling for a ceasefire.

"Stop. I have Parker!"

I spotted Slate, blood on his face, Loweck limping beside him. They were both armed, and I locked gazes with my commander. He shook his head once, but I didn't know what he was trying to tell me.

"You're going to let me out of here, and you can have

your captain," she said, shoving me into the hallway, still clutching my collar with a strong, sticky spider's hand. We almost tripped on the big Padlog dead on the floor.

Slate nodded at her, holding his gun at his side. "We'll lower our weapons." He started to crouch, and I felt Foral relax. The knife dropped from her grip a second later, and she fell over, knocking me to my knees. The gunshot hit her in the back, and Sergo stood behind her with a pulse pistol raised.

"Any others?" he asked, glancing into the room.

"Not in there." I took Slate's outstretched hand, letting him help me to my feet, and stared at Foral's dead eyes. "Dammit. She was going to come clean. I had her hooked," I told them.

"Boss, we rescued you. Would you believe they let Loweck get close enough to one of their guns?" Slate beamed at his wife.

"This was a big waste of time. We need to check for any pertinent information on them and get the hell out of here before reinforcements come. If we're on Bazarn, you have to be sure someone from PlevaCorp is watching this place," I said.

Sergo was still standing there, staring at his old companion's body. "I killed her."

Walo buzzed beside him, pulling the gun away from her boyfriend. "You're going to be okay," she assured him.

"Let's move." I shook my head. What a waste, but hopefully, we'd learn something from their belongings. Otherwise, I'd risked our lives for nothing.

FIFTEEN

The memory of the Deity's conversation with Jules was fresh, but with Patty in front of her, it felt like a distant event.

"Tell me everything," Patty said as they sat around the crackling fire. Dal'i had forced them to relocate from the peaks, worried the resting god would be eavesdropping on their conversation. Dean kept glancing at Jules, as if urging her to steal Patty's powers and be done with it, but Jules didn't want to act so rashly.

"Why did you do it?" Dean asked Patty.

"We've been through this," Patty told her older brother. They sat beside one another on a fallen tree, her feet dangling on the tall seat.

"Enough with the sob story about never fitting in on *Horizon* or the Academy. You abandoned your family," Dean told her.

"Not like you cared that much," she told him.

"Patty, he's been out there all alone for the last seven months, trying to find you," Jules assured the girl. Dean's sister hushed up at that, and a smile broke over her face.

"You did that?" she asked.

Dean nodded, mumbling under his breath. "I did."

"You still haven't told me what happened," Patty said, and from the look on Dean's face, he was in no shape to tell her. Jules rested beside Dal'i across the fire, and she sat up straighter, deciding to be the storyteller.

She informed Patty about the Arnap, and how they'd invaded the Ritair. How the beings had been chased from Sterona and later tracked down by the same Arnap, and that *Horizon* had been sent to investigate rumors of genocide. Patty remained silent as Jules described the scene of Papa and Slate fighting off the Arnap on the bridge, while Jules and her mother saved Leslie and Natalia.

Lan'i stood, his pacing behind them kicking up dust. "We need to find these Arnap. We'll destroy them for what they did to your father, Patty."

Jules glanced at him, recalling the *L & P* etchings on Patty's childish drawings.

"You don't need to do that," Dean told them.

"Why not? He's right. We have to avenge…"

"Jules killed them."

"But there are more. We can free the Ritair…" Patty was cut off again by her brother.

"Jules killed every one of them." His head hung low as he rested his elbows on his knees.

Patty grew silent, and her gaze fell on Jules through the fire. It was so strange, seeing her old friend with bright purple eyes. "Thank you, Ju."

That day came rushing into Jules' mind, the sheer power she'd unleashed, and she glanced at the other Zan'ra, recalling what the Deity had shown her. Ja'ri had killed her own people. This god had said she wasn't really one of the Four. That she'd been created to fool them, and that Jules was supposed to free the Deities. Could she do this?

"Do you feel anything of O'ri in there?" Jules asked Patty.

The girl shook her head, frowning. "No. It's all me. I

do feel different, but that's just the powers, I think. These gifts are wonderful. I can't believe you moaned and complained about them for so many years. If anyone doesn't understand you, then screw them."

"I'm bringing you home," Dean told Patty, grabbing her by the arm.

She tugged it free, shaking his grip. "I don't think so."

"Mom is worried sick, and you didn't even say goodbye to Dad," Dean said.

"Does it matter now? I have too much to do," she claimed.

"Like what?" Jules asked softly.

"Sealing these Deities. Jules, you saw what they did on Uleera, right?"

Jules had seen only too clearly, but that had been Ja'ri. These three had fallen in line, but why had they done it? Did they feel remorse? She couldn't bring it up, not without giving it all away. She still needed to learn how to free the Deities, and that meant she had to learn how to seal them.

"I know. Let's go there, to Desolate… I mean, Uleera. Show me how to help," Jules told them, and Lan'i smiled, his white teeth turning orange from the flames' reflection.

"That's my girl," he said, catching a jealous glance from both Patty and Dean, though for different reasons.

"Jules, we have to return to *Light*. We promised your dad," Dean said.

Patty rose, floating up from the log, to land beside Lan'i, who put a protective arm over her shoulders. "We're not going anywhere. You can go. You shouldn't be here with us. It's the Four, not the Five," Patty told her brother.

"Jules, can I speak to you for a minute?" Dean asked, and Jules nodded, stepping from the fire with him until they were out of earshot. "We found her. Can you use that crystal bracelet thingy and steal the essence or whatever so we can get the hell home?"

She stared into his big pleading eyes and stepped onto her toes, kissing his lips. "I'm sorry, but I can't. Not yet."

He spoke soft and slow. "Jules, you promised me."

"I know, but there's more to this than bringing Patty home. I need to stop them," she said.

"The Deities?" he asked, glancing in the direction of the mountains they couldn't see in the night sky.

She peered over his shoulder, toward the flickering fire. "No. The Zan'ra."

Dean would have a million questions, but now wasn't the time to discuss them. She kissed him again and whispered in his ear, "Trust me, okay?"

"What choice do I have? I'll trust you," he said, giving her less of a fight than she'd expected.

They returned to the fire and sat down, Patty staring at them. "How sweet. You two are finally a couple."

Jules was glad no one could see her reddening face in the darkness. "Tomorrow, we'll hit the coffins and make sure none of them ever leak out again."

The Zan'ra smiled widely. She could only hope she wasn't being played for a fool by a lying god.

"She was telling the truth," Rivo said.

"She was?" I leaned over the table, staring at the screen.

"Yes. PlevaCorp delivered the funds and the instructions. They were basic, nothing we didn't suspect, but the key is, we have a contact. A way to communicate with him," Rivo told us.

"We need to find this executive at PlevaCorp first. Why haven't we destroyed them yet?" Slate asked.

"First of all, we don't know where their head office is. They moved years ago, and they're more clandestine than Sergo's love affairs," Rivo said, inciting an annoyed buzz from our Padlog friend. She lifted her hands. "No offense."

"None taken." Sergo slumped in his chair, visibly deflated after killing someone from his past, and a Padlog at that. It was a reminder of his former life, one he'd left behind to work with me on *Light,* but he was lucky to have Walo at his side.

"Will you guys leave him alone? He's had a bit of a tough day," Walo said, and Rivo nodded, continuing.

"They made contact with him on Bazarn. I've always suspected they had some form of operation here, but there was no proof. Now we have it." Rivo exited the program, activating a map of the planet we were on. It revealed the region where the executive had instructed Foral to meet him at the start, and Rivo pinned it.

"This is an island: not a floating one, but a real island in the Solemn Seas. It's a very affluent area, and each island is customizable to one's needs. This one is owned by an unidentified shell company, but they paid in full and have never been late with a tax payment. I suspect it's connected to PlevaCorp. There will be guards, and shields, but if we hit them quickly and silently, we should be able to catch them off guard," Rivo said.

We were inside her offices in a floating island high above the oceans. It was well protected, far more secure than when her father Garo had lived here.

We'd managed to escape the underground bunker, which had been deep in the Duup mountains. We were lucky enough for Rivo to be able to contact her shuttle pilot to find us, and a couple hours later, we were cleaned up and ready to strike PlevaCorp.

"What are we waiting for?" Loweck asked.

We all rose, heading out of the fancy boardroom past a bunch of Molariun employees, each with glowing HUDs floating in front of their eyes as they talked with business partners around the universe. Their cubicles had sound-dampening fields, and Rivo waved and smiled at them as we walked through with purpose. Slate looked like a giant compared to the short workers, and his gun was out of place, but we exited quickly and were ushered outside, where the pilot awaited us.

Slate let out a whistle, eyeing the ship. "This isn't any normal transport shuttle, is it?"

He was right. The vessel was smooth, matte gray, with countless weapons systems jutting from the underside and wings. It was about four times the size of a normal shuttle, yet manageable within a planet's atmosphere. As we entered the craft, I asked Rivo if I could see about getting my hands on one of these for Haven's defenses.

"We'll talk." She winked one of her four eyes, and I smiled, trying to convince myself I wasn't nervous about the upcoming attack. We were taking our feet to the street and invading the private residence of a PlevaCorp executive, one that was connected to Lom in the future.

Mary was going to have a heart attack when I told her about our adventures on Bazarn. I'd have to leave some crucial details out, depending on how this went.

Once we were loaded in, sitting facing one another on the long white benches, four more arrived. They were the huge Duupa beings, the giants from the mountain regions, and they wore massive armored suits. Their guns were taller than I was, and I swallowed hard as one came to sit beside me. The bench groaned under the duress, and Rivo greeted them affably.

"These are my friends, and friends, these are my personal guards," Rivo said.

"Nice to meet you," I said, and one giant only nodded, speaking in English.

"Likewise."

The ship rose from the parking pad on the edge of the office's floating headquarters, and we moved toward our destination.

"From our surveillance, there's one vessel docked at the island, and it's a yacht. I suspect there will be defenses, but nothing this baby can't handle." Rivo patted the wall with her glove, the metal reverberating at the touch.

Rivo was in her element here on Bazarn, and I decided then and there to give her more responsibility on *Light*. Either that or I'd have to dismiss her so she could return home where she belonged.

Slate spoke up, and we listened with anticipation. "We're going to head in the back entrance. The pulses on this ship will disrupt the shield just long enough for us to sneak through. Of course, that will alert them to our presence pretty quickly, which means we won't have much time to access the building." Slate flipped his tablet around, showing us an image of the property from above. "We're going to the courtyard and entering through this side entrance. The servant halls will have less security, and we can gain entry to the main offices from there. From what we can tell, the executive spends most of his time here." He pointed a big finger at the top right of the screen.

"We need him alive," Rivo said, glaring at Sergo.

"I'll do my best," the Padlog man buzzed.

"Any questions?" Slate asked.

"What are they going to do?" Sergo asked, jabbing a thumb toward the huge soldiers beside me.

"They clean up any messes," Rivo said with a smile.

My body thrummed with excitement. We were getting closer to having some information on Lom. I'd already spoken with him in the nether region of the portals, and had verified he wanted me at Udoon. If there was a way to track him through the timelines, we might have the upper hand. Or at least, sabotaging his network here would hurt him in the long run.

We stayed quiet, Walo and Sergo talking softly across from me, and Loweck stared toward the pilot's bench, where a Molariun soldier flew us quickly over the tumultuous waves of the Solemn Sea. Today, it was anything but solemn. I hoped this wasn't an ill omen.

"Prepare yourselves. We're heading in," Rivo advised us, and I clutched my pulse rifle, my hand starting to sweat. I'd taken something for my headache from earlier, but the back of my skull was still tender from the beating it took as I was knocked out. We could have all used a night's sleep, but word would spread fast to this PlevaCorp exec, and we didn't want him to be able to scatter before we intercepted him.

I heard our ship's pulse blasts, and glanced toward the viewscreen, seeing a sphere around the island flicker and fail. The island was a couple of miles in radius, but it was covered in tropical trees and greenery. We entered it, landing behind the central building that took up a tenth of the land.

We jumped out of the ship, the Duupa giants heading out first. They moved far faster than I'd expected, and given their girth, their footsteps were oddly silent as they rushed through the knee-high grass toward the rear of the structure.

I followed, Slate at my side, and peered to the sky, seeing a drone heading in our direction. I began to point to it, and one of the Duupa soldiers dropped to one knee, aiming his huge gun straight up. He pulled the trigger and the drone exploded, pieces raining behind us.

"Good shot," I mumbled, running once again. I wore an armored vest, making my body weight a little heavier, but it was far less cumbersome than a full EVA. Once we landed at the rear of the four-story building, we reset our composure, letting everyone take a breather.

Slate lifted a hand, motioning us to follow the building toward the courtyard. We obeyed, and seconds later, we entered the open space near the side of the mansion. It was quiet here: too quiet, by my estimation. Just when I thought we were in the clear, a Molariun girl walked out of the servants' section, carrying a basket. She dropped it when she spotted us, and Rivo raced to her side, a finger on her own lips, silencing the girl.

We entered the building, the big soldiers staying outside. They were too large for covert action, and I let Slate and Loweck take the lead, doing what they did best. They moved with purpose through the halls, sweeping open doors and placing timed electrical locks on others. If someone was inside, they wouldn't be able to escape for half an hour.

When we passed through the servants' area unscathed, we found the entrance to the main house. Slate made room for Sergo, who managed to break the lock code in an impressive forty seconds. He smiled and shrugged as I walked past him into the main foyer.

"I've been expecting you," a voice said, and I turned to see the silhouette on the second balcony moving closer to us. Everyone's guns tracked the form, and when she stepped into sight, I lowered my weapon.

"Janine?"

SIXTEEN

The air was chilly, and Jules glanced at the other Zan'ra, none of whom used a visible shield like hers. "Why is your shield not colored like mine?" she asked Dal'i.

The girl smiled, pointing to the ground. "I don't use a sphere like you. My barrier covers my body an inch out, preventing injury. You can make it clear; you just have to concentrate and imagine it there, but not visible. Try it."

They were right outside of the lake near Desolate's portal, and Dean had watched with interest as Jules pointed to the bones of the Zan'ra along the underwater cliffside. Now he chatted with his sister as they waited to head across the countryside to the ocean.

Jules focused, picturing the sphere as invisible, and the green lights flashed, then faded. She could tell it was still activated, and she smiled at her accomplishment. "Thank you."

"There's a lot we can teach you, Jules."

"I know. Let's finish this, and then I need to get home. I promise I'll be back soon, and we can continue the training," she told Dal'i, only because it was what the Zan'ra wanted to hear. It was unclear who or what she could trust.

The Deity had given her one truth, and the Zan'ra had showed her another, but Jules almost bet the true answer lay somewhere in the middle. It was going to be tough to decide which side to land on, and that was why she needed to speak with her dad, not to mention the fact that they were heading to Techeron. Once Papa was within his Kraski ship, she would no longer be able to reach him with a portal, and she wasn't going to miss that mission. He'd been clear she had to be there.

Seeing Dean and Patty laughing and talking made it all the more difficult. Dean wasn't going to budge without bringing Patty along, and it was clear his sister wouldn't leave the other Zan'ra, especially Lan'i.

"Ready?" the blue-eyed boy asked them, and they nodded in reply. Jules moved to Dean's side, but he shook his head.

"Patty's going to bring me, if that's okay with you," he said.

"Oh, sure. No problem." Jules stepped away, watching as Patty lifted her brother inside an invisible sphere, carrying him along as she floated higher into the sky, moving in the direction of the ocean.

Jules couldn't help but feel slighted at the action, even though they were siblings with a lot to discuss. She shoved the hurt aside and took to the atmosphere, racing high at a forty-five-degree incline until she caught up to the other Zan'ra. For a moment, she was free, speeding over the bleak landscape, and she joined in the other Zan'ras' cheering.

They acted different once all four were together. Gone was the sullenness, the anxiety. She could understand the chemistry between them when they were nearby. Jules didn't know what to think, and the words from the Deity on Boria dug into her mind. *We guided you there to free us.* And lastly: *You are one of us.*

The other three's elation stopped as they neared the city: once their people's capital, now a ruined pile of rubbish. The memories the Deity showed her of Ja'ri destroying it filled Jules' thoughts, and she glanced at Dal'i, who stared at Lan'i, him nodding slowly and frowning at Jules before racing away. So they thought she was Ja'ri, and from the hurt in their eyes, they recalled that day so long ago as well.

The group hovered over the barren rocky ground, through low-lying white patches of fog, and eventually, they slowed and descended toward the water. It was calmer today; no black storm clouds threatened to fire lightning at her.

Once they landed, Jules noted how the two Zan'ra had paled at seeing their old city. Patty didn't seem to notice any change, and this proved to Jules that O'ri was buried deep inside her. For a moment, she considered using her hidden bracelet on Patty, to steal the Zan'ra's essence and bring the siblings to *Light*, while leaving these other two behind. But she needed to know how to rouse the gods.

"Dal'i said you spoke to him?" Lan'i asked, pointing to the light waves.

They were on the shoreline, at the bottom of the crag, and water lapped against the rocks, sending mist over them. "I did."

"How can this be? We've never spoken to them before, not through the traps," the blond boy said.

"Ja'ri was the one to seal him here. Maybe that's why?" Patty suggested.

"Could be. You didn't hear anything on Boria, did you?" Dal'i asked.

Jules shook her head, but was aware she'd already told the girl about speaking to the Deity under the giant tree on the other world. She didn't bring that up.

"Can you imagine?" Lan'i asked.

"What?" Dean stared toward the water. It was his first

time here, but Jules had described it in detail to him.

"They're asking *her* to free them? They really are mad, right, Ja'ri?" Lan'i asked.

"Jules," she corrected him.

He raised his hands, laughing. "Whatever you say. Let's redo this. With all four of us, it'll ensure he stays buried forever. We used to have a tool to hone our powers for this purpose."

"What happened to it?" Jules asked.

"I think you had it last… or Ja'ri did. Must have been lost. We can make do, it just takes some effort," Lan'i said. The boy rose into the air, and Jules did too, shrugging an apology to Dean, who stayed behind. She watched him climb to higher ground to avoid the dangerous water, and a second later, he sat down, staring in their direction.

They flew over the water until they arrived at the spot where the Deity was submerged below, and Dal'i was the first to plummet into the ocean. The others followed, Jules going last. The water was clearer this time, less ominous, and Jules had a sudden panic that the Deity was gone, vanished from the coffin it lay trapped in. But when they arrived a moment later, it was there, the chains clinking underwater as it waved from their movement.

"Anything, Jules?" Dal'i asked, and Jules stared at the box.

They could hear one another under the ocean, which surprised her too. "Nothing."

Lan'i floated closer, his hands burning bright and hot. The water bubbled near him, and Dal'i came to the opposite end of the wooden box. The circle burned into the center of the coffin started to glow green, and Jules' hands took on the same color as she floated to the long side. Patty stared at her from the other end, eyes pulsing purple.

Lan'i spoke ancient words—Zan'ra prayers, Jules

thought—and soon they were all saying them. Something urged Jules to join in. She memorized the phrase, a simple mantra repeated over and over: *Sealed for eternity. Banished from time.*

It felt oddly parallel to their plight with Lom, and she wondered if he could be trapped in the same manner. She didn't think so. She'd need to kill the man instead. He was mere flesh and blood, mixed with some cybernetics. Nothing like the Deity inside this underwater box.

Jules saw the shadow emerging from the circle on the coffin, but none of the others seemed to notice it. They acted elated as they worked to secure their trap.

It isn't time, but return when you can. Thank you, daughter. The words had much less ferocity to them now and took on a comforting, soothing tone. The dark shadow withered into the coffin, and the circle stopped glowing green.

"We are done. Good work, Four," Lan'i said with pride.

Jules followed them, glancing over at the box. The Deity was confident they would meet again.

---

*S*he was the spitting image of Janine before she'd become sick. Her hair was past her shoulders, the exact same tone of brown. It even curled out at the bottom over her right side, just like Janine's had. Those eyes penetrated mine, and she passed a smile, one I'd seen so many times during our marriage. But this wasn't Janine or Mae; they were both dead. I'd been a witness each time.

"Dean Parker," she said, her voice sweet. It was the same tone Janine used to have when she wanted something from me. *Let's go to the country for the weekend.* Or *I don't want ham, can't we just order takeout?*

The hair on my arms stood straight up, and I walked closer toward her, Slate aiming his gun directly at the hybrid. "What do I call you?" I asked her.

"I'm Katherine, and as you know, I work for PlevaCorp." She started for the staircase that curved to the foyer from the balcony.

"How did you hear we were coming?" I asked.

"I had no idea when you'd arrive, but Lom told me to be cautious. I guess I wasn't careful enough. I thought the Padlog woman could manage your ragtag group," Katherine said.

It was a shock seeing a hybrid after all these years. Sure, there were other models living on Haven, since they only had a handful of variations. Leslie resembled Janine and Mae as well, but she'd aged slightly, and her scars and haircut made me forget they were from the same mold.

"I'll show her a ragtag group," Slate muttered beside me.

"Are you going to cooperate?" I asked her, and she nodded, a wry smile still on her lips.

"What choice do I have?" She shrugged, and I noticed her clothing. She was in business attire, similar to what a female executive would have worn to the office in the States. Black slacks, white blouse. Flats for shoes. Something she could run in if she had to. Sensible.

Someone banged on the front door, and Sergo moved to it, checking through the window before opening the ten-foot-high slab. One of the Duupa entered, his head nearly hitting the doorjamb. "Clear," he told us.

"I guess that means you're coming with us," I said, pointing to the exit.

"Where?" she asked.

"Why, you're going to have the pleasure of rotting in a

cell aboard my starship, *Light*."

"I've been itching for a change of scenery," she said, winking at me. I didn't like how easily she was giving in, but what else was I going to do? Torture her?

"I don't like this," Rivo said, mimicking my own thoughts.

"She's our link to Lom. We need to find out everything we can," I told her. "And I don't want to worry Mary and stay on Bazarn any longer than we have to."

Katherine walked across the foyer, and my team watched nervously as she strolled outside. I glanced up at the balcony and at the corners of the rooms. "Make a quick sweep of the place. Take any electronics: tablets, disk drives, headsets. There has to be something here that can aid us."

They listened, Sergo and Walo rushing up the stairs, Loweck and Rivo moving through the main floor. Slate and I stood guard, watching as the Duupa soldiers led Katherine toward our ship.

"That was easier than it could have been," Slate said when they were out of earshot.

"If I know Lom, which I'm beginning to think I do, this isn't a coincidence," I told him.

"Which part?"

"The woman. She looks like my wife. Not only the same hybrid model, but every detail is Janine. He's messing with me. But the good news is, I don't care. It changes nothing." I glanced at Slate, who'd been the one to kill Mae at the Bhlat outpost many years prior.

"Good. We'll find out more from her," Slate said.

"We'll have to err on the side of caution with what she feeds us, because Lom is behind it all. He's the puppet master tugging on the strings."

The others arrived almost at the same time, each

carrying some electronics, and we left, heading for Rivo's killer craft.

"Let's go home," I said as the door to the vessel slid closed.

"I can't abandon her here," Dean said.

Jules let out a frustrated breath. "You aren't leaving my sight."

"But…"

"But nothing. They trust me—and you, apparently. We're going home, then we'll meet up with them later as we planned. Patty will be fine," Jules told him.

"What if you use that device? We'll grab her and rush through the lake into the portal room, before they have a chance to fight us," Dean suggested.

Jules shook her head, knowing it wouldn't work. "I have to tell you something, but I can't here." She peered over his shoulder, seeing the other three chatting amicably a good twenty meters away. They weren't paying any attention to Jules and Dean's conversation.

"I don't want to separate from her. What if I never see her again?" he asked, his big eyes pleading. Jules' heart ached at the sound of his voice, but she had to stand firm on this one. She needed the Four to think they were in control, that they were a solid alliance with the same goals.

Now that she thought about it, she hadn't figured out what those were. All this action, and they hadn't discussed the future. "Give me a minute, then we leave, okay?"

Dean hesitantly nodded and followed her to where the others formed a circle. "How do I reach you?" she asked.

Dal'i walked over and grabbed Jules' hand. "The Four

are inside you. Imprinted. It's difficult, and takes a lot of energy. To do a full projection like the first time we met, I had to sleep for a day after. Can you feel me? Can you see me when you close your eyes and imagine my form?"

Jules pressed her lids shut, concentrating. She understood then, and focused, finding Dal'i's essence. "I can do it." She sounded more confident than she felt. "We're going to *Light*, but will return. What's the plan?"

"Plan?" Lan'i asked.

"You've ensured the Deities are sealed, and the Four are reunited. What's the end goal?" she asked.

"I haven't given it much thought," the blond boy said, causing Dean to bristle at the use of Patty's Zan'ra name.

"We'd better figure that out," Dal'i said. "I'm tired of hiding."

"I expected Ja'ri to have our mission set," Lan'i finally said. "You were always our leader."

Jules nodded, realizing it would be best if she took charge. If she was going to pull the impossible off, she needed them to think they were on the same side. "Stay close. I'll be in touch."

"When?" Patty asked, glancing at her brother.

"A couple of weeks. We have somewhere to be," Dean told her.

Patty walked over, hugging Jules, then Dean. Jules was close enough to hear her muted words. "I love you, Dean. I'm sorry I wasn't there."

He squeezed her tight, replying too quietly for Jules to make out what he said. They broke apart, and Jules grew her sphere, this one not green, and circled it over Dean.

She gave the other Zan'ra a wave and saw how difficult it was for Dean to leave his sister so soon after finding her.

They lowered into the water, and she stared at the mass graveyard here. According to the Deity, this had been Ja'ri's work. Could she trust them?

They found the Shandra, the lights illuminating their passage into the waterlogged stone-walled room, and Jules located the symbol for their ship. It had only been a couple of days, but she felt like a lifetime had passed.

SEVENTEEN

I paced our suite, finding the entire situation difficult to focus on. "You're telling us that Ja'ri was evil?"

Jules and Dean were beside one another on the couch, and she looked fresh after a good night's sleep and a shower. I'd tossed and turned, only catching pieces of Jules' muddled story after they'd arrived safely on *Light* ten hours ago, but it had been enough to scare me.

"There are two sides to this," Jules started. She lifted her left hand. "On one side, we have the Zan'ra. Right now, the Four include Lan'i and Dal'i, who are both original Zan'ra, or claim to be."

"Are you suggesting they're lying?" Mary asked her daughter, but Jules shook her head.

"I don't think so. Then you have Patty and me, who are holding the essence of a Zan'ra inside us, giving us these powers. We don't have the memories of O'ri or Ja'ri, and that's for the best, because when the Deity showed me what the girl had done, it was atrocious.

"We make up the Four, and their main objective is to hold these Deities so they can continue to live," she finished.

"And what's your thought on these gods?" I asked her, stopping my incessant strides.

She peered over the couch at me, pointing to a chair

across from her. "Papa, can you have a seat? You're making me nervous."

"Sorry." I shifted around the furniture, taking the chair next to Mary. She'd already visited Katherine, but we were waiting to interrogate her. I hadn't told Jules about our guest quite yet.

Jules glanced at Dean, who'd slunk on the couch for most of the conversation, and continued. "I don't know who to trust. They could be fooling me, but she told me something interesting."

"What's that?" Mary asked.

"That I'm not one of the Zan'ra. I'm different. She called me special and said I was one of them, placed on Lainna to find a host some day."

"What's Lainna?" I asked, but the second the question was out, I understood. "The crystal world."

Jules nodded, and Mary's eyes went wide.

"They put something there, hoping it would be their savior. I was intended to be created to trick the Zan'ra into trusting me; then I was told to free the Deities."

"Jules, are you kidding me?" Dean asked. "I thought we could trust the Zan'ra with Patty. Now you're telling me they committed genocide on their own people, and that these gods are the good ones?" He started to stand, but Jules grabbed him by the shirt and hauled him down.

"They aren't aware of this. They can't speak with the Deities like I can. They think I have Ja'ri's essence, and that I'm on their side. You saw that, right?" Jules asked, and Dean finally agreed.

"I did, but will you promise that whatever happens, Patty makes it home?" he asked.

"I promise," Jules said, and she locked gazes with me, her lips pursed.

"Then it's settled. We have to use the bracelet to grab

O'ri from Patty, then free the Deities, let them clean up their mess of the other two," I told them.

"Papa, they might be…"

Dean frowned, drumming his fingers on his knee. "If the Zan'ra really did that, we need to stop them. And if that means freeing these gods, then so be it. What's the worst that can happen?"

I laughed out loud, catching them all off guard. "I think a lot of terrible things can occur from releasing these ancient beings, but first off, we're just a short time from reaching Techeron. Once we arrive, a few of us will be heading to Fontem's collection."

"What do you expect to find?" Jules asked.

We'd been through this countless times, but I played along. "Something to aid me in defeating Lom of Pleva. His mission must be thwarted."

Mary picked up her mug of tea and wrapped her fingers around it, holding it close to her chest as if she were suddenly cold. "Anything to avoid sending you to Udoon."

She'd let it slip and seemed to catch it right away, but the damage had been done.

It was Jules' turn to stand up in outrage. "What are you talking about?" she asked Mary, but when her mother didn't reply, she snapped her attention on me. "Papa, what does she mean?"

I relented, resting my hands on my thighs. "I saw Lom."

"I know, I heard that…"

"No. I went through the portals, searching for him. He came, and he issued an offer. He wants me, and me alone." I hated seeing the pain in her eyes.

"You can't be considering it—"

Dean cut in. "No way Mr. Parker gives in to anyone."

I appreciated his confidence, but that wasn't true.

"Honey, we'll know more after Fontem brings us to his cache. He claims to have objects to assist our mission."

"And if he doesn't? You go to Udoon? Then what?"

"I meet someone named Viliar, and he brings me to Lom."

"Into the future?" Jules asked.

"Into the future."

"And you believe him? That he'll stop his plan to merge our timelines?" Jules was the one pacing now, and I kept my eyes on her.

"I'll only do it if I have no other choice," I told her.

"No. You. Won't."

"Honey, it's not up to you," I said, but she was fuming. Her eyes were glowing a darker green, burning hotly as her fury increased.

"I'm not a child!" she screamed, shaking the table. She floated without the green sphere, and my jaw dropped. I swore there was a dark shadow around her, and for a moment, I thought she was bigger, but then her feet landed and she shrank into herself, collapsing into a ball on the couch. Dean held her, staring at the girl.

"Jules, I think the Deities might be right," Mary said.

"That I'm one of them?" she asked, sitting up straight again. "Good. Then maybe I take care of Lom myself."

My laugh was sharp and cut the tension in the room. Soon Jules was laughing too, and Dean joined in. Mary remained quiet, watching us like we'd gone off the deep end.

"If you had a way to stop him, I wouldn't object," I told her.

"Let me work on it," she said, standing up and moving to the kitchen. "Anyone want some coffee?"

"Since when do you drink coffee?" Mary asked.

"Papa lets me," Jules said, outing me.

Mary was about to speak, and I cut her off. "Is this the

battle you want to win?"

Now she did smile and raised her hand. "I'll take a cup."

———————

*J*ules woke from dreams of her childhood. She'd been on Earth, playing with Maggie in the grassy field behind their farmhouse. The air was thick with the scents of summer: growing plants, freshly watered soil, and bloomed flowers. Her mother loved perennials, and Jules preferred the opposite. Through the eyes of a child, she'd thought the annuals were much prettier. It was the kind of garden a princess might have. Now, seeing the images so vividly through her dream-eyes, this older version of Jules understood.

The perennials were rooted, tougher, and they returned every year, stronger with each passing cycle of the seasons. It was how her mother lived her life, and Jules wiped a tear from her eye as she made the realization. She needed to make moves that would keep her family rooted, not the quick and easy choices.

Her room was too hot, and she tossed the blankets aside, letting the climate-controlled temperature blow cool air on her pajamas. There were another four hours before her parents would be waking, but Jules was restless and unable to sleep.

She folded her legs over the edge of the bed and glanced at the mirror. Her hair was a mess, and she took out her brush, going over the curls with long strides. She knew what her next move was.

Jules slid from her pajamas and opted for a Gatekeeper uniform. It sat pressed and ready to wear in the corner of her closet, and she went to the bathroom, cleaning up. She had to look older, more professional, if she was going to pull this off.

If only there was something she could do about her eyes. She closed them, picturing them brown, not green, but when they blinked open, they still glowed. Maybe it was impossible to turn them off; otherwise, the other Zan'ra would do the same.

Jules was never one for wearing makeup, but she applied enough to do the trick, lining her eyes and adding mascara. She felt foolish, but in the end, she was confident she didn't look quite as much like a kid playing dress-up. She exited her room, tiptoeing to the suite's exit, and she glanced at Dean's suite's door as she went. He'd be deep in slumber. She almost stopped to see if he wanted to join her but didn't. This was for her to do alone.

Jules passed a couple of decks and smiled at the crew that greeted her along the short trip. She eventually found the cell block where their prisoner was being held. There was a guard stationed there, and Jules walked up to Plinick, an Inlorian crew member. Her lower arms were crossed as she snapped awake at Jules' presence, using her top hands to click discreetly at a keyboard, pretending she hadn't been dozing off.

"I need to see her," Jules said.

"Your father gave implicit directions not to let anyone inside," Plinick said.

"He sent me," Jules said.

She stared at Jules with a doubtful gaze. "Should I call to confirm?"

Jules leaned closer, lowering her voice. "I'm sure you don't want him to find out that one of his guards is sleeping on the job. This prisoner is important, and there might even be someone on board that wants to free her."

"That person isn't you, is it?" Plinick asked with a

raised eyebrow.

"Nope. I'll be ten minutes, and it'll be like I was never here," Jules said.

"Fine." The energy barrier disappeared, and Jules stepped through the entrance, smiling at the woman.

"I'll be quick," Jules told her, and stood taller, composing herself.

There weren't many cells, and it was obvious which one was occupied. A soft blue light lit the exterior, holding Katherine inside. Jules stopped at the edge and pulled a chair from a closet across the hall. She flipped it open and sat on the molded plastic seat.

"Katherine, is it?" she asked.

The woman was lying down, sleeping facing the ceiling. She jerked awake and sat up, looking around.

"Over here," Jules said, and they locked eyes. She reminded Jules of Leslie, only she seemed younger, more… perfect. A newer hybrid, according to her mom.

Jules knew the story about Papa and the hybrid named Janine, and about Mae, the other woman who'd initially been sent to infiltrate Papa. They'd replaced her a year in with someone more pliable. It turned out they'd both betrayed her father: Janine with the Deltra, and Mae with the Bhlat.

"It's you," the woman said, her voice smooth as silk. Katherine walked over, her appearance somehow well-maintained despite not having a shower for three days.

"Hello." Jules shoved her hands in her pockets, watching for a reaction.

"It's about time they sent somebody. I didn't expect to be left here so long without anyone coming to interrogate me," she said.

"They found a lot of valuable information at your office," Jules told her. "Dean Parker doesn't think you're necessary, but I convinced him you might have something we need."

Katherine had a chair inside her room too, and she dragged it across the white floor, sitting on it and facing Jules through the transparent blue-hued barrier. "He's misguided if he doesn't think I can help him."

Jules didn't let the words strike a chord. "We know everything."

"Child, I doubt you do."

Jules faked a smile, inwardly bristling at the term. "Lom wants to merge the timelines. He destroys Hanrion's facility, stealing a version of the man and his nullifier so he can create his own in the future. Only to do that, he needs something massive. A planet full of the crystals that fuel the device." Jules paused, and the expression on Katherine's face finally cracked her perfectly poised façade.

"What do you want?"

"I want you to help me. Not my father, me."

Katherine recovered some of her color, but it was obvious they were on the right track with their assumptions. Perhaps Papa's plan to destroy Lainna was going to work. Even so, Lom had ways to communicate with people like Katherine here, and Jules couldn't let him live.

"Just tell me what you're after," Katherine said, some bite returning to her tone.

"How do you talk with him?" Jules asked.

"He'll kill me," she said.

Jules sighed, watching the woman, and she waited a moment before speaking again. "I'm aware of the stories, Katherine. About Lom and PlevaCorp creating hybrids to do their dirty work. They sent the pitiful creatures to Earth knowing full well the *Kalentrek* placed there by the Delta hundreds of years earlier would destroy them. People like Janine and Bob, my mother's fake husband, were sent there to trick the humans into helping their cause. They all died.

"The Deltra then sacrificed the rest of the hybrids, convincing them to fly into the sun. Lom was the one who sold them to the Kraski. This has been proven, and Haven is full of hybrid refugees that survived the Event." Jules watched closely while she spoke to Katherine, and the woman swallowed hard, the masseter muscles clenching in her jaw.

"There's more to it than that," Katherine said.

"So you're okay with the making of a race in a lab, and the subsequent selling them off like slaves to the Kraski, as long as you're in a cushy office out of harm's way. Is that it?" Jules was being a little harsh, but it was necessary.

"Lom has treated me with respect—"

"Sure. He needs someone obedient to do his bidding while he's gone. You do understand he can't win, right?"

"Once he finds out I'm not answering, he'll move ahead with his plans," she told Jules.

"The thing about megalomaniacs like Lom is that he was always going to follow through, no matter what. He *is* going to attempt to destroy the universe, because once he suggested it might happen, he was tied to it. A man of Lom's stature has everything, but after my dad shot him twenty years into the future, he was at a loss. He wanted reparations, and regardless of what happens to you, he will try to kill us all.

"What I need you to do is tell me how you talk with him. He won't ever find you, and you can move on to a new life. I promise."

Katherine was scared now, and she nervously glanced toward the end of the corridor and then over to Jules. "How can I trust you?"

"Because I know my father, and he won't let you out of here. Ever. I can make you a deal," Jules said, hoping she'd be able to back this one up.

"What kind of deal?" Katherine asked.

"When it's all over, I'll bring you to Haven, where you can live out your days among others like you. If you choose," Jules said.

"He's going to kill me," she said softly.

Jules shook her head. "No he's not."

"How can you be sure?"

"Because he'll still be in the future, and he'll be dead," Jules told her, goosebumps covering her arms as she said it.

"Okay." Katherine leaned forward and told Jules everything she asked.

EIGHTEEN

*T*echeron. The planet was two days away, and from there, we'd finally use the Kraski ship to head to some remote world Fontem wasn't giving us the name of. From what we understood, there were three systems within three days' FTL from Techeron, but we didn't have many details on any of them. From Sarlun's records, the world acted as a trade hub for this distant region, and we were going to use that as an excuse for our arrival.

"Fontem, you sure you won't tell me what we're going to find?" I asked the Terellion again, and he smiled at me from behind his facemask.

"Soon enough. My secrets will be revealed," he told me.

"Boss, you ready for this?" Slate arrived, Karo behind him.

"Suma should have the nullifier up and ready to test," I told the group.

"Where's Jules?" Fontem asked.

"She didn't want to come. Said she needed to see Regnig about something," I told them. Jules had been acting fishy for the last week, but learning you might be a Deity would do that to any teenage girl.

"What's this place called again?" Slate asked.

Karo answered. He knew, as a Theos. "Lainna."

"Lainna," I said, the name sounding funny off my tongue. I'd always thought of it as the crystal world, but giving it a name seemed to increase its peculiarity to me.

"Why did the Theos choose that planet to make the Iskios graveyard?" Slate asked him.

"We were drawn to it. Now it's clear why. The crystals power the portals, they hold essences of the Zan'ra, they power time-distortion nullifiers. The place is very potent, and quite amazing," Karo said.

"Sorry we need to destroy it," I told Karo, but he understood.

"No need to apologize to me. I only hope it doesn't have any ill effect on the portal network," he said.

I'd asked Jules for her opinion, and she didn't think they were linked. The core on the Theos' work acted as the central focal point, and Jules would know better than any.

"Can we interrogate this Katherine when we return?" Slate asked.

"Maybe." I'd been putting it off. I wanted to rid the universe of the planet that could fuel Lom's dimensional merging technology. Once that was done, I could breathe a little freer.

Things were progressing. The last seven or eight months had moved quite slowly as we took the long trip toward Fontem's destination, but we were finally seeing some traction. With Lom's Padlog contact dealt with, and his present-time contact from PlevaCorp in our possession, we were getting somewhere.

We started into the Shandra room, when I heard someone calling from down the hall. "Hold up! Mr. Parker, I'd like to join you!" Dean arrived, holding his helmet under his arm, looking like a high school football star posing for a picture after the big Friday-night game.

"I thought you'd be with Jules," I said, raising an

eyebrow. They were rarely apart.

"She told me she wanted to go to the Academy solo, so I thought I'd come with you guys," Dean told us.

"Okay, what the hell." I clapped him on the shoulder and ushered him into the room.

Slate stepped toward me, speaking low. "Are you sure about this?"

"The kid needs to be involved, and he's a smart young man. Better having him under our watchful eye than letting him leave again," I told Slate, and he nodded.

Natalia had been keeping busy, and she'd even offered to be part of the bridge crew during the last few weeks. She was spending more time there than I'd expected, and was looking better after having something to take her focus off the loss of her husband. We'd seen Leslie take a long time to acclimate to her new life after Terrance had died, and I didn't want Nat to end up isolated and alone.

We piled in, the room feeling full with all of us in EVAs. There was no breathable atmosphere on Lainna, and I found the symbol for the temporary portal Suma had brought with her to the crystal planet. When we'd first visited the world, the only option was to fly there, but the Alliance had since created a portable Shandra that could be moved and delivered by ship, making this trip a lot easier. It also gave Suma the ability to leave quickly when she was finished.

Luckily, Lom didn't try to stop me this time, and our group arrived on Lainna. The portal room looked much like the others, but half the size. It was built into a mid-sized Shimmali cruiser, and we were cramped inside the space.

Fontem was the first to leave through the doors, and I waited until everyone was out to exit behind them.

"Captain, it is good to see you," a robotic voice said,

and I peered to my right to see W the android pilot walking toward me from the bridge.

"Dubs, how are you doing?" I asked.

"Well, considering. Suma and Hanrion aren't much for company." Dubs greeted the others.

"We're about to check out the operation, if you're interested," I offered, but he declined with a shake of his head.

"I've been instructed to have the ship ready at all times, in case a quick escape is necessary. From what I hear, the machines they are constructing are temperamental and extremely volatile," Dubs instructed me.

"Then maybe you'd better stay put. See you soon," I told him, and he turned away, lumbering toward his pilot's seat on the bridge.

We left the cruiser, and I grimaced as I saw the world waiting for us outside the spacecraft. I didn't have fond memories of this place. Leonard had also been taken captive here by a remaining Iskios, but we were confident they were vacated by this point. I warned the others to be cautious, regardless of our assumptions.

This sector of the world was green, reminding me of Jules. Varying shades of the color imbued each crystal shard jutting from the hard ground. The rock formations were erratic, forming sharp ridges and flamboyant mountain peaks.

I didn't have to ask where Suma was. The thrumming of energy from their creation sent vibrations through the gemstones and resonated towards us, and Slate pointed to the source of the sound we heard carrying across the landscape.

"It seems they're making some progress." Slate's voice traveled through my earpiece.

"Let's check it out." I took the lead and noticed that

Dean stayed close to me. He stared at everything around him with a genuine interest, or perhaps fear. I knew he was thinking about my daughter when he saw the emerald crystal formations.

Suma and Hanrion's device was directly on the planet's equator, and it was larger than I'd expected. The nullifier was positioned at least thirty meters in the air, with drones surrounding the structure. Harvested local gemstone sat in organized piles outside, and I spotted Suma in an EVA, studying a tablet with the four-legged Hanrion beside her.

I used my arm console and searched for Suma's connection. When I found it, I spoke softly so I didn't startle her. "Suma, look behind you."

Her head swiveled around, and it was hard to miss her beaming smile, even from fifty meters out. She waved us over, and our group picked up the pace. Dean nearly tripped on an upright piece of clear stone, but I caught him to avoid injury. He acted sheepish as we kept going, his gaze stuck to the ground.

The entire building shook constantly, and I felt the vibrations in my hips. "Suma, how are things?"

She looked tired, but the erratic Hanrion seemed calm and collected behind his facemask. "We're almost there, Dean. We've had a couple of setbacks, but…"

"But what?"

"Hanrion created a time bubble again, optimizing our efficiency," she told me.

I stepped closer. "What do you mean?"

"We've been working on this for over a year," Suma told me.

"What?" Dean blurted beside me, but I ignored it.

"That's dangerous. Was it the only way?" I asked.

Suma nodded, holding the tablet out to me. "It was. This was far more complicated than creating a nullifier to pause a research building. You wanted to create something colossal enough to envelop a planet, and we've managed to do just that." She indicated we should follow her to the structure. Hanrion remained behind, continuing to work on a tablet.

She led us inside a doorway, and my visor's auto-tint kicked in immediately. The room was so bright.

Before any of us could ask a question, she continued, "This is the inside of our nullifier. The crystals you saw outside were used to make the bubble, but with this, we're going to harness the world itself. With the amount of energy stored here, we'll have no issues fueling our merger."

"Walk me through it," I told her.

She strode deeper into the space, where whirring electronic panels and ten-foot-high black boxes with blinking lights sat in long rows. "We'll activate the device remotely."

"From orbit?" Slate asked.

"Even farther," Suma answered. "We've dug into the core of the world, and it will utilize the power of the planet to bring the nullifier to life. We've set the parameters at five hundred kilometers on each side of the world's diameter." She pressed on, and we all followed, stopping at a screen along the rear wall. A table of computers with two chairs sat there, and she used one of the keypads to bring up an image. "We've also set the explosives within the core, and in ten locations around the world, for good measure."

Slate grinned at this. He would always appreciate a big explosion, no matter how old he was. The image showed a map of Lainna with ten surface icons blinking, and one large one in the center of the 3D picture.

"When we activate the device, it will pull every version of Lainna from each dimension. Hanrion thinks there might be millions of them. They'll unite in the same time-line momentarily, long enough for us to destroy them all."

Suma turned to us, her snout drooping.

"You don't want to do this, do you?" I asked her.

"It's not that. This technology is terrifying, Dean."

"We're not going to use it again. It'll be destroyed with the planet," I reminded her.

"I know."

"How long before it's ready?" Karo asked, staring at the paused image on the screen.

"We can have it done tomorrow," Suma said.

"Meaning you'll still be in the time bubble for a while?" Dean asked.

"You pick up quickly. Yes, I guess it'll be another month inside our bubble," she said. "I could possibly finish it in the next five minutes, but every few days inside, I need to come out. Otherwise…" Suma didn't have to finish. This was taking a dangerous mental toll on her.

"Can we do anything to help?" Slate asked.

"Hanrion and I have a surprisingly good system, and the drones complete our instructions quickly. We'll have it done. If you want to stay on the ship, I'll come find you in the morning," Suma told us.

"Good work here, Suma. I'm proud of you," I told her.

"Me too," Slate offered.

The three of us had been through a lot, and I was asking even more of Suma now. I made a mental note to force her to take a long break after this. An extended vacation. Her father would love to spend some quality time with his daughter.

We left, heading for the ship. Hanrion scarcely noticed us as we passed by, and I saw Karo was trailing behind the group. I slowed my pace, waiting for him. "You okay?"

"This place was once important. I find it hard to believe we're going to destroy it." Karo kept walking, not meeting my gaze.

"Do you have another suggestion? If we managed to remove Lom's possible fuel source for his merging device, he won't be able to win," I reminded him.

Karo shrugged. "Even so, changing the universe is a big deal."

My old friend Teelon's words echoed through my mind the second Karo said it. *Change the universe.* Was this what he'd meant? I didn't think so, but the parallels were there. This would disrupt a lot of things, and not only our timeline. But given the dire circumstances, if Lom were able to create a device like this to accomplish his goals, we had to beat him to it.

"I learned a long time ago that change is a part of our lives. If we don't change and adapt, we die," I said, point-blank.

"You're right, Dean. If I hadn't met you, I'd never have discovered pizza," he said, laughing to break the tension.

We piled onto the ship, waiting for tomorrow, when we could finally thwart Lom of Pleva's master plan.

---

*J*ules hated lying to her parents, and the way her mother trusted her so implicitly made it even worse. But now was the perfect timing, with Dean with Papa and the others, so she'd told them she was off to see Regnig, rather than to Katherine's secret ship. It was close to Bazarn, and Jules hoped this wasn't another elaborate ruse where she'd be trapped. No one would even know where she'd gone.

The promenade on Bazarn was busy, and Jules wiped a bead of sweat from her forehead. She was in casual clothing: a gray hoodie with leggings and white sneakers. She looked like a normal human kid on vacation, and she wore wide tinted sunglasses to hide her obvious eyes.

She moved to the edge of the space, behind a Padlog dining vendor. The smells of roasting food were strong here, and she glanced around, making sure no one was paying any kind of special attention to her. Jules activated her shield, leaving it invisible as Dal'i had shown her, and she raced up, moving from the crowds and into the sky. She went as fast as she could and doubted anyone even noticed her small form arcing from the surface.

Jules thought about the other Zan'ra as she traveled through the clouds, pushing out of the atmosphere and into space. She flew around the countless satellites in orbit and avoided one of the many defense drones Rivo had installed after her father had passed.

Katherine had given her specific instructions to find her vessel, including the exact coordinates of the system's tiny moon it was nearby to. Jules slid her sleeve up, observing the round screen strapped to her wrist. She was getting closer.

Bazarn was beautiful from above, the perfect place for opulence and wealth. It wasn't necessarily Jules' style, but she could appreciate people wanting to escape here for a few nights.

The star was bright and orange, and gave Bazarn the perfect climate for tourism. She turned her back to it and raced away, heading for her destination.

Convincing Katherine to turn on Lom had been too simple, but Jules thought perhaps the woman had already been thinking all of the things she'd brought up. Deep down, Katherine knew she was nothing more than a slave, and she was caught in a cell on an Alliance vessel. She was in self-preservation mode, and Jules had done her best to persuade the PlevaCorp executive she wouldn't let her boss do any more harm.

Papa was going to be so angry with her, but in the end, he'd agree it was the right action to take. She hoped.

Even at her fast speed, it took two hours to find the right moon. It was a small and misshapen hunk of rock, and the ship was right where Katherine had described it. Jules approached with caution, searching for signs of life. It was dark, powered down, and still. No defenses attempted to stall her as she neared the exterior.

Jules had pushed through walls before, when she'd stopped the Arnap from killing her father and Slate. At that time, she'd been filled with fury and rage, but now she felt none of those things. Could she still manage the feat? She closed her eyes, visualizing moving through the hull. Her entire body began to vibrate, the shield with it, and she floated forward, passing through the metallic barrier with ease. When she was inside, she cut the power off and laughed out loud.

The life support was on inside, but she still kept her shield up as she exited the storage room she'd arrived in. This ship looked identical to the PlevaCorp freighter Patty and Lan'i had stolen from *Light* months ago. Something shifted, and Jules glanced to her right to see one of Lom's robots rolling toward her.

She shot a tendril of energy at it, frying the circuits. Its face screen flashed as the green beams flickered over its surface before stopping in place. She continued through the dark corridors. Tiny lights glowed from their recessed positions along the walls, and she followed them, heading for the room Katherine had told her the device was inside.

The ship was quiet, and Jules moved stealthily, anticipating more robots attempting to block her. By the time she reached the crew quarters, she'd stopped another two of the bots with ease. She opened the door to Katherine's suite. Everything else on this ship was plain and robotic, but the interior of the room was adorned with bright art, lush bedding, and fancy glasses. Katherine had good taste and hid her personality here. Perhaps there was more to the hybrid woman than met the eye.

She stepped over to the desk and found the drawers were locked. Jules gripped the handle tightly and tugged, adding her power behind it. The lock snapped, and she saw the device inside.

This was it. Her way to communicate with Lom from the future.

Jules sat at the desk, tapping the flat device to life. There was a message waiting. She read it and smiled. She waited a moment and keyed in a response, pretending to be Katherine.

NINETEEN

$\int$uma had come in the early hours of the morning, after we'd managed three or four uncomfortable hours of sleep. The portal ship wasn't built to house as many guests as us, and we were sprawled out across any available space. I slept near Dean on the bridge, while Dubs stood on his charging station.

When Suma arrived, we all had something to eat, and several hours later, we set course. "Dubs, can you go here first?" I pointed at the map, and without a word, he shifted our trajectory.

"Where are we going?" Dean asked.

"I have to see it one last time," I told the young man.

Slate stood beside me. He'd been there that day, and I knew he understood why I had to return.

We arrived twenty minutes later, and it looked the same as it had. The crystal mountain was formed like a pyramid, and the symbol was embedded along the ground, water still filling it. The entire region was blue.

"This is it," Dean said quietly. He'd been a little boy when Mary was taken, so he'd have no memory of that tumultuous time in my life. "This is where they took Mary. With Jules inside her." Magnus' son stared at it, jaw open. "You ended up finding her."

I nodded along, feeling every memory of that day

course through me. Those had been the darkest months of my life. "You know, things have a way of working out, Dean." I told him this, hoping it would make him think of his Zan'ra-infused sister.

"Thanks."

We slowly flew around it, and a minute later, I asked Dubs to take us out. "No more trips down memory lane. Let's do what we came here to accomplish."

He pressed the throttle, racing through the atmosphere, and we distanced enough from the nullifier's range to feel safe.

Suma stared out the viewscreen at the planet beyond, and I couldn't believe she'd spent a year of her life inside that time distortion to make this happen.

"Thank you, Suma," I told her, putting an arm over her shoulder.

"You're welcome. It was quite the experience working with Hanrion on this," she told me. "He's eccentric, but brilliant. I learned a lot from him."

"I can imagine. What will he do after this?" I asked.

She glanced over at the man. "He wants to go home."

I nodded, not blaming him one bit. "To continue his research?"

"That's what he said."

"This is the best move, right?" I asked Slate on my other side.

"Cut the supplies, remove the threat." He nodded in agreement.

We gathered in the rear of the ship, where Hanrion was already bent over the complex controls. Karo and Fontem were there, letting the mad scientist take the lead.

"Is it ready?" I asked Hanrion, the words translating through a speaker attached to the ship's wall.

"It is. Would you care for the honors?" he asked me,

pointing to a round icon on the screen. It pulsed slowly, and I couldn't believe we'd managed to create this in time. I really hoped it worked; otherwise, we were destroying this world for no reason. It held a lot of bad memories, and the evil energy of the dead Iskios, so I didn't think it would be missed by many.

I stepped to the console and peered at Suma, who gave me the slightest of nods. I scratched at my chin, my fingers rubbing the stubble. This was it. I took a breath, and before I exhaled, I touched the screen, turning the giant nullifier on.

A clock countdown began in alien digits, and our equivalent appeared, telling me there were five minutes and eleven seconds before it was done.

Suma walked over, describing what was happening. "The device is utilizing the power of the world, sucking the energy from the core. Once we've ascertained that the many worlds have merged, we'll detonate the explosives. They're not something to be trifled with."

"Where did you get them?" I asked, and Slate answered.

"The Empress was kind enough to donate them to our cause," he told me.

"She has the power to destroy planets so easily?" I asked, not liking that one bit.

"We already knew that," he reminded me.

Suma activated a screen on the wall, which now showcased Lainna from our current position. It was quite the vision from here, the colors merging and cascading into wave-like patterns below. It didn't seem real.

The timer counted down, and I grew more nervous with each tick of the clock. When it reached ten seconds, I was dripping sweat. The others shifted on their feet, fidgeting with their hands, no one speaking.

When the timer chimed, the planet shook, and it became blurry. "That is the merging. It is complete," Hanrion informed us. I gaped at it, seeing countless versions of the same world from multiple dimensions.

"Do it," I ordered, and Suma hit the next icon.

The screen turned red, flashing as the pre-set explosives began to detonate. The surface bombs hit first, breaking the crust apart, and a moment later, beams of orange shone from the axis as the core exploded, sending a shockwave over the planet.

"Are we out of harm's way?" Fontem asked, and a moment later, the ship shook violently. We were tossed around the space, and I bashed into the wall, hitting the floor right beside Dean. By the time we'd composed ourselves, I thought something was wrong with the screen.

"Is it done?" I asked, and Slate used the console to zoom in. There was nothing there but billions of fragments of clear crystal, the stones devoid of color now.

Lainna was gone, and with it, Lom's hope of creating his destructive tool.

––––––––––––––

"Your dad's home!" Mary shouted from the hallway. Jules heard the pitter-patter of Maggie's claws rushing for the door, but she remained seated on her bed. She felt terrible for keeping this from them, but there was no way they'd agree to it. The mere fact that she'd messaged through the device to the real Lom of Pleva felt wrong.

It was concealed in her room, and she wished there was a better place to hide it. She'd never given her parents a reason to snoop through her stuff, and she wasn't about to now. She left it under some books in her desk's bottom right drawer and wiped her sweating palms over her jeans.

Jules caught her reflection in the mirror and wished this was over before it began. That she had never heard of the Zan'ra, the Deities, or Lom of Pleva. There were people out there living their lives, hanging with friends on Haven, going to the lake to swim on weekends, not concerned about the fate of the universe. It was all too much. She stared at herself, wondering if she could be one of them someday.

"Jules?" Papa's voice carried through her door, and she opened it wide. He must have seen the emotions on her face, because he grabbed her into a hug, kissing the top of her head. "Honey bear, are you okay?"

"Yeah, I'm fine. I worried about you two," she said, which wasn't a lie.

"We're fine." He looked tired, his eyes puffy, his skin sallow.

"Is it done?" Mary asked, and Jules followed her dad into the living room.

He fell to the couch, still in his dirty jumpsuit. "Lainna is no more." The words held power, and Jules felt her knees weaken.

"Lom is going to be furious," Mary said, taking a seat beside Papa.

"Good."

Tears of relief flooded her mom's face, and Jules rushed over, squishing in. They hugged on the couch. "I hated that place," her mom said.

"I know. So did I," Papa added.

"Do you think Lom's done, then?" Jules asked.

Her dad nodded. "He won't be able to hurt us."

Jules went rigid. "He's waiting out there. He can meet you in the portals. Do you really think that someone like Lom will let this go, just because he can't make this nullifier?"

Papa frowned at her while clenching his jaw. "What do you propose?"

Jules' heart pounded, and she shook her head in an exasperated gesture. "I'm not proposing anything. I'm saying he's not dealt with. You've only managed to create a roadblock for him."

"She's not wrong, Dean," Mary said.

"We'll figure it out. One thing at a time. We'll be at Techeron tomorrow, and then we can finish this mission and regroup. Does that sound fair?" he asked them, and Jules had no choice but to agree. There was no way she was missing out on Fontem's secret stash. Not after all the hype.

"Will the Zan'ra be fine for now?" Her dad jumped to his feet, heading for the kitchen.

Jules joined him, sitting at the island while he started to make coffee. "They said they'd stay low-key for a while. I asked them to wait for me."

"Do they think you're going to join with them after this?" Mary asked, taking the stool next to Jules.

"I haven't said as much."

"And what do you suppose will happen?" Papa asked.

Jules had to be sure first, so she left it open. "We'll see. One way or another, I'm bringing Patty home, that much is certain."

"And the other two?" Her mom was trying to pull more information out of her, and Jules didn't want it to seem like she was hiding her own secrets.

"If I can negate their powers, I will."

"How could you do that? Are you strong enough?" Papa asked as the machine sent water over the ground beans, sending a wonderful aroma into the kitchen. Jules was already hooked.

"I will be if I'm a Deity," she told them quietly.

"Do you think that's possible? I mean, I understand these ancient gods tricking people. The Iskios did it with us, but if you're one of them, wouldn't you know it?" Papa asked.

"No. From what I gather, they covered my true powers with the fake layer to match the Zan'ra, who were likely created in their own image. Strip that away, and I might have some other abilities hidden within," Jules said. "I may wake one."

Her dad turned toward her, stopping what he was doing. "Jules, you can't be serious."

"It's the sole option," she told him. As long as they were distracted by the whole Deity thing, they weren't going to think she was dwelling on anything else.

"We'll talk about this later. Dean said he'd like to speak with you. He'll be at the diner in twenty minutes," her dad said, changing the subject like he always did when he didn't want to discuss a topic any further.

"Thanks." Jules sauntered off, hearing her parents argue in hushed tones. She glanced at her door as she passed it in the hall, thinking about Lom and wondering if he'd replied yet.

Instead of checking, she departed their suite, walking past Dean's door and continuing to the restaurant where they'd once shared fries and talked as if they were more than friends. It felt like so long ago.

He was inside, and the place was busy at the moment. She waved at Walo, who sat across from Sergo, his back to her.

Considering he'd arrived at the same time as her dad, he looked far fresher than she'd expected, one of many advantages of youth. He smiled at her, his eyes crinkling slightly. His hair was nicely styled, and for some reason, seeing him made Jules more nervous than if she'd been meeting Lom of Pleva for a burger.

"Hey, Ju," he said.

"I heard the trip went well." She sat beside him on the bench, instead of on the opposite side, and he turned slightly to face her. He was trapped but didn't look too upset about it.

"It was intense. I'll tell you one thing. Time travel and multiple dimensions aren't something I want to think about for too long," Dean told her.

"Have you ordered?"

"I did. Got you the usual," he said.

She was a fully independent woman and wanted to stay that way, but there was something special about Dean taking charge and presuming what she wanted to eat. He was right, though. She was suddenly ravenous, and the thought of a juicy burger made her stomach rumble softly.

"Listen, I have something to say," she told him.

He rubbed his forehead, breaking eye contact. "No. I don't want to hear it. I can tell from your expression it's going to be heavy, and I'll have to keep a secret, and lie to cover it up, and then your dad will hate me, and…"

"I'm going to kill him," she whispered.

Dean stopped talking, turning to face her again. "Kill who?"

"Lom. I'm going to kill Lom of Pleva."

The serving robot arrived, setting two plates on the table. "Order up."

The burger had a single cake candle burning in the center of the bun, and Dean smiled at her, despite the dire subject matter of their conversation.

"What's this?" she asked.

"I missed your birthday. A girl's sixteenth is important." He reached below the table and brought a box up, sliding it toward her.

"You didn't have to do this." But it felt great that he had. Her entire body felt warm, euphoric, and loved. Thoughts of Lom and Zan'ra vanished from her mind as she accepted the small gift-wrapped box.

"I did. You'd better blow out that candle before it ruins your dinner." He grinned at her, and Jules puffed her lips, sending a gust of breath over the flickering flame. It snuffed instantly, casting the familiar scent of birthdays from years gone by.

"What's this?" she asked, rotating the present in her hand.

"You'll have to open it to find out," he told her.

It was wrapped in pink paper, a tiny silver bow on the top. She dug into it, finding a wooden box below the covering. It separated on hinges, and she stared at the earrings.

She removed one, dangling it in a tight grip. "They're beautiful." The jewelry was shaped like stars, shiny white-gold in color. Each was set with a diamond inside, and she returned the earring, clutching the box to her chest. "Thank you, Dean."

"Happy birthday."

TWENTY

Techeron was a busier hub than most. Considering the population density of this quadrant was far less than any Alliance member sectors, this place had a lot of traffic through it. It was one of the only major trading hubs within a month's travel, making it everyone's primary destination.

"It was a dive last time I was here," Fontem told me. He sounded worried.

"No big deal," I assured him. "We'll let the crew have a few days on the surface, and Mary's going to talk to the locals about joining the Alliance. It's the perfect cover. No one will ever know our true purpose for taking the eight-month trek."

"Thanks, Dean. I hope my stash remains untouched," Fontem said.

The bridge was full of our primary crew members, and Mary took her seat to my left, with Slate to my right. Jules and Dean were on the secondary helm consoles behind Rivo and Suma, with Walo, Sergo, and Loweck rounding out the team.

Everyone here understood our real mission and had explicit instructions to act natural on Techeron. I'd intended to keep our team small when we traveled on the Kraski ship, but Dean was asking to come and I didn't want to leave him behind, not after the year he'd had. With

Karo and Fontem, along with Slate, that made our group a solid six. Suma was glad to be staying here, especially after the countless hours she'd put in on Lainna with Hanrion. We'd already delivered the scientist home, and he'd seemed ecstatic to return to his usual work.

"Entering their range, sir," Sergo told me.

There were two space stations here, each as significant as Udoon, and I counted at least forty ships of various shapes and sizes docked or waiting to dock in patient lines.

"We're not sticking around. Sergo, get clearance for the surface, and we'll disappear before you enter the atmosphere," I ordered, and the Padlog buzzed his acknowledgement.

Mary turned to me and forced a smile. "I hope this is worth the trip," she said.

"Good luck with the locals. This could be a big win for the Alliance. A hub like this would give us more credibility and increase our trade routes substantially," I said.

"I'll do my best." She leaned in, kissing me on the lips before moving aside while I rose from the captain's chair.

"Anyone coming with us, it's time to go," I told them, and everyone joining us rose.

"Suma, you're in charge here while the others are on the surface protecting my wife," I reminded her, and she nodded.

"Be careful," she called as we exited the bridge.

In a few minutes, we were walking through the hangar past a Padlog vessel, an Inlorian ship, and to my Kraski vessel. It was outfitted with the same cloaking tech we'd used in New Mexico, but this version was modified, cleaner and more effective.

I waited while the others boarded: Karo, then Fontem, followed by Jules and Slate. Dean stopped at the ramp, glancing at me. "Mr. Parker... I mean, Captain Parker, thank you for letting me join you."

He reminded me so much of his father at that moment that it broke my heart. I could picture the man he'd become in twenty years and smiled at him. "I'm glad you wanted to. Now let's hurry, before they leave without us."

Slate took the pilot's seat and activated the cloaking device. We didn't want to alert anyone that a Kraski vessel had been at Techeron, and we sure as hell didn't want someone following us. Six people on a ship this size was a little crowded, but there were enough beds to sleep two, with an extra cot. We'd take two shifts, with Slate teaming up with the kids, and me with the Theos and Terellion.

Techeron continued to be abuzz with activity, and I watched as *Light* was ushered forward in a lineup to orbit the planet of commerce, where Mary would take a shuttle to the surface to have a meeting with their government. It could be a good opportunity for the Alliance, but all I wanted to do was visit Fontem's secret destination.

After travelling for a while, I finally asked, although I wasn't confident he'd give me a firm answer. Fontem stood behind Slate, hands on the headrest, and stared into the blank space through the screen. "Now will you tell us where we're going?" I asked him.

Fontem smiled, his tanned skin crinkling at the eyes. "Slate, there's a system called Tutep. Set course for the fourth planet from the star. It's named Cubus."

Slate keyed something into the computer and glanced over his shoulder. "I don't see any Cubus."

"Then it's been preserved. Good. Make for Tutep. Fourth planet."

Slate entered the matching coordinates, and I saw our ETA appear on his console. "We'll be there in three and a half days, Boss."

"Good." I patted Fontem on the back and hoped we

were about to find something useful to assist us.

———————

"*A*re you certain you should do this?" Dean asked Jules. They were in the kitchen, sitting across from one another at the table. Jules peered toward the door, checking for the tenth time if anyone was up and about. Slate was on the bridge, and the other three were all sleeping, so there were no prying ears.

Jules sipped the coffee, wishing Dean would be more supportive of her decision. "It's my only choice."

"And what happens if you can't get home? Lom hasn't been able to." He had a good point, but Jules wasn't going to let that stop her.

"I'll figure it out," she assured him.

"And if you don't?"

"Then the universe will be safe, and I'll be gone," she told him.

Dean averted his gaze, gripping his empty cup. "This sucks."

"Agreed, but he's not going to stop until he's dead." Jules was tired of arguing, so she brightened and changed topics. "We're arriving tomorrow. This could be fun."

"Fun? You have the strangest idea of a good time, you know that?" Dean asked, finally breaking his solemn mood.

"Maybe you should remember that when this is done and you take me on a date," she told him.

"A date? Okay, if you manage to go ahead in time, kill Lom of Pleva, get Patty home, and settle the Deities, I'll take you anywhere you want to go," Dean said quietly, and she jutted her hand out, nearly knocking her cup over.

"What am I supposed to do with that?"

"Shake it. We're making a pact."

He took her offered hand, mechanically pumping it three times. "Fine. It's a date."

It was a shame Jules might leave in a few days and never see him again. He seemed to notice a shift in her mood, and he stood, crossing the table to lean over and kiss her softly. "Come on. Let's see what Slate's up to."

"If I know Uncle Zeke, he's flying on autopilot, and we're cruising into an asteroid field while he sleeps." Jules darted through the hall, amped up on caffeine, and found Slate sitting straight up. "Maybe he's not asleep."

"You think so little of me?" Slate asked with a laugh. "I woke up five minutes ago."

Jules grinned at his joke and took a seat beside him, staring at the visuals outside their ship. A bright purple and yellow nebula was directly in front of them: far away, but close enough to see the beauty of it.

The map flashed once, and Slate zoomed on the image. "Dean, go wake the others. We've entered Tutep."

Jules watched as Slate targeted the fourth world. "This can't be it," she said. The planet was devoid of any life. Judging by the picture, the place was bone dry, lacking anything resembling an atmosphere. It was gray and black.

"No kidding. But maybe it's a good hiding place?" Slate shrugged.

"Good morning," Jules' dad said. She offered him her spot, and he shook his head, pointing to the chair. "You stay."

He chose to stand and absently petted his newly-trimmed beard. Jules knew that habit well; it meant he was anxious. Fontem and Karo arrived a moment later, each wearing white jumpsuits.

"Fontem, this isn't a very hospitable system. Good

choice," Slate said.

"All is not as it seems, my friend." Fontem's eyes danced as he spoke.

"Can you cut the riddles? What are you talking about?" Papa asked.

"Continue to the fourth planet and you'll see," Fontem advised them.

Jules disappeared, using the hour or so to make some food for their small group. It wasn't often you had any alone time on a ship this cramped, so she took her time, thinking about her plan. Reaching Udoon wasn't going to be a problem, but making Viliar use the device to send her to Lom might be tricky.

The message she'd sent Lom had been simple. *We have the girl. We'll use her as bait.*

Lom hadn't replied, and she was nervous, thinking that the device was sitting on *Light* in her bedroom right now. If her mother stumbled across it, it would ruin everything. She was happy to see her dad pleased with his progress as they'd destroyed Lainna, but it was only a matter of time before Lom stopped him again, threatening his family. He'd eventually go to Udoon Station and sacrifice himself for their sake.

Her father was too important to too many people. He wasn't just a figurehead; he was a leader. Whether he liked to think so or not, he was in charge of the Alliance. Dean Parker called the shots on Earth, New Spero, Haven, and in the Academy. Indirectly, they all took his lead. The other Alliance members considered him the face of humanity, as well as the head of the Alliance. Regnig had also dubbed him a Recaster. The Theos called him the True. Teelon had said he was special and told him to change the universe. He was important, more important than Jules could ever be. She would take his place at Udoon.

"Jules, we're arriving!" Dean called from down the hall.

She brought a couple trays with eggs and a carafe of coffee to the compact bridge, and handed the dishes out. Everyone took the offered food with a thank you, and they ate while Slate guided their cloaked Kraski ship toward the world.

"This place is terrible. I guess we'd better suit up," her dad said.

"That won't be necessary." Fontem turned to face them. "Slate, take us into orbit and slowly lower through the atmosphere."

"There's nothing but rock there," Slate told him.

"Just do it," Fontem ordered. Slate glanced at Papa, who nodded once, saying it was okay.

One moment, Jules was seeing the uninhabited bleak surface; the next, it was a lush and vibrant landscape, full of life and sunlight. "How is this possible?" she asked softly.

"I hid it from outside eyes. Kind of like how you have a cloaking device on this ship. I tricked any randomly passing vessels to continue on. Nothing to see here." Fontem sounded proud of himself.

"Let me get Regnig," Papa said, and Jules felt a thrill as she saw the gorgeous planet through the screen.

"Let's wait for Regnig. There will be some walking first, and his legs aren't up for the challenge, I'm afraid," Fontem told them.

Slate let the Terellion advise him where to land, and the ship lowered, setting in the center of a mountain range.

"We're here." Fontem started down the corridor, and Slate powered off the ship, peering at her dad.

"Careful where you tread. I have a feeling we're missing something," Slate whispered to Papa, loud enough for Jules to hear.

I hoped Slate was being overcautious, but I knew he was right. Fontem had left too many things out, told me too much out of convenience over the last couple of years since he'd been saved from the Collector's ship. The stories from Regnig about his obsession with returning to his dead wife's side lingered in my thoughts, and I couldn't blame the man for wanting that life again. I'd probably be the same way.

Regardless of him telling us the planet's atmosphere was fully breathable for all of us, we waited until our probes returned, displaying a positive result. We exited the ship to find a wonderful day. This place wasn't overly hot, not like some of the planets we tended to visit. Rather, the weather was perfect, twenty Celsius with a light breeze.

After experiencing our cramped vessel for three days, being outside was a pleasure. The sky was immense, only dwarfed to my left by the massive mountainside. Thick coniferous-like trees covered the landscape below and up the side of the peaks, creating a dense valley of green vegetation.

"This is a nice place," Dean said, standing beside me. We were all armed, and I noticed that Dean had taken one of the heavier packs.

"How far is it?" I asked Fontem.

He was already trekking away, long strides carrying him toward the valley. "A day's walk," he said.

Slate groaned, picking up another pack of supplies. "A day? Couldn't we have flown closer?"

"No. I made it impossible to randomly locate. The odds of finding it here are astronomical," Fontem said, his voice growing quiet as he gained distance.

"I guess we'd better go. Jules, you good?" I asked her.

Her eyes were glowing darker in the bright sunlight, and her hair was pulled into a curly ponytail. She was so grown up these days. When I pictured her in my head, she was still this little kid with thick curls, spinning around and saying things like "I can help." Here she was, almost a fully grown woman, and it pained me to think she'd eventually leave the nest.

"I'm glad to be here," she said, starting off. Karo stayed close, passing me a smaller pack, and I slid it over my shoulders.

"This better be worth it," I told him.

"I hope so too. Can you believe he had the technology to cover the entire planet with a false front? How long has it been like this?" Karo asked, walking with me toward the others.

"A long time. Fontem has a few tricks up his sleeve."

The air cooled as we dropped in elevation, and since there was no pathway built into the forest, the climb down was extremely slow. Fontem led us to a flowing river directly in the middle of the copse, and he stopped at it, bending over to touch the moving water. "This funnels from multiple tributaries around the mountains. We're at the lowest point of the region. The water is fresh, and you can drink it." As if to prove this, he pulled a canteen from his pack and filled it up, drinking deeply.

Slate tested it first, and stuck his thumb up in the universal gesture, signaling it was good. I tried it, finding the liquid chilled and almost sweet.

"We have a long way to go. Let's continue," Fontem said.

By the time we took a break, my legs were aching fiercely, and despite the cooler temperatures in the tree cover, I was soaked with sweat. Slate looked about as bad as I felt, but the kids were doing much better. Jules acted like she was out for an evening stroll, and Dean seemed bored, even though he had the most to carry.

Fontem and Karo unpacked some food sticks, handing the flavored bars out, and we sat on the ground. Everything smelled hearty here, and I heard the sharp trilling of something resembling a bird from above.

"You sure there's nothing dangerous here?" Slate asked, slinging his pulse rifle over his shoulder to set it on the forest bed.

"Nothing we need to concern ourselves with. They only come out at night, and something our size is too large for them," Fontem said, not expanding on what exactly these predators were. No one asked.

"How much farther?" Jules asked him.

"A few hours. Trust me, it'll be worth it," he assured us.

"How long did it take you to accrue all of your items?" I asked him.

He bit into his bar, chewing it a few times before answering. "Years. Centuries, really. Once I had enough funds, and somewhere to store them, I may have gone a little overboard. I still have a lot of artifacts I don't understand, but I've decided to give Regnig access here when we're done. He's expressed interest, and someone should have eyes on them."

I listened, picking up on the subtle nuances in his statement. It sounded like he wasn't going to be around for long. I filed that bit of information away for later. I didn't want to grill him in front of the group. It reminded me of the way my grandmother used to point at things in her house, telling us grandkids what she was leaving us when she died.

"I'm sure he's going to love that," Jules said. "Regnig is obsessed with ancient civilizations and all their contraptions."

"I'd be so bored," Dean said. "I need to be out like this, exploring planets, racing through space on important missions."

I smiled at his enthusiasm. Had I ever viewed my life with the same kind of courage? I'd been a mediocre student and had gone straight from high school to college, majoring in accounting. While some of my hometown friends went to Europe on backpacking adventures, I was doing my best to set myself up with a modest career, something stable. I'd never felt like I was missing out, and then I'd met Janine, and everything had seemed to be on the right path. How wrong I'd been.

"Sometimes we need to study what's been to see what's coming," Karo said, with the wisdom only a Theos could muster.

"I can see it both ways. While I like researching with Regnig, I love being out here. I don't know which path I'd choose," Jules said.

I did. She'd choose to be out in the universe, assisting others. It was her nature. Hell, it was in my blood too.

"You have to be kidding me, Ju. You're not the 'stay-behind-a-desk' kind of person," Dean told her, tossing a broken twig at her legs.

"Maybe I am. There are lots of intricacies that make up Jules Parker," she said lightly, throwing the stick back at him. "What about you, Uncle Zeke. Were you ever a nerd?"

He laughed at her choice of words and rolled his eyes. "Do I look like a nerd?"

"Well…" Dean laughed.

"I didn't have time to be a nerd. I was too busy trying

to make money, and then when I enlisted, it was all get up and go," Slate said.

He'd told us his history, about how his brother was killed in the line of duty overseas, and how Slate had joined the army to avenge him, nearly losing himself along the way.

"There's still time, Slate," I told him. "I have some great books on Ainter Eleven archaeology, if you want to read them."

"Sounds like a hard pass," Slate said.

"Imagine the undiscovered secrets out there…" Jules stared toward the sky. "Millions of planets, each with their own stories. Studying Earth history was a literal career for some back home, right, Papa?"

"That's right."

"We had classes at the Academy, but they were quite basic. I mean, take this planet, for example. It's been around for billions of years. It's transformed many times. Each world has dozens of layers of history, so many cataclysmic events, plagues, fires, ice ages, all sparking the next era. It's fascinating." Jules closed her lips as she realized all eyes were on her.

"Eloquently put," Karo said. "You're right. Each life is important, and we often forget how many are lost with the passing of every era."

"That's part of the reason I was so captivated by my artifacts. I have things long forgotten by every single person in the universe. There's something special about that, even if I don't understand the function," Fontem told us.

"Time to continue?" I asked, knowing my protesting legs were asking to rest. The longer we waited, the more that would become true.

"Yes, let's move." Fontem rose and started the journey, pressing deeper into the valley's forest.

TWENTY-ONE

*I*t was dark by the time we stopped again. Fontem led us to the edge of the mountain, along a rocky cliff face. Most of the range was sloped, full of trees and growth, but here it was a solid drop, almost a straight ninety-degree escarpment.

"We've arrived," Fontem advised us.

The noises around us had changed, the birds growing silent and another animal sending shrill songs through the night air, mixing with dueling insect wails. Overall, it was soothing, and I almost wished we were camping here for the night. But curiosity had me filling with adrenaline as I peered across the stone wall, searching for an opening.

"How do we access it?" I asked.

Fontem's teeth were bright as he smiled, and he pointed above, some thirty or forty feet up. "There are rungs dug into the stone, hidden behind another device." He moved his hand over the surface, and it disappeared behind a fake rock overlay. "The opening is up there."

"Great. Climbing invisible steps in the dark," Slate muttered.

"Can you shut the device off? Make it easier?" I asked him, but he refused.

"These are my rules," he said plainly.

The tree cover was less dense here. It had thinned out

as we'd climbed from the middle of the valley where the river had expanded. Here, it was mostly rocky ground, leading to Fontem's cliff. This allowed the sliver of a moon to cast sufficient light to see what we were doing.

I unslung my pack, letting it drop to the ground, and the others followed suit. I felt lighter on my feet without the added burden.

"We'll need water and sustenance," Fontem said. "I'd suggest someone stays behind to make camp as well. Perhaps two of us."

I waited for volunteers, and when none came forward, I asked Slate. "Do you mind?"

He shrugged. "This is more your thing. I'll stay behind, but I'll need some company. Dean, how about you?"

Dean grunted and began removing some camping gear from his bag. "No problem. It's probably just a bunch of dusty glass vases up there anyway."

"Thanks, guys. Jules, Karo, are you ready?" I asked.

Jules was staring at the spot Fontem had pointed to, and I bet she wished she could just float up there ahead of us. She was being a good sport about it. "Sure thing, Papa." Her words were rushed, full of excitement.

Fontem took the first steps, demonstrating that the rungs were three feet apart in a straight line. "You can feel them, so grab the next before you release the first one." He moved up slowly, half of him disappearing behind the fake wall of stone.

Karo went next, and I set a hand on Jules' shoulder, leaning in. "I'm glad we're here together."

"Me too, Papa." She began climbing, and I went last.

"See you guys soon," I told them, grasping at the first hidden rung.

---

*F*irst Fontem then Karo vanished into an invisible opening in the rock wall, and Jules took one last look at Dean on the ground. He stopped what he was doing with Slate, and waved at her. She waved back, holding herself up with one hand, before turning to the final section. She climbed it slowly, pretending she couldn't just drop free and float the last few meters.

Her dad was close behind, making good time. Jules felt no more handholds, and she saw an arm extend out from the rock to help her. She took Karo's assistance and was pulled through the opening. It was dark, but Fontem had activated a light on the circular corridor's wall. He pinned the glowing device to his collar, and Jules stepped to the side as her dad came through after her.

"That was... interesting," Papa said, dusting his hands off. Jules glanced around the tunnel, only seeing for a few yards before the light beams died off. "How far does this go on?"

"There are a few different paths to take in here. I used digging bots to create an intricate tunnel system that would be easy to get lost in. I suspect at least a few people have sought my treasures over the years, so even if anyone found this opening, the chances they discover my cache is once again..."

Jules finished the sentence for him. "Astronomical."

"Right. You've been paying attention." Fontem's eyes twinkled.

It was obvious the Terellion was thrilled to be here. She suspected he'd been itching to return to this place since she'd freed him, and it was evident he didn't want further delays.

Fontem started forward, having to crouch for the first

twenty paces or so until the tunnels split, giving them two options. "Left. Left. Right. The entire time. Do that, and you can't lose your way."

Jules repeated it. Left. Left. Right. The tunnels grew wider, until she could stand without ducking, but Karo was two feet taller than her, and by the time they'd walked in- side for a half hour, he'd asked to take a break.

Jules wondered how deep into the mountain they were, and she inhaled deeply, the air so musty, she almost coughed some dirt out. Her uniform was covered in grime now, but all of them were in the same boat.

"Not much farther, Karo. I'm glad you came, Theos." Fontem turned, and Karo glanced at her dad, who shrugged in return to the unasked question.

Another ten minutes moving through the passageways, and they arrived at the end of this tunnel. It separated into three options. Fontem turned to them and grinned. "This is the end. Take the center."

Jules glanced to the tunnel near her and saw something inside. She pushed some green light from her hand, light emerald flames licking from her fingers, creating a make- shift torch. "Papa, what's this?"

He followed behind her, and she nearly tripped on them.

"Bones," he said, bending down to observe the pile.

Fontem's voice startled Jules as she stared at the re- mains. "I suspect there are more inside here, though that one would have to be semi-fresh to not be fully decom- posed by now. They were close. Come. It's time."

Jules left the bones uncovered and joined Karo beside the middle entrance. Fontem leaned against the dark stone wall and urged Karo in first. "After you. As a Theos, I think you'll appreciate this."

Karo took a step. "It's just more…" His voice cut off,

and Jules saw he was gone. She went next, hand out-stretched. Without thinking, she shot her shield up, forgetting to turn the green off. It glowed, lighting her path as she passed through some invisible barrier. When she emerged on the other side, she gaped at the sights.

Karo stared toward the clear-domed ceiling. The pale blue star was close, filling half of their sightlines. The dome overhead was tinted, helping block any retinal damage, and Jules couldn't help but feel like she was at the edge of the universe.

"What is this?" her dad asked. She hadn't even heard him enter the room.

"This is Reonis. It's millions of light years from the nearest Shandra, and so distant that none within your Alliance have ever seen anything remotely near it. This is what I call Ubos, my antiquities assemblage." Fontem walked past them, and for the first time, Jules took stock of the room. The ceiling dome was at least a hundred meters tall, making it twice that wide, with a golden floor speckled with something resembling diamonds, glinting light as Fontem activated digital torches around the space.

There were rows of shelving, each glass, meticulously devoid of dust. Jules passed by them, looking at the odd assortment of goods here. She stopped at one, where something resembling a shrunken Padlog head sat attached to a wooden mount.

"You don't want to touch that," Fontem warned her.

"Why not?"

"It's cursed." That was enough explanation for her.

"Regnig!" Papa shouted. "We forgot him."

Jules continued walking through the endless rows of treasures while Fontem and her dad activated the portal sticks. They filled the edge of the dome with the beam spread, and Fontem marched through, returning in a few minutes with a disheveled Regnig.

I was sleeping, he told them, making Papa laugh.

"Would you like to return home?" he asked Regnig.

I think not. Hello, Jules. Hello, Karo and Dean. Fontem, so this is the fabled Ubos, is it? Regnig walked over, hobbling with his cane, and he stuck his tongue out, peering toward the blue starlight with his one red-rimmed eyeball.

"It's pretty cool, isn't it?" Jules came over to his side, helping prop him up.

Is there somewhere to sit? he asked, and Fontem guided him to the middle of the dome. There were two plush chairs, complete with footrests, and a golden candelabrum that looked like it came from Earth's medieval time period. He tapped it, and a projection of a fireplace lit up, phony flames dancing near the resting spot.

"I used to come here to think at one point, but eventually, it was too much to bear, once I lost my wife for good," Fontem said.

Jules helped Regnig onto the chair and noticed the painting along a pony-wall built to give this section of the dome a homey ambiance. The woman was the same species as Fontem, and she was beautiful. "Is this her?" she asked, walking toward the image. The shelves here were each eight feet high, and because they were made of glass, combined with the clear dome, they gave the space an open feeling.

"That's her," Fontem said softly. "But I didn't come here to relive my past. I have things to show you."

Was it difficult to reach this place? I hadn't heard from you for a while.

"Sorry we haven't been by lately. Jules visited the other day, at least. You did say hi for us, right, honey?" Papa asked.

Jules' eyes sprang wide in fear of being caught. She'd

lied to her parents and was about to get caught in the cross-fire. "Sure I did. Right, Regnig?" She tilted her head as she stared at him, willing him to understand she wanted him to play along.

Of course. She's an upstanding daughter, and she would never forget to obey her father.

She smiled and mouthed the words "thank you," receiving a private thought from the telepathic bird-man. *We'll discuss this later.*

Jules nodded, not wanting to have that talk with Regnig now, or ever. If he learned about her plans to stop Lom, he'd tell her parents for sure.

"What did you want to show us?" her father asked, and Jules searched for Karo, who was nowhere in sight.

"How about this?" Fontem said, leading them two rows in, to the third shelf. He picked up the box, opening it to reveal a ring. "This ring fools people into thinking you're dead. Try it."

Papa shook his head. "I don't think that's necessary," he said.

Fontem shrugged, slipping the thick white-gold band over his pinky finger. Instantly, his skin turned a grayish hue; his hair became thinner, greasy, and his hands appeared bent and gnarled, like cold death had set in. "No heartbeat. No vitals. It's quite the piece of technology."

"Where did you find it?" Papa asked.

"You don't want to know." Fontem set it down, continuing on. Jules stared at the box, and when no one was looking, she slipped the ring into her jumpsuit pocket. That might come in handy.

"Fontem, is there anything that might be related to the Zan'ra?" she asked. "Four circles with an X through them, maybe?"

She thought she saw something spark in his eyes,

maybe fear, but it passed quickly. "I don't think so, but feel free to check."

Jules continued through, hearing Fontem as he talked about various other useful tools. Karo was nearby, and she crept over to him, checking what he was doing.

He looked pale, and she saw why. The marking of the Iskios was embedded on a piece of metal, sitting on the shelf. "They're gone, Karo. And because we've stopped Lom from having a fuel source for a nullifier, the Vortex will never be returning."

"You're right. Thanks for the reminder. It's hard to imagine devoting one's life to these artifacts, isn't it?" he asked her, and she slowly nodded in agreement.

"He's lived a long life."

"So have I, and all I have to show for it is a wood-burning pizza oven," Karo said with a laugh.

"Not to mention Ableen and the teens," she reminded him.

"And them too."

Regnig had recovered from his daze and was walking toward Papa and Fontem as they quietly discussed something. When Jules was nearby, she heard the tail end of the conversation. Her dad was moving his arms around, speaking softly. "… Delineator?"

"No, not like you think. This won't work either," the Terellion said, and when they spotted the others arriving, Fontem hastily set the rectangular object on the shelf.

"If it's the same to you, can I take it?" her dad asked.

Fontem nodded. "You may take anything you desire."

Jules doubted that was true, but at least he was being nice about it. Fontem tossed her dad a colorful bag. "Use this."

Papa slid the tool into the bag, and they continued on. "What about weapons?"

Fontem raised an eyebrow and waited for a nod from Dean Parker before agreeing. He led them to the opposite end of the room, and Regnig and Karo joined their group as the Terellion motioned for them to stop. This section of the domed room was bereft of furniture, and Fontem waved his hand, bringing a projection to life two feet in front of him. He pressed a code, and Jules peered over his shoulder, memorizing the pattern. It didn't seem like anyone else was paying attention, and she repeated the code in her head a few times, making sure she had it right.

The floor descended, revealing a stairwell.

"What's down here?" her dad asked.

Fontem descended the steps. "Something to turn the tides."

TWENTY-TWO

I'd begun to doubt the value of this journey, but Fontem wouldn't have brought us here for nothing. He was invested in our plight, as he'd become one of us over the last year or so. Regnig used the railing on the steps, and I slowed, assisting him to the bottom of the stairs.

The others were already down there, waiting in the orange glow of the recessed lighting. This room was nearly as vast as the one above us, and the moment I stepped foot on the grated metal floor, I felt the power of the space. There had to be over a thousand artifacts here, many of them locked behind glowing forcefields.

This is not a safe place. Fontem, why have you collected these?

He shrugged as he stared toward his horde of weapons. "It started because I knew people would be willing to spend a lot on these devices, but it ended up becoming an obsession."

I walked beside Jules, the light of her eyes reflecting from a dark shelving unit's door as we stopped at it. "Where did you find them?" I had yet to see underneath his domed room, but it seemed enough to start a war... or end one.

"All over. Many of these were excavated from vanquished worlds, some from epic space battles from millennia ago. I had a few crews of salvagers seeking out ancient rumored wars, and they found most of this. Technology so alien, I've never been able to make sense of it. Perhaps you and your team will have better luck," he said.

I blanched, wondering what we would do with so many armaments. The Alliance was seeking peace among space dwellers, but there would forever be need for defense, and occasionally, offense.

Karo's footsteps clanged against the floor as he walked through the bunker, spinning to face Fontem when he came to the end of the room. There was a door there, and he laid a hand on it. "Fontem, what's behind here?"

"I have a few secrets for me alone. Please, respect my privacy. Everything else here is at your disposal," the Terellion said, and we all gawked at the towering black door.

Jules nudged me with her elbow, leaning in. "This is insane. What do you think this one does?" She pointed at a shiny cylindrical object behind one of the barriers. The energy was woven together, making it impossible to breach the barricade.

Fontem emerged from the shadows, resting his hand on my shoulder. "That melts metal. It'll liquefy anything metallic within a ten-foot radius instantly."

"Why is that stored here? Shouldn't it be in a mechanical shop, or with a construction crew?" Jules asked. I knew the answer but waited for Fontem to tell her.

"It has a timer. See how small it is? It looks like you could leave it in a pantry and someone would think it was a can of food," he said.

"What good would that do? You want to melt all the soup containers?" Jules asked.

Fontem tapped his chin. "Good point. But what if that pantry was on a space vessel, and the kitchen was near the hull?" He waved his fingers and smiled. "Goodbye crew."

"That makes sense," she said in reply, and we continued to the next object. "How about this?"

"This is a little different. Not everything here is destructive. That will copy any device." He released the barrier from this locker, the energy field vanishing, and reached inside, hauling out the box. "Stick any electronic device in here"—he slid the top level open—"and it's replicated on the bottom. Complex 3D printing, including whatever software is on the gadget. In a rush? It only takes two minutes. You sneak the stolen device back, and you have its doppelgänger, with all the information you need."

"That could come in handy," I told him.

We continued on, Fontem showing us the few items he fully understood, and I quickly realized he had far more firepower in here than I'd thought at the start. There were things too dangerous to ever reveal to the Alliance, and I decided some of them, like the star harnesser, would need to be dismantled safely.

It was good of you to hold on to these. If anyone else had access to this, it would be bad. Regnig's beak opened and shut as he shuffled to the next display case.

"My sentiments exactly. I was hoping Dean would be able to help dispose of anything he deemed excessive," Fontem said.

"I'd say most of it is extreme, but we'll do our best," I admitted. Fontem was acting peculiar, and it was hard to miss. Karo and Regnig walked off, chatting enthusiastically, and I held Jules' arm while Fontem followed them.

"We need to watch him," I whispered to my daughter.

"I was thinking the same thing. Did you see him when I asked about the Zan'ra symbol? He was guilty, and what's behind that door? If he's giving us full access here, why the secrecy?" Jules spoke so softly, I could barely hear her.

Fontem's voice cut into our private conversation time.

"Jules, there's one more thing I think you might want to see."

"What is it?" she asked. The ceilings were shorter here: not so much to feel cramped, but as we arrived at Fontem's side, it seemed like the walls were shrinking around me. My head pounded as I spotted the wood grain, the shape of the object, and the symbol burned into the top of it.

But Jules was the one who spoke when Fontem opened the storage container, revealing his prize. "It's a coffin. You have a Deity here?"

———————

*J*ules' skin crawled the moment Fontem had opened the container. It was concealed at the darkest corner of the room, and for a second after seeing it, she thought her eyes were deceiving her. But this was no trick of light. This was one of the Deities' coffins.

"Alas, there is no ancient god trapped inside. It's empty," Fontem said, using his fingers to pry the lid open. It was hinged along the far edge, and Jules leaned over the eight-foot-long coffin, making sure there was nothing lingering within.

She touched the interior, resting a palm on the coarse wooden grain. "How did you find this?"

"Be careful, Jules," Papa warned her, but she was confident there was no threat remaining, if there ever had been. Plus, she didn't actually believe the Deities were a danger to her, not if they were telling her the truth. She might even be one of them. It was too much, so she removed her hand, waiting to hear Fontem's answer.

"I'd heard of them for years, only snippets of information, but nothing substantial. They were like rumors on the wind, never landing anywhere long enough to grasp. Word of the Zan'ra was just as fleeing, but it was said that some dangerous people from a devoured race had sealed off their creators, fearing their own deaths. When I heard a coffin mentioned, it lingered in the recesses of my mind, because it was almost too unbelievable.

"One day, one of my salvage crews brought a haul to me, and we sorted through the goods. I didn't find much of use, but this was inside. When I saw it, I knew. This was one of the coffins. But did that mean one of the Deities was loose? Quite the mystery."

Jules thought about it. If there was a loose god, wouldn't someone have spotted it by now? And why hadn't the Zan'ra explained that to her? "It might have been a failed attempt, before they figured out how to permanently trap them."

"Can you confirm this is similar to what you've come across?" Fontem asked, his eyes suddenly wild as he stepped toward her, his hands nearly grasping her collar. He composed himself and returned to normal, but there was a change in his tone. "I mean, I've always wondered, and this would be quite the find if it was touched by a god."

Jules absently moved from him and the coffin. "This looks like one of them to me."

Fontem nodded, lightly closing the casket before slamming the door to the container. "As you can see, we have a lot of important artifacts here. Perhaps we can call it a night and continue tomorrow."

I think that's a good idea. We can have a fresh start in the morning. Regnig started toward the stairs.

Jules didn't want to leave. She was too excited about everything in here. There had to be devices that could aid her fight against Lom, but everyone else was already exiting the basement floor. The room almost thrummed with power, even if the weapons were inactive and safely stowed behind high-energy shields. These goods had been here for countless years, and as they began up the steps, Jules was reminded just how far they truly were from the planet Dean and Slate were on. The blue star burned hotly through the dome. Fontem was a challenge, and Papa was right. They needed to keep a close eye on the man.

With a last glance at the room full of sacred tools and artifacts, Jules stepped through the portal, returning to the tunnels on Cubus.

Walking through the same corridors was slower with Regnig, and when they emerged outside again, it was nightfall. Camp was set up, and Slate and Dean sat on the ground next to a burning fire. Their eyes glowed orange with the reflection of the flames as they stared toward the people climbing down the hidden rungs.

"Regnig, care for a ride?" she asked the elderly man.

Please. I'm afraid my wings aren't what they used to be.

She picked him up awkwardly and jumped from the opening in the mountainside, slowly floating toward the camp. She arrived first and set the birdman on the ground. He shook his feathers off and moved toward Slate.

Hello, friends. Do we have anything to eat?

"Sure, Regnig, we caught something that looks like fish," Dean said, and Jules noticed how hungry she was as she smelled the cooking meat.

Slate rose, dusting the dirt off his pants, and walked over to her dad. "You took a while. Everything kosher?"

"There's a lot to see. We'll be returning tomorrow. You can join us, if you like," Papa told him.

"Can I come too?" Dean asked as Jules plopped to the rocky ground beside him.

"Sure thing, kid," her dad said, and Dean grinned at Jules.

"Anything good?"

Jules wanted to tell him about the ring she'd jammed into her pocket, but kept it to herself. "He has a Deity coffin in there." She said it quietly enough that the others couldn't hear her. They were huddled around each other at the edge of camp, discussing the stash and the plan for tomorrow.

"Are you kidding? What does that mean?" Dean asked.

"I think it's part of his plan."

"How?"

"The reason Fontem made us come in the first place. He thinks the Deities can help him," she whispered.

"Why? Who petitions a god?"

Her dad arrived, frowning toward them. "Dinner almost ready?" he asked, making Jules wonder how much he'd heard.

"Sure thing, Mr. Parker." Dean plucked the scaled creature from the flames, and the others joined them around the fire.

They ate crusted bread with the meat and talked about how many things could assist the Alliance, but Jules could only think about that coffin, and what she was going to do when they returned to see the rest of the Zan'ra. She needed to figure that puzzle out before she departed for Udoon. She was running out of time.

Jules finished her food, watching Fontem from the corner of her eye. He was acting normal, as if there was nothing out of the ordinary, but his façade had been cracked inside his private cache. There was something devious going on, and she was going to find out what.

One by one, their group headed for the comfort of the erected tents, and Jules waited until Fontem had retired to bed to leave the fireside. Eventually, she entered the tent she was sharing with her father, but kept her eyes peeled and her ears open.

"Good morning, boss." Slate's voice woke Jules from a deep slumber, and she opened her eyes, blinking at the bright morning light pouring through the open doorway.

She'd fallen asleep! Jules ran her hands through her hair, tugging at a couple of knots, and climbed from the sleeping bag. No one was freaking out, so that meant Fontem was probably at the fire with the rest of them, having breakfast. She'd worried for nothing. She still felt the crystal bracelet around her wrist under her jumpsuit's sleeve, and she kept it there. Its presence was oddly comforting.

The air was crisp at this early hour, and she scanned the area, giving Dean a little wave when she spotted him. His hair was a mess, but she thought it was kind of adorable. Regnig's beak jutted from the tent he was sharing with Fontem, and he exited, flapping his wings a few times.

Has anyone seen Fontem? Regnig asked, and Jules' heart pounded.

"I thought he was here…" Slate spun around, then shrugged. "Guess I was wrong. Maybe he's at the lake for a bath."

"Papa…" Jules' breath caught in her throat. She should never have fallen asleep, but she'd been so tired, full of a great dinner.

"What is it?" her dad asked, chewing on a protein bar.

"He's gone," she told him, so sure of it.

"Who?"

"Fontem."

His face changed, shifting to a concerned expression she'd seen many times in her short life. "Are you certain?"

She nodded.

"Fontem! Where are you?" Papa called, but no one answered.

"Boss, he's probably at the lake. Let's go check," Slate told Karo, and they started off.

"They won't find him there. Papa, I have to go," she told her dad.

He grimaced but nodded in agreement. "Be careful. Left, left, right," he reminded her, not that she'd forgotten the instructions from yesterday.

"What are you doing?" Dean arrived, jogging over from near the fire he'd started again.

"I have to go too." She grabbed his collar, standing on her toes to peck him on the lips.

"Where?"

But she was already gone, floating toward the hole in the cliffside.

The trip through the tunnels took far less time when traveling surrounded by her green sphere. She kept it glowing to give her light along the trail, and five minutes later, she slowed and settled near the three tunnel entrances, opting for the center one.

"Please be open," she muttered, praying Fontem hadn't deactivated their access from this side. She walked through the portal barrier and arrived within the dome. "Thank you."

She shot into the air, moving for the peak of the dome, and searched for Fontem. The room was vacant.

The stairs were closed, but she recalled how Fontem had activated them. She waved her hand in the air as he had, but nothing happened. Jules moved to the same location he'd been standing, trying the motion again, and the keypad projection illuminated. Nervously, she ran the pattern she'd watched Fontem use over the air, and the floor began to shake, revealing the stairs.

Jules hurried down them, floating the entire time. The space felt ominous alone, and she felt the threat of every dangerous item here. Fontem was nowhere in sight. "Where are you?" she shouted, receiving nothing in response.

Jules glanced at the door he'd told them was off limits, and it became clear. He'd tricked them into coming to this place. He had no means to travel so far, but he still could have found a ship to give him passage to Techeron, she was sure of that. But... he'd needed to know something first. All the time spent with Regnig, researching the Zan'ra and the Deities; it hadn't been for their benefit. It had to be for his own objectives.

Jules floated past the rows of devices, the containers with dangerous artifacts locked behind their walls, and landed at the black entrance Fontem had ordered them to keep away from. She set her palm on it and instantly sensed the portal behind it. "Damn it."

Jules peered over her shoulder and found one of the tall locker doors wide open. She ran for it and grabbed the empty box inside. It was twice the size of her hand, and the symbol carved on the top was only too familiar. Four circles with an X overtop. He had a device belonging to the Zan'ra and had taken it through the portal.

She was about to force the door open when she remembered something from the day before. Jules returned upstairs, grabbing a leather bag she'd seen, and added a couple of items to it. She clasped the flap and slung it over her shoulder.

Jules was angry she hadn't felt the pull of the portal stone the day before, but with everyone around her and all the talk about weapons, she hadn't noticed. Now it was like a tuning fork, vibrating in her hand.

The door wouldn't open. She searched for a keypad, but there was none. Jules closed her eyes, feeling the need to follow Fontem. Whatever he was after wasn't good, and she suspected the fallout was going to be disastrous. She passed through the entryway, her body turning into another state for a split second. When she materialized fully, she took stock of the cramped room. The crystal lit up at her presence, but this was unlike any Shandra she'd ever seen.

Jules pressed a hand to it, feeling its core. There was no icon table here, no option to choose where you traveled to, but Fontem had clearly used it.

"This is a one-way trip," she said slowly, her realization of the crystal's power difference filling her. This Shandra might bring you to another portal. You could never travel through this one to arrive at Fontem's collection. He was protecting his treasures, but also gave himself a quick escape, which he'd done this morning while the rest of their camp was fast asleep.

Her mouth was dry, and she pressed her lips together, wondering for the first time if Fontem had drugged them during last night's meal. Where had he gone?

She stood over the rounded waist-high crystal, still touching it. Where had he gone? He had a Deity coffin, the Zan'ra symbol on the empty box, meaning he'd taken something that involved them.

Lan'i's words from when they'd chanted over the Deity's underwater grave filled her mind. *We used to have a tool to hone our powers for this purpose.* That was it! Fontem had the device the Zan'ra had operated, the one that had been lost with Ja'ri.

That meant…

Jules activated the portal, urging it to bring her to Desolate.

TWENTY-THREE

The storm was fierce. The moment Jules emerged from the thrashing lake's surface, she had to brace herself within her energy shield. Wind gusted against her, battering her defenses, and she peered in the direction of the ocean, seeing the unmistakable black skies. It was past dusk, and from here, she spotted a handful of stars where the clouds had parted enough to reveal the time of day.

Fontem was here.

Her heart raced, and she tried to focus on her mission. She needed to stop Fontem from rousing the gods. Jules had considered doing this very thing, but not for her own selfish interests. The Zan'ra were dangerous, and if she was truly infused with the spirit of a Deity, she had an obligation to assist them. The urge constantly tugged on her subconscious, compelling her to free them as ordered.

She sped toward the ocean, only pausing to hover over the destruction of the Zan'ra city below. Ja'ri had done the ultimate selfish act, killing her people to preserve her own life. Jules hated the Zan'ra she was impersonating.

By the time she neared the churning oceanside, the sky was so black, she struggled to see. There was no hint of moonlight through the dense clouds, and Jules searched for Fontem. Lightning forked through the air, more hostile than the day she'd spoken to the Deity. It was down there.

She stared through the giant waves, water splashing over her as they crested, striking the cliff's face.

Jules felt the others arrive. This was a new sensation, or an old one that she hadn't recognized before this moment. The Four were here. She had to act fast, before they came and distracted her. Jules jumped over the cliff edge and crashed into the ocean.

Inside the protective barrier of her sphere, she swam toward the coffin.

She was too late. Fontem treaded the water near the coffin, and the circle on the box burned bright yellow. The shadow began pouring from the lid's edge, and Fontem didn't notice her as she approached.

He wore an advanced scuba outfit, his face concealed with a mask, eyes wide as he stared at the Deity thrashing from the inside of the tomb.

"Fontem! Stop this!" she screamed, and even under the surface of the water, he somehow heard her words. Another one of her gifts, she suspected.

"How did you... leave me alone. This is my right. I found him, I have the right to petition him!" Fontem swam away from her, the shadow solidifying more with each passing breath.

"You don't know what you're doing! It's too soon!" she shouted, but Fontem didn't care.

Jules moved closer, trying to grasp his arm, but he recoiled. "I need this. You should have left me frozen in time. I can't stand this! Let me ask my boon, Jules." His face was slack, his words heart-wrenching.

"They're coming!" she told him, but he didn't seem to understand.

"Who is?"

"The Four. Or at least, the other three of them," she said.

"Then I'd better be quick!" Fontem moved closer to the figure. She noticed the green gemstone in his hand, which had to be the device Lan'i had mentioned the last time she was here. The misty black vapor drifted in the water, moving in swirling patterns as a body began taking shape. Jules had only thought of the Deities as ethereal, and hadn't expected them to be made of flesh and blood. He took on the color of the ocean, sharp protrusions forming at his shoulders, a bald head erupting from the shadows.

You have done well, my daughter. The voice was jarring, stronger and crisper than before.

"It wasn't me!" she told it, but her denial felt irrelevant.

"It was me! I demand something of you," Fontem told it, and Jules cringed as the huge head turned to face Fontem. The Deity stood on the bottom of the ocean now, its immense height making its eyes level with Jules. They were bright, each one half the size of her body.

Why do you speak to me? Daughter, remove him from my presence.

"I can return you to the grave I freed you from!" Fontem raised his hand up, showcasing the pulsing green crystal.

He laughed, the sound booming and terrible. Jules noticed she no longer bled as a result of her close proximity to the Deity, and briefly wondered what had changed.

The Deity raised its giant arm. The water shifted and sent Jules and Fontem away, as if an intense current had taken hold of them. The device in the Terellion's grip fell loose, moving toward the ocean bed far below. He scrambled for it, but the Deity rushed toward him, grabbing the man with a massive hand. Fontem fought to escape, but it was pointless. Jules assumed the god would kill him, but it didn't.

I thank you for releasing me. What is it you seek? the Deity asked.

Fontem ceased his thrashing. "My wife… I… I need to return to her. To grow old with her in her timeline. To do it over again, but without my genetic flaw."

Jules heard the pain in his voice, and at once understood his reasoning for everything he'd done. If she'd encountered that with Dean, would she not want to do the exact same thing Fontem was requesting of the god?

Is this all you seek?

The question appeared to shock Fontem, and he stared into the god's white eyes. "It is my wish!"

Jules swam over to them, waiting for the Deity's response, and it came very soon, with little deliberation. *I shall make it happen. Go to her. Live out your days. I will replace the other version of yourself. You will have no memories of this timeline. You will grow old with her. Your genetic advances will be removed. Do you agree to this?*

Fontem's eyes were wide, his mouth ajar behind his EVA mask. He nodded. "I agree to your terms!"

Let it be so. The god released Fontem, and further black mist poured from the god's fingers, swirling around the Terellion.

"Goodbye, young Jules. Thank your father for me. Take care of my things. They are yours now," Fontem told her as he spun, and seconds later, he was enveloped by the underwater whirlpool. When the waters calmed, he was gone.

Jules shed a tear behind her shield: not for the loss of the man, but for what he'd just gained. It had been his single focus for so many years, and now, even though he wouldn't remember it, he'd fulfilled his lifelong goal. He could reunite with his wife.

"You can send people in time," she told the god matter-of-factly.

Does this surprise you? he asked.

"It does. Am I truly one of you?" She was nervous for the answer. "If I go to the future to kill someone, can I return here, to my family?"

Of course you can. I will have to show you, though. Release me.

She was about to tell him he was free already when she felt the presence of the rest of the Four. The Zan'ra had arrived, and they weren't going to be happy.

Do not be fearful, child. I will handle them.

The god crouched and sprang upwards, leading for the ocean's surface. If he was going to stop them, she needed to help Patty before he did something irrevocable.

Jules rocketed after the Deity.

———————

I couldn't wait any longer. It had been two hours since Jules had set out, and that was disconcerting. Our entire group was determined to find her, Slate armed and taking the lead. Karo carried Regnig, and Dean guarded the rear of the group, a pulse pistol gripped in his palm.

"Slate, it's left, then left, then right. I think you screwed up the last one," I told him, and the big man stopped, Karo bumping into his broad back.

"I don't think so… jeez, I hate these tunnels. They're too small. Remember how I feel about confined spaces, boss." Slate spun around, as if searching for the answers.

"You're right. I think I know where we made the mistake. Everyone follow me," Dean said, reminding me so much of a younger Magnus. Dean was a lot thinner, but he was growing, and he was taller than I was now, his shoulders broader.

"Lead the way, kid," Slate told him, and we returned to

the previous split-off in the corridor system, opting for the other entrance. With Dean guiding us, we arrived at the portal in the center hole sooner than I'd expected, and we all piled in.

"Jules!" I shouted as I ran into the domed room, which sat on an asteroid in some distant unknown system. The pale blue star hung above us, and Slate and Dean gawked at the immense beauty and power of it.

"Jules!" I shouted again, scouring the room, running through the many rows of intricate artifacts. She was nowhere to be seen.

"Over here, Dean!" Karo called, waiting for me at the stairs. We rushed down them, ending in the hidden basement where the weapons were kept. A couple of the crates were open, but there was no Jules or Fontem.

I set a hand on the black entrance and rested my forehead on it. "They went this way."

Karo mimicked my movement and shook his head. "I should have sensed the portal yesterday."

"There's a Shandra?" I asked.

"The same, but different."

"Slate, we need to get at it!" I yelled to my commander, who was just arriving at the bottom of the stairwell. His gaze scanned the room full of armaments, and he whistled.

"What do we have here?" Slate asked.

"We have a dilemma." I rapped my knuckles on the door. "We need inside."

"Any ideas how we do that?" Karo asked.

Regnig hobbled over the last step, nearly tumbling over it. He caught himself on the wall and opened his beak wide. *See the left edge? That's a keyhole.*

I glanced at it, running a finger over the dark surface. He was right. There was an indentation, and I bent over, trying to peer through the tiny hole. "Everyone, scour the room. We need to find the key."

The Zan'ra hovered above the water's surface, the waves higher than ever as the massive storm expanded around them.

Patty moved toward her as soon as the girl spotted Jules, but Lan'i was quick to order her to his side. Jules needed to touch her, to steal her essence before the Deity killed them all.

"What have you done, Ja'ri?" Dal'i asked, her face contorted in anger. "You've sealed our fate!"

"It wasn't me, and stop calling me that!" Jules shouted in return.

"You need to accept who you are, Ja'ri. You're one of us. You're one of the Four. Our leader. We followed you then, and we'll do so now. Own the position, and together we can rule this universe," Lan'i said, a confident grin cast over his face.

Your time is over.

The others began to bleed from their noses, and Jules saw blood welling in Patty's ear, even from twenty meters away. Patty's hand rushed to her face, and she dabbed a finger over the blood on her lip.

"It's not over!" Lan'i shouted. "You see, we embedded a special layer of defense." He flew higher into the sky, and the Deity followed. He swam upward, then floated toward the blue-eyed boy. Water poured off him in droves, creating more waves, but something stopped him. The moment his foot breached the ocean, Jules saw the chain attached to his ankle.

It can't be! I was released!

"Ja'ri is the key. She made these coffins, and only she can free you!" Dal'i laughed, and Jules realized what she had to do.

"I'm sorry, guys. I'm with you. The Terellion stole the crystal, used it to ask a favor. I tried to stop him, but I was too slow," she told them over the wind.

"Good. I knew you wouldn't fail us, sister," Lan'i said.

She floated near them, the Four in a line facing off against the Deity. He seemed to be assessing them, calculating, and Jules raised a hand, her left one. She felt the weight of the crystal bracelet that had once stripped her of her powers. She'd been a little girl then, and not having the gifts had seemed like such a terrible thing. The truth was, she'd managed to stop the attack regardless, and it had given her the confidence that she could still accomplish things without her abilities.

Patty had a taste for the power now, but Jules would be there for her after this. She would be the friend she'd stopped being years ago and support Patty through it all.

The Zan'ra filled with power, each of them taking on their colorful ambiance. Jules joined them in her ploy, green energy crackling around her. She wondered if the Deity recognized what she was doing, but didn't have time to consider it as Dal'i shot an orange pulse toward the god. The beam disintegrated before striking him, but another followed. Soon Lan'i added his, and Patty kept frozen, glancing at Jules as if she was unsure what to do.

Jules waved her over while the others were distracted, and Dean's sister obeyed, eyes wide and full of fear.

The Deity raised one of his arms, sending an invisible battering ram at the two offensive Zan'ra, and they shot away, their shields temporarily breaking. Jules had to disable Patty's shield if she was going to be able to touch the girl's skin.

"Patty, we need to attack!" she shouted.

"Do we?" Patty asked.

"Help them!" Jules moved in front of the girl, trying to mentally send a message to the huge god. *You have to take the purple one's shield down! We don't have much time!*

There was no indication he heard her pleading thoughts, but she began firing at the god alongside Patty. The others arrived, their shields up once again, and blasts erupted from their hands, sending orange, blue, purple, and green spherical pulses at the Deity.

For a moment, Jules dreaded that they'd won and killed the god, but it began laughing, a terrifying and menacing sound entering her mind. *You cannot harm me!*

A wall of smoke poured from the god, racing toward them like a tidal wave. It struck, cutting their power. Jules felt it the instant the mist hit. All four of their shields faltered, and they plummeted toward the ocean.

Jules hit it painfully, the waves pulling her under the water. Her abilities were still there, just the shield gone, and she opened her eyes, searching for Patty. Lan'i was already swimming for the surface, and finally, in the roiling water, Jules spotted her friend.

Patty was sinking, and Jules swam for her, grabbing the girl. She tugged her arm, dragging her to the surface, and she smiled at Patty, who was struggling to regain her composure. Jules slid her sleeve up, activating the bracelet. She mouthed two words at Patty before using it: *I'm sorry.*

The Zan'ra essence slipped from the girl, entering the clear crystals around Jules' arm, filling them with the bright purple color of O'ri.

Her shield reactivated, and she pulled Patty inside her bubble, flying out of the ocean and high into the angry night sky. Lightning continued to dazzle the eyes, thunder booming almost constantly.

The two Zan'ra fought with everything they had, but the Deity blocked their assault with grace.

"What have you done?" Patty asked her, the energy drained from her.

"The Four are done. I saved your life."

The Deity increased in size, fins jutting from its neck. Its white eyes glowed as it raised both hands.

It ends now!

"This isn't good," Patty whispered.

TWENTY-FOUR

"How about this?" Karo asked, and I tried to jam the long tool into the keyhole. It didn't work. None of the artifacts had.

I leaned against the door, hoping my daughter was safe.

"We could leave, go for *Light*, try to see if she contacted Mary," Slate suggested.

Dean shook his head fiercely. "What if she returns here and we're already gone? No way. We can't leave her."

"The kid's right. I'm not risking it," I said.

Regnig was full of energy, and he was hardly using his cane as he searched the upstairs level. *Perhaps this will do the trick.* He waved his little wing at me from the top of the stairs, and I jogged over, seeing a black object in his talons.

He leaned to the side and tossed the key down the steps. I caught it deftly and smiled. This felt like the same material as the door. This had to be it.

The others grew silent and made room for me as I ran for the doorway. The key trembled in my nervous fingers as I lifted it toward the keyhole. It was long and skinny, with no traditional key head, only a finger loop. It fit perfectly, and I stuck my right index finger into it, tugging to the side. The door clicked open, swinging outward on interior hinges.

"Regnig, you did it!" I could have kissed him right on the beak, but we didn't have time for that. The Shandra stone was round, and it glowed as I neared it in the cramped closet-like room.

"There's no table," I said.

"Have no fear, boss. Remember that tool J-NAK the robot gave us?" Slate rushed to his pack and opened it, setting aside countless objects.

"You were a Boy Scout, weren't you?" I asked, unable to keep the mirth from my voice.

"Never leave home unprepared, Dean." Slate smirked, bringing me the tool that would aid us in recovering the last location the Shandra provided. Since we couldn't plug it in, I activated the wireless sensors, and it somehow locked to the gemstone. It flashed, showing the previous symbol. Four circles. An X over them.

"She went to Desolate." I set a hand on the stone and pictured the symbol. Before it sent me anywhere, Dean ran into the room, jumping toward me with his palm out.

The small room went white.

---

*T*he Deity's powerful scream permeated Jules' ears, but Patty didn't seem to notice that she was bereft of the Zan'ra essence. The other two were still fighting, but their efforts were useless. They were too weak. Blood poured from them like an endless river, and Jules almost felt sorry for the duo. They'd done terrible things in their lives, even if it was their nature, but Jules didn't believe in that. They had free will.

Both of them had allowed Ja'ri to kill their own people, to destroy their cities and lay waste to Desolate. That couldn't be forgiven. Jules believed everyone had their own life choices, and regardless of the situation, she would never have permitted something like that to happen. Not on her watch.

"Ja'ri, assist us!" Lan'i ordered, but she didn't intervene. If any trace of O'ri's essence was in Patty, Jules was positive the Deity would be targeting her at this moment too, so she'd acted just in time.

You are gone! The god clapped his hands together, and their shields vanished. Mist circled over their floating bodies, and when it departed, the Zan'ra disappeared. Jules glanced at her wrist, finding the crystal bracelet didn't hold O'ri. His essence had vanished.

Her body grew tired, the weight of the Zan'ra off her shoulders, and when Jules glanced at Patty, she found the girl was curled into a ball at the edge of her sphere. Jules crouched near her, and saw her eyes were rolled back in her head. She was breathing, though.

Set her down. We have much to discuss, daughter.

The storm subsided, casting the clouds apart, revealing a star-filled sky. The moon was nearly full, making the night beautiful. The waves slowed, shifting in a rhythmic and mesmerizing fashion, and Jules wanted to curl up beside Patty and sleep.

Instead, she moved for the top of the cliff and settled to the surface, Patty rolling out as she cut of her shield. The god walked toward her, and she to it, standing on the edge of the rocky crag.

You did well, bringing them to me. The Four are no longer.

"Good. I'm glad." Jules knew this didn't make up for all the dead Zan'ra on this world, but it would have to do.

You haven't finished releasing me, daughter. I still need your assistance. Then there's the matter of the others. His voice was deep but not threatening anymore.

"I can't."

What? He grew taller, his ankles firmly under the

ocean's surface. *This is your burden. Free us as we planned millennia ago,* he demanded, but she shook her head.

"I have something to do first. Then I'll return and release you, I promise," she said.

What is your duty?

"There's a man, a very bad one, and I need to kill him," Jules told him. "But I need to be able to return when I'm done. It's the only way I can release you from your bonds." This had to work.

His giant hand lifted toward her, water dripping from his fingers. He stepped forward, leaning over to touch her on the head with his finger. *It is done. You can find home when your mission is satisfied. Perhaps you'd rather I send you there now?*

She shivered at the thought. Could the Deity make it so easy? Could he kill Lom and fix everything? She asked him, and he shook his head. *There is much we can accomplish, but I'd need to be there in his timeline to perform this task. You will do well to remember you are one of us: a Deity.*

"How can this be? I'm a human girl," she told him.

You're much more. He began to leave, but stopped. *I nearly forgot. You do not need these.* He tapped her head again, and Jules felt something shift inside her. It was like her soul was being torn from her body, and she fell to her knees, screaming into the night sky.

"What have you done?" she begged, the pain beginning to subside.

I've removed your Zan'ra powers. You have no need for them.

She held a hand in front of her eyes, seeking the green glow's reflection, but it wasn't there. "Does this mean I won't be able to do things like I before?"

He shook his head, his white eyes dimming as he started to lower into the water. *No, but you are a Deity. You have no need for parlor tricks. You have much more inside you. Use it. Return to me. Finish your duty.*

He continued to lower, but she had so many questions. "Wait! How do I use them? I don't understand!"

You do. Look inside. And with that, the Deity was fully submerged, once again returning to his underwater prison.

Patty remained unconscious, and Jules grabbed the girl's hand. If she didn't have her powers, what was she? Could she fight Lom? Were her plans unraveled?

Jules stayed on the rocks, thinking on it for some time before remembering what he'd told her. *Look inside.* She turned her reflection inward, seeking what it meant to be a Deity. Something snapped, a lock in her mind, and information flooded her brain.

And she knew what she had to do. Jules rose in the air, still clutching Patty's hand. She might not be a Zan'ra, but she could emulate their gifts, and that would have to be enough until she fully comprehended her capabilities. She partly wished he'd wiped them all, making her a normal teenager, but there was too much to do to ensure her friends and family's safety. When it was over, she'd make a final request of the gods, as Fontem had.

She cradled Patty in her arms and spun around, stopping to stare at the calm ocean. "I'll keep my promise."

Jules hurtled toward the lake.

---

*I*t wasn't easy arriving in the middle of an underwater portal room, but I'd known what to expect. By the time we climbed out of the lake, we were both on our backs, groaning in pain and gasping erratically.

"That wasn't very fun," Dean said, managing to catch his breath.

I rolled over, getting to my feet. I was soaked, and the

night air was cold. I helped Dean up and set a hand on his shoulder. "You should have stayed behind."

"Not a chance, Mr. Parker. If Jules is here…" His eyes grew distant, and he smiled, pointing past me.

I spun to see a familiar shape arriving, and she carried Patty in her arms. Jules settled to the lakeshore, and Dean rushed over, grabbing his sister from her grip.

"Papa! Dean!" Jules said, tears streaming down her face.

It was astonishing. For the first time since her powers had faltered as a kid, her eyes no longer glowed.

"What happened?" I asked her, pulling her into a firm embrace. I was soaked, but she didn't seem to care, nuzzling into me.

"They're dead."

"Who?" I asked.

"The Four."

Dean was beside Patty, one knee on the ground, and I saw her eyes blinking open. "Where am I?"

Dean laughed, helping her into a seated position. "You're safe. That's where you are." He hugged his sister, and she sobbed into his sleeve.

"I'm sorry, Dean. I didn't know… I had to…"

"We saw the drawings," Dean told her.

Patty looked surprised, and I had no idea what they were referring to. "What drawings?"

Jules reached into her pockets and pulled out a piece of paper, handing it to Patty. She unfolded it under the moonlight. "Who did this?"

"You. I found them in your room on New Spero," Jules told her. "L and P. Lan'i and Patty. You had drawings of him everywhere."

Patty accepted her brother's hand and rose to her feet, staring at the child's drawing. "I hardly remember that. It's like a dream."

"Jules, are we done here?" I asked her, not wanting to linger any longer than we had to.

She nodded. "We're done."

"And you're certain the Zan'ra are gone?" I asked.

She slid her sleeve up, revealing an empty crystal bracelet. "The Deity made sure of it. They're gone."

It was Dean's turn to ask a question. "If that's the case, where's the god?"

Jules averted her gaze, the tell-tale sign she didn't want to tell us the truth. "He's underwater. I didn't finish freeing him."

"Honey, something doesn't add up. If the Zan'ra are gone, why can you still fly?" I whispered.

"Can we talk about this later?" she asked, and I agreed, but only because she didn't look capable of staying on her feet much longer.

I glanced toward the lake. "Let's head to *Light*. It's time to go home."

———————

The others arrived a week later, returned from Fontem's secret dome, though Regnig had remained behind. Karo had set up the portal sticks in his suite, so Regnig could come and go as he pleased, but so far, he was too intrigued by everything to leave.

"You did well," Mary told me, hugging me. She rested her head on my shoulder, and stared out the viewscreen in our suite toward Techeron below.

"From the sounds of it, so did you. They're really going to join the Alliance?" I asked, and she released me, coming to sit on the couch. I joined her, kicking my feet up.

"And we have a meeting set up with three other races from out here, who expressed interest." Mary looked so beautiful, her skin aglow after we'd returned home safe and had a long steam shower to wash off the trip. I hadn't seen her smile so much in years.

The doorbell rang, and Jules popped her head from her bedroom, shouting at us from across the hall. "I'll get it!"

I grinned at Mary as I heard Natalia's accent greeting Jules at the door. Charlie and Carey rushed into our suite, tails wagging, bodies wiggling, and Maggie romped around with them, circling the kitchen table, then the island, as they played excitedly.

Dean and Patty trailed after their mother, and it warmed my heart to see their family together. It would never be the same without Magnus, but they'd make do eventually. The most important thing was that they were all here.

Natalia looked healthier after a couple of weeks on *Light*, and the kids were smiling, chatting with Jules in the kitchen.

"Nat, can I bring you anything?" Mary asked. "Wine?"

"Sure, that sounds great." Nat took a seat across from me, and my wife returned with three glasses of red from our favorite vintner on New Spero.

"How are they doing?" Mary asked, facing toward the kitchen where the three teenagers talked.

"Better than I expected. Thanks again for taking a special interest in them," Nat said, not meeting our gazes. "I've been a terrible mother. Without Magnus, I just couldn't…"

"Don't worry about it, Nat. That's what family's for. We support each other when we need it most. We're glad we have Patty and Dean back too," I told her.

"How's Jules?" Natalia asked, taking a sip of her wine.

I peered at her, seeing the beautiful young woman she was becoming. Jules looked different without the glowing eyes, almost like I didn't recognize her. She wore a t-shirt, jeans, her curly hair pulled into a loose top bun. She seemed so normal.

"She's got some things to work out, but I guess… she appears really happy," I admitted.

"She's a special girl, that one. I knew it the minute I met her," Nat said, and Mary beamed proudly.

There were so many uncertainties, but we'd managed to destroy Lainna to prevent Lom from creating his nullifier. We'd found Fontem's goods, with countless artifacts that could assist our futures, and we'd ended the Zan'ra threat, returning Patty home where she belonged.

Jules was confident the Deities were under control, but she was going to need to deal with it eventually. She hadn't mentioned Lom in a while, and that was good. I wanted to put him out of my mind.

"What about the executive in your cell?" Natalia asked, and my eyes sprang open. I looked at Mary, whose expression matched mine.

"I forgot about her. With everything going on…" I set my glass down.

"Me too. We were so worried about Patty, and then we had these meetings, and Fontem…" Mary said.

"I'll go see her later tonight. I'm sure there's no news there," I told them, hoping I was right.

"When are we going to eat?" Jules asked. "I'm starving over here."

I laughed, rolling my eyes at her impatience. Sometimes, she could bear the weight of the universe; other times, she was a kid again. I preferred this version of her. "Right now. Can you set the table?" I asked her, and she nudged Dean.

"Give me a hand, would you?" she asked, smiling at him.

I could tell they had feelings for one another and tried not to worry that she was too young, or that he was vulnerable after the death of his father. Truth was, I loved Nat's kids like they were mine, and Jules and Dean's futures were in their own hands.

We ate, had a glass of wine, and enjoyed one another's company like old times. Tomorrow, we were starting the long journey to Haven, but tonight, we were a family.

"Plinick, good to see you," I greeted the guard. Her eyes opened, and I watched as she dabbed some drool from the corner of her lips.

"Captain Parker, I wasn't expecting you," she hastily replied.

"I'm here to visit the prisoner," I told her.

"Yes, sir. Go right in."

The energy field faded, and I stepped through, heading for Katherine's cell. She was wide awake, sitting on her bed, reading a tablet.

"I see we've given you some privileges," I told her.

She dropped the tablet in surprise, but it landed softly on the bedding beside her. "Dean. I was beginning to think you'd forgotten about me."

"You've been treated well?" I asked, not sure I wanted her to be.

She peered up at me with Janine's eyes and smiled. "Better than you probably think I deserve."

I didn't take the bait. I squinted, looking at her well-furnished room. Someone had taken it upon themselves to improve her situation.

Neither of us spoke for a minute, me waiting for her to spill the beans without me asking. "Your daughter is quite the girl."

My breath caught in my lungs, and I cleared my throat, playing along. "I know. I sent her here."

"Then you heard about her plan? Did you use the communication device?" she asked, and I nodded along.

"Sure. We used it," I said, trying to sound relaxed.

"It's dangerous, but when she offered me sanctuary on Haven, I had no choice. I want Lom to die," she told me.

The picture was growing clear. I turned, rushing from Katherine. "Was it something I said?" she called after me, but I hardly heard her over the thumping of my own heart.

I raced through the corridors, straight for our suite, and when I arrived frazzled and worried, I found Jules' room empty. "Jules! Are you here?"

Mary stepped from the bathroom, a glass of water in her grip. "What are you shouting for?"

I ran my hands through my hair, feeling my world fall apart. "Jules…"

"What about her?"

I crossed the room, heading for the console embedded in the kitchen wall. With the quick tap of my finger, one of the guards' faces appear on the screen. "Captain Parker, what can we…"

"Did my daughter use the portal?" I asked, cutting him off.

"Sure. She was through about fifteen minutes ago," he told me, and I ended the call.

"What is this about?" Mary asked me as she grabbed hold of my shoulders.

"Jules. I think she's heading to Udoon. She's going for Lom."

EPILOGUE

*T*he planet near Udoon was nothing but a stepping point for Jules to reach her goal. A long time ago, before she was born, her father had come into this same Shandra room, meeting with someone named Cee-Eight, who'd flown them to Udoon Station. It was her dad's big plan to capture Lom and deal with him. She found it ironic that sixteen or so years later, she was using the same portal to move for Udoon with the exact same goal in mind.

Jules felt different since her experience with the Deity. More herself now, not the Zan'ra imposter. She flew through space, spotting a handful of starships as she neared Udoon. Loweck had lived on this planet for a time, even though she wasn't of their race. The locals were squat, four-legged creatures, with protruding bellies and mist to assist their breathing away from the surface.

The station was about the same as her father had described it. Seedy. It facilitated trouble. People only came to Udoon Station to gamble, drink, find drugs, or hire killers. It wasn't a good place, but today, she had need of it.

Jules hated leaving home behind like this, but she didn't have a choice. She'd brought Patty home, fulfilling her promise to Dean. He was going to be so upset with her, but this was for him and for her family. Lom wasn't going to stop because of a setback.

Jules moved for the station's outer hull, far from the

docking bays where a hundred various spacecraft were parked. She touched the metallic station and pressed through the wall, creating her own entrance onto the station.

The room was busy, lights flashing, and she stepped from the corner, raising a hand over her eyes to stop the blinking light show. Music was pumping through speakers, and Jules removed her pack, holding it near her chest to keep from being pickpocketed.

There were numerous unrecognizable beings, but she spotted an Inlorian, as well as a Kraski, here. So they weren't all gone.

Jules walked right by a giant bouncer, who shouted after her in a foreign tongue, but she kept walking, heading for the rendezvous spot. The lounge was half-full, various people sitting across from one another, speaking in hushed tones. Two unfamiliar aliens rose, one taking a swing at the other, and she ignored them, heading for the back of the room.

Jules was about to ask someone how she could reach Viliar, when she spotted the hooded man across the lounge, sitting at the bar sipping a drink. It couldn't be him. There was no way.

I felt every ache in my body as I waited for her. I knew she was coming, but the exact date was unclear. I'd seen her only nine of her months ago on New Spero, during Magnus' wake, but she hadn't seen me. Another two of my years had passed. Two long and miserable years.

I patted my pocket, ensuring the Delineator was safe and sound, and took another drink from my mug. This was my life now. Waiting. Boredom. Loneliness. I should have done it all differently, but it was too late for me. My Jules was gone, but this one… this Dean's daughter could make it. I felt it in my throbbing joints. I kicked a leg out, knocking my metal knee against the bar, and glanced around. Someone was starting a fight behind me, but that happened so regularly here, I paid it no mind.

I finished my drink off, wiping my mouth with my sleeve, and lowered my chin.

"Want another one?" the barkeep asked, and I shook my head, dropping a credit on the table. It was time to go. Maybe Jules wasn't coming after all. Maybe she was smart enough to stay behind. To live her life while she could.

"Who are you?" The voice cut through me, her voice so familiar, yet so distant.

I stood, my balance uneasy after the drinks, and I turned toward her, my hood exposing half of my face. "Jules…"

She reached up, snatching my hood off, and staggered back, hand flying to her mouth. "How?"

"We'll have time for that later." I pointed at the doorway. "Your contact just walked in."

I watched as her gaze drifted to the tall man in a gray suit near the entrance. "What are you doing here?" she whispered.

I longed to hug my daughter, to tell her everything, but this wasn't her. She wasn't mine.

"I'm from the future. And I'm here to help you kill Lom of Pleva."

Her eyes glistened with tears and she took my hand, squeezing it tightly. "What do we do?"

THE END

ABOUT THE AUTHOR

Nathan Hystad is an author from Sherwood Park, Alberta, Canada.

Keep up to date with his new releases by signing up for his newsletter at www.nathanhystad.com

Sign up at www.shelfspacescifi.com as well for amazing deals and new releases from today's best indie science fiction authors.

Made in the USA
Las Vegas, NV
06 December 2023

82161596R00163